The Wave Runners

Kai Meyer

Volume 1 of 3
Translated by Anthea Bell

EGMONT

EGMONT

We bring stories to life

First published in Great Britain 2007
by Egmont UK Limited
239 Kensington High Street, London W8 6SA

First published in Germany 2003
under the title *Die Wellenläufer*
by Loewe Verlag GmbH, Bindlach, Germany

Die Wellenläufer text copyright © 2003 Kai Meyer
English translation copyright © 2007 Anthea Bell

The moral rights of the author, the translator and the
illustrator have been asserted

ISBN 978 1 4052 1635 7

1 3 5 7 9 10 8 6 4 2

A CIP catalogue record for this title is available from the British Library

Typeset by Avon DataSet Ltd, Bidford on Avon, Warwickshire
Printed and bound in Great Britain by the CPI Group

CONTENTS

THE POLLIWIGGLE

Jolly ran across the ocean, striding freely. Her bare feet only just dipped into the water. Its inky blue depths yawned beneath her, going down and down to the sea-bed lying far below, several hundred times deeper than the height of a man.

Jolly had been able to walk on water from the moment she was born, and over the years she had learned to move easily on the rolling surface of the sea. It felt to her like running through a puddle. She leaped nimbly from wave to wave, avoiding the breaking crests, which could sometimes make her stumble.

All around her a sea battle was raging.

Cannonballs whistled past her ears, but few came close enough for her to feel the draught as they shot by. Acrid smoke drifted over the water between the two sailing ships, blurring Jolly's view. The creak of planks and the flapping of the great sails mingled with the thunder of the guns. Gunpowder smoke burned her eyes. She had never liked its aroma, unlike the other pirates: her friends on the *Maid Maddy* claimed to love nothing better than the smell in the air after cannon had been fired. And when the sides of enemy ships exploded in the distance, and the screams of their enemies echoed across the sea, they said, it was better than being in any tavern drinking gin and rum.

Jolly didn't particularly like rum, any more than she liked the gun-smoke of the cannon on board. But whatever her nose thought of it, she knew her job and she'd do it.

It was another fifty paces to the enemy vessel, a Spanish three-master with two gun-decks and three times as many cannon as they had on the *Maid Maddy*. The whole galleon was magnificently decorated with ornate carvings: wooden faces that peered through the clouds of smoke now and then like strange, fabulous beings. Some looked so real, even at this distance, that you felt they might come to life at any moment. The Spaniards' boats were hoisted along the sides of her hull; a cannonball from the *Maddy* had brushed past one of them, shooting away some of the cordage from which it hung, and now the little boat swung against the mighty hull with every shock the ship suffered, making a dull, hollow sound.

Jolly was running with the current, which took her towards the galleon even faster. She had only to set foot on the water to feel which way the sea was moving; sometimes she could even tell if there were storms brewing or high winds blowing out beyond the horizon. She couldn't imagine ever spending long on land. She needed the familiar ocean, the feel of the bottomless abyss beneath her feet. Just as some people feel dizzy at great heights, Jolly panicked if she went too far from the sea and its roaring breakers.

She was crouching slightly as she ran now, although no one on the Spaniards' deck seemed to have noticed her. Curiously enough, she saw not a human soul behind the carved posts of the ship's rail. A galleon like this carried at least two hundred men, and they must all be expecting the pirates of the *Maid Maddy* to try boarding her. So why were none of them on deck?

Captain Bannon, commander of the pirate ship and Jolly's best friend, would normally have kept well away from a vessel like this: too large, too strong, too heavily armed. Not to mention the fact that the *Maid Maddy* had room for just seventy pirates, so the Spaniards would greatly outnumber them in hand-to-hand fighting.

All the same, when the ship appeared on the horizon there had been some reason to think it might be a good prize. Captain Bannon himself had climbed to the crow's-nest of the *Maddy* and studied the silhouette of the galleon through his telescope for a long time. 'They've reefed in sail,' he called down to his crew. 'Looks like they're in difficulties.'

The sea was too deep here for a ship to cast anchor, which meant that in spite of favourable winds the Spaniards were drifting – and that made no sense. But Bannon wouldn't have been one of the wiliest pirates in the Caribbean if he hadn't let his nose and his curiosity guide him in such cases.

'There's something odd about it,' he'd said before he sent his men to the guns, 'but maybe we'll all do better out of this business than looks likely now.' Captain Bannon often said such things, so no one was surprised. His crew trusted him – most of all Jolly, to whom Bannon had been something like mother and father combined ever since he bought her as a small child in Tortuga slave market and made her a member of his crew.

The thunder of guns, louder than before, made Jolly jump aside. She felt the wind of the heavy iron ball pass her and thought she saw it whistling by hardly an arm's length away. When she looked round, her worst fears were confirmed.

It had hit the *Maid Maddy*.

A great jet of water and splintered wood rose from the stern of the racy xebec, not a type of ship often seen in this region. The *Maddy*'s rail had no decorative carved posts like those on the galleon, but was a plain, waist-high wooden wall with openings in it for the gun barrels. The ship was painted blood-red, and Bannon had had white fangs painted on the front of the hull to make the bows look like the open jaws of a beast of prey.

Angry shouts reached Jolly's ears, scraps of voices making their way to her through the billowing grey smoke between the two ships.

Jolly half turned, and hesitated. She couldn't see from here whether the *Maddy* had suffered serious damage. Oh, please, Jolly silently begged, let her be all right.

But then she remembered Bannon's orders, her duty to him and the others, and turned to move forward again. A few steps took her to the hull of the Spanish galleon. She ran along the ship's side until she was standing under one of the two gun-ports at the stern. The lower gun-deck was about three yards above the surface of the water. Jolly wasn't even five feet tall, but it would be easy for her to throw one of the missiles from the bag slung around her through the opening.

She opened the flap of her leather bag and took out one

of the bottles that clinked alarmingly inside it at every step she took. They were filled with a bronze-coloured liquid, and their necks were sealed with wax.

Jolly took aim, drew a deep breath – and flung the bottle through the first gun-port, past the mouth of the cannon. Someone gave a cry of alarm, loud enough for her to hear it out here. Then a cloud of green smoke shot from the port, so dense and evil-smelling that Jolly quickly ran on to the next opening. There she took out a second bottle and threw it. She worked her way on, from gun-port to gun-port, until green vapour was billowing from most of them. None of the cannon on the lower deck were firing now. The gunners behind them must be blinded by the smoke, and Jolly knew from experience that the stink of it would turn the stomach of even the most hardened seaman.

For a change, she tried throwing the next bottle at the upper gun-deck. Once again she aimed it accurately through one of the gun-ports. If this went on her mission would be a total success. With a little luck, she could put the entire crew of the galleon out of action all by herself. Then Bannon and his pirates would only have to board the ship, take their coughing, half-blinded adversaries prisoner on deck, and no serious resistance need be expected.

But Jolly's attempt to hit the upper gun-deck was less

successful. The bottle flew through the gun-port just as the men inside were pushing out the cannon to fire the next shot. The glass smashed on the steel of the gun-barrel, the liquid inside splashed over the hull of the ship and immediately turned to caustic vapour. Jolly raced forward and threw herself flat on the surface of the water to escape the fumes. At the same time the Spaniards fired the cannon above her. A split second later she heard it score another direct hit on the pirate vessel. Wood splintered, and then there was an explosion – the cannonball had gone right through the hull of the *Maid Maddy* and struck the ammunition store.

Tears came to Jolly's eyes as she saw flames leaping from the yawning hole. She knew what a hit like that meant – she'd seen it often enough, and before today it had always been enemy ships that suffered such a fate. But now there was no doubt about it: the *Maddy* was going to sink. How could Bannon have made such a mistake? In her time as the captain's protégée Jolly had lived on three ships, but the *Maddy* was the one she knew best. To see her go down was like losing both her home and a good friend at the same time.

There was only one hope for the pirates now: in the little time still left to them they must capture the Spanish galleon, or they'd all sink to the bottom of the sea with the *Maddy*.

Desperate determination brought Jolly to her feet again. She took another bottle out of her bag, and this time it hit the mark. So did the next, and the one after that. Still none of the Spanish gunners were leaning over the rail to turn their fire on her. But then someone did put his head through one of the gun-ports, saw Jolly, and yelled, 'Hey, they've got a polliwiggle! They've got a damn polliwiggle with 'em!'

A second head appeared. 'There's no polliwiggles left no more. They was all . . .' Then he saw Jolly. His eyes, already rimmed with soot, widened. 'Oh, by God, curse it, they do have a polliwiggle!'

Jolly gave the men a grim smile. Taking careful aim, she threw a bottle past their faces – it missed them by a hair's breadth – and into the galleon. Swirling green vapours rose behind their heads. A moment later they had disappeared from sight.

Jolly ran on. Threw. Ran. Threw again. The thought of her friends drove her forward. She wasn't bothered about possible enemies now, or about keeping in cover, or even the shapes of the sharks that had appeared a few minutes ago beneath the surface of the water. Here and there she saw silvery-grey dorsal fins cut through the water like sword-blades, but she wasted no time thinking about that. Instead, she flung bottle after bottle into the ship until the bag slung around her was empty.

She had almost reached the galleon's bows by now. Bright green smoke was billowing out of all the upper gun-ports. No more cannon were being fired. The Spaniards' deck was swathed in dense vapours that made fighting impossible. Even the carved figures around the rail seemed to be pulling faces in the thick smoke.

If only Bannon could manage to get the *Maddy* –

A crunching sound made Jolly spin around. She let out a cry of delight and relief. The sinking pirate ship was making for the stern of the Spanish galleon with all sails set. It looked as if the mouth painted on the bows of the *Maddy* had rolled back its lips to show its bared fangs in derision one last time. With a couple of swift leaps, Jolly got into safety on her own ship. Soon stern was battering against stern. Grappling hooks and ropes flew across to the Spaniards' deck. A wild horde of pirates with scarves tied around their mouths and noses to protect them from the green smoke were clambering up the hull of the larger ship. Jolly knew every one of them, had known some all her life, others only a few months. The pirates wore clothing from every country in the world: baggy Turkish trousers, cotton shirts from the colonies, Italian waistcoats, garments patched together from the remains of Spanish uniforms. Many had tied wide sashes around their waists, and one even

9

wore a discarded skull and crossbones flag as a cloak. They swarmed up the wood like brightly coloured ants, made their way hand over hand along ropes, or swung from the spars of the *Maid Maddy* into their adversaries' rigging.

Very briefly, Jolly caught a glimpse of Captain Bannon, hair yellow as straw and raging like a dervish as he swung himself across to the Spanish galleon on a rope, sword between his teeth. She felt as if their glances met in that short moment, and it seemed to her that he was smiling down at her, in spite of the scarf around his face. She could tell from his eyes alone. They could look so friendly that Jolly was sometimes surprised his victims didn't hand over their ships of their own accord, just because of the warmth in that gaze. It didn't fit with his wild determination and unscrupulous nature.

Jolly raised an arm in triumph, cheered out loud, and then she too was beside the bows of the enemy galleon. She seized one of the ropes hanging down and clambered up it as nimbly as a cat.

The green smoke on deck dispersed quickly. Even as Jolly climbed the rope she heard the fighting end before it had really begun. The coughing, spitting Spaniards surrendered, with streaming eyes and dripping noses. Hardly any of them raised a weapon against the pirates, and if they did it was only a weary reflex, not done with a real will to fight.

Jolly swung herself over the rail. Bannon, seeing her, strode quickly over. 'Well done,' he said, slapping her so hard on the shoulder with his mighty hand that her knees almost buckled. He turned to his men, who were just herding the captured Spaniards together amidships.

'Cut all ropes to the *Maddy* to keep her from dragging us down too. The rest of you, disarm our friends here. This is our new ship now!' And with a grin for the girl at his side, he cried in an even louder voice, 'I'd say this vessel needs a new name. From now on she's the *Jumping Jolly*!'

Jolly felt quite dizzy with pride as the pirates shouted with jubilation around her.

At the same time they heard a creaking and crunching noise from the *Maddy*. The painted muzzle of the beast of prey was grinding its teeth as it died.

Ten minutes later the *Maid Maddy* had still not sunk entirely. She stuck out of the sea at a slanting angle like a rock, an ominous monument against the setting sun. The superstructure at the stern was almost level with the surface of the water, but the bows with their painted fangs still jutted well above it. The ship's figurehead – a dark Neptune with his trident – rose against the deep blue sky as if to hurl a last proud cry of defiance into the world.

Even as the pirates were herding their prisoners together on deck, something seemed to be wrong. Captain Bannon acted like a happy, victorious man, but Jolly was perhaps the only one to notice the concern in his eyes.

There were too few Spaniards here.

The galleon had only forty seamen on board. Not even enough to man all the guns, let alone deal with everything else that was necessary on a vessel like this. Even Bannon with his crew of seventy wouldn't find it easy to get the galleon under way. But forty Spanish sailors? It was impossible.

And there was something else strange about them.

'They're not Spaniards,' said Cristobal, Bannon's steersman. 'Most of 'em speak Spanish, a few look like Spaniards, but if you ask me they were born here in the colonies.'

'So?' asked Jolly pertly, earning herself a stern glance from the steersman before he turned to his captain again.

'They've a cut-throat look in general. See those scars? And their boozy faces.' He grinned, showing a blackened canine tooth. 'Fact is, they look like us.'

Bannon did not return the grin. He anxiously scanned the deck, briefly inspected the prisoners, and then looked at the empty horizon. 'What does all this mean?' he whispered in a toneless voice, so low that only Jolly and Cristobal heard him.

A shiver ran down Jolly's back. Was it a trap?

'They've searched the whole ship, our men have,' said the steersman. 'No one else aboard, no explosives nor other tricky stuff. No cargo neither.'

'We'd better get out of here,' Bannon decided. 'And fast.'

With unaccustomed haste, he gave orders to the first mate. Soon a loud cry of, 'Clear the decks to set sail!' rang out. A dozen pirates clambered up the rigging like spiders.

'What about them?' Jolly pointed to the bound prisoners. Cristobal had gone over to one of them, seized him by the collar, and was talking to him.

'We'll put them ashore somewhere,' said Bannon, going over to the rail. He sounded thoughtful. There were no enemy ships anywhere in sight.

Jolly looked at the sinking *Maddy*. She still lay at an angle in the water. The current had carried the galleon thirty or forty feet from the wreck, and the distance was increasing with every passing moment.

Cristobal came back to the captain.

'Well?' asked Bannon. 'What do they say?'

'Seems they were prisoners. Every last man jack of 'em condemned to death. They were offered their freedom if they'd go aboard this ship and do all they could to defend it.'

'Forty men? On a ship like this? That's ridiculous.'

'I guess whoever thought this up didn't expect any of these fellows to survive. Seems they've got one thing in common: they were all once gunners. They weren't picked to tackle men in hand-to-hand fighting – they were meant to destroy us from a distance.' The steersman rubbed his stubbly chin. 'And another thing. Seems like some other vessel towed 'em here. They were never under full sail . . .'

A loud flapping noise drowned out his words as the pirates in the rigging unfurled the sails. The mighty bundles of fabric shook out within seconds.

'No!' cried Bannon.

Jolly saw what he meant, and at the same moment she heard it too.

Pitchers fell from the sails. Large, brown clay pitchers which smashed into thousands of pieces as they hit the deck. There must have been two or three dozen, now breaking with a hollow sound everywhere on board as they struck each other. Some fell in the middle of the screaming group of prisoners, another hit Trevino, ship's cook aboard the *Maddy,* on the head and felled him.

And there was something inside the broken pitchers that

at first sight looked like dark tangles of thick threads – until they disentangled themselves of their own accord, and fell apart into hundreds of little balls scurrying away in all directions on their thin legs.

'Spiders!' screeched someone, and others took up the cry. *'Spiders . . . them pitchers are full of spiders!'*

Bannon shouted orders that no one could hear in the outbreak of panic on board. The prisoners screamed blue murder as spiders positively erupted among them. The pirates ran around on deck, some trying to stamp on the creatures, but they soon gave up when they realised how hopeless it was. Ten and then twenty scrambled over the body of the unconscious cook, others found their way up boots and trousers, into the rigging and on to the rail. The spiders might be as panic-stricken and confused as the men on board, but they were faster – and above all, they were enraged.

Jolly hauled herself up into the shrouds. Her hands were damp with sweat and her breath came fast. Everywhere the pirates were yelling, stamping, shaking off spiders. Cristobal brushed several at once off his body, but he hadn't noticed a particularly fat spider crouched at the nape of his neck. He screamed when it stung him.

Bannon laid into the spiders first with his sword, then with his bare hands. He tried to follow Jolly up into the shrouds, but then he too was stung several times, and the pain made him lose his hold on the ropes. Cursing, he fell back on the deck.

'Those dogs!' he cried with a failing voice as the spider venom took effect. 'Jolly – the figurehead. Remember the . . . fig–'

He collapsed. Jolly stared at the lifeless form below her, and tears shot into her eyes.

She must do something, for heaven's sake, she must help Bannon and the others somehow! She looked desperately around for a weapon, knowing at the same time that anything she did would be useless. No one could get the better of those spiders.

She suppressed a sob as she began to clamber down the shrouds.

Jolly knew exactly what Bannon had been trying to tell her.

From up in the rigging she had a clear view of the wreck of the *Maddy*. The figurehead at the bows rose like a pointing finger to show her the way.

She avoided several spiders, ran to the rail, and stood on it, swaying. There were spiders everywhere now, a teeming dark carpet of them covering the deck and all the men on board. Most of them were no longer moving. Several had almost entirely disappeared under the scrabbling, hairy bodies. A few were still calling for help up at the tops of the masts, but hordes of the eight-legged creatures were approaching them too.

Jolly looked back at Bannon for the last time, and then leaped into the depths below. She fell rather than jumped, and it was like crashing down on a stone floor as she met the surface of the water without sinking into it. She was lucky not to break every bone in her body. She rolled over, was tossed violently back and forth by the waves, but finally she got to her feet.

Silvery triangles glided towards her, circled around her. Jolly, who had been at close quarters with sharks more than once before, knew that they saw only the soles of her feet outlined on the surface, and wouldn't recognise her as worthwhile prey. She forced herself not to think of the men who had jumped overboard to get away from the spiders. They certainly hadn't had her luck. Jolly ran fast over the water, striding towards the *Maddy*. This time she was running against the current; her breath came fast, her heart hammered in her chest, but finally she saw the pirate ship ahead of her – or rather, what was left of it.

The Spanish galleon rose against the twilit sky behind Jolly. From a distance it looked as if the wood itself had come alive. The dark surface moved, covered with teeming life that kept changing colour.

The water around the *Maddy* was choppy. Jolly had difficulty avoiding the white crests of the waves. You couldn't trust the sea foam; the surface under it sometimes gave way, sucking in your feet like quicksand, and then you had to make sure you pulled yourself out in time, before the water solidified around you and held you fast.

She managed to seize the edge of the ship's red rail and hauled herself up by it. As soon as the superstructure at the stern had sunk completely and the interior of the ship filled with water, the *Maid Maddy* would go down like a stone. Not even a polliwiggle like Jolly could escape the deadly current then.

Jolly must be faster. Even faster than the water.

Gasping, she swung herself over the rail and up on deck, where she immediately lost her footing on its wet slope and slid a couple of paces down. Flailing her arms wildly, she caught a rope and tried to hold it – but it gave way and fell to the deck beside her. Jolly slid on, feet first, and now she was coming dangerously close to the foaming, turbulent water. At the last moment her hands and feet got a grip on one of the gratings above the hatches to the hold as she slid over it. It was some three yards from here to the raging water, but the ship was going down all the time. In less than a minute the grating would be under water, and by then Jolly must have reached the figurehead, the one place that still held out any hope of safety.

She could, of course, simply have run for it across the open sea, but to move over the rocking, surging waves took ten times as much strength as covering the same distance on land, and Jolly hadn't seen an island anywhere on the horizon. At some point she would collapse from exhaustion in the middle of the sea, would have to lie down – and then she would look the same as any swimmer or any large fish to the sharks below.

She *must* reach the figurehead. It was her only hope.

A mighty tremor ran through the ship, and then, with a groan, she settled at a steeper angle. Every degree the *Maddy* rose further in the air made it harder to clamber over the deck.

And Jolly became aware of something else, at first only on the edge of her field of vision, but then, as she looked more closely, she saw it with dreadful clarity.

Among the whirlpools and spray at the foot of the sloping deck, a shape was moving in the water. A figure that was almost human but had long, thin limbs, skin with an oily sheen shimmering in rainbow colours, and a hideous face that was only a great maw and half a dozen rows of razor-sharp teeth. Jolly saw the creature's jaws snap open and shut, biting angrily, menacingly at the foam and the waves.

A kobalin! A real live kobalin! Jolly had seen one before, but some time ago, two or three years back, and that had been only a young one. The pirates had dispatched it with a few well-aimed shots into the water.

But this kobalin was fully grown, raging down there in hopes of its prey as if it hadn't eaten for months. The noise of the battle must have lured it this way. Kobalins loved carrion, particularly human flesh, and there were tales of shipwrecked crews torn apart and devoured within a few minutes by a handful of them.

Jolly felt as if her body wasn't hers any more. As if losing the captain and all her friends wasn't enough, and being shipwrecked with her strength gradually failing – now one of these brutes had to turn up!

She began climbing again, more carefully this time. First over the grating, then hanging on to a rope, and from there – at last! – back to the rail. The sound of the kobalin's jaws snapping behind her back drowned out even the tormented grinding of the wreck and the roaring of the sea. The dreadful creature was lying in wait down below, baring its teeth, just waiting for the moment when Jolly finally lost her grip.

Kobalins feared leaving the water. Only the bravest among them sometimes put their heads or claws above the surface; most preferred to look for food down below. It was unusual for the kobalin down there to be reaching its arms out for Jolly, even if it couldn't get at her. For it to raise its torso above the turbulent waves now and then was nothing short of sensational.

Jolly climbed on and reached the figurehead. More than once, on quiet nights when only he and she were still awake on board, Bannon had told her how the mechanism worked, letting her into the *Maddy's* best-kept secret.

The figurehead with its grim Neptune face was hollow, and would hold a grown man. Provisions to last several days were stored in waterproof compartments inside it. It could be released from the ship's hull with the help of two metal bolts, and made a perfect lifeboat for its occupant. Hidden weights ensured that it would keep facing up as it drifted, and there was a hatch that could be opened to let in fresh air.

The kobalin uttered a dreadful scream as one of the masts broke and the entire weight of the wood fell on it. Out of the corner of her eye, Jolly saw the mast crash straight into the monster's open jaws, thrusting it down into the depths.

She gave a grim snort of satisfaction, but she no longer had the strength to feel glad. With the last of her will-power she opened the hidden trapdoor in the back of the figurehead, wriggled in with difficulty, and closed it again behind her. Any cracks in the wood were sealed by leather padding. For the fraction of a second, Jolly felt as if she had been put into a coffin alive. Her throat tightened in panic. She'd rather go down with the *Maddy* than be shut up like this. But then reason got the upper hand again.

The wreck was rising at a steeper and steeper angle. It could begin its final fall to the bottom of the sea any moment now.

Jolly pushed back the two bolts. They slipped easily out of their fittings, as if Bannon had oiled them only recently. There was a cracking sound, and for a moment Jolly thought the *Maddy* was breaking up. But no — it was the figurehead coming away from the hull. She didn't even notice its free fall to the depths below, only the impact, which sounded like a hundred hammer blows on the figure's wooden exterior. There was a droning in Jolly's ears; she almost lost consciousness. Then the waves caught the figurehead. A deafening screech came up from the depths, perhaps the dying kobalin, perhaps the *Maddy* as she sank. Jolly could only hope she was far enough from the wreck by now not to be dragged down into the depths in its wake.

It was pitch dark inside the figurehead, and the air smelled musty. Jolly dared not open the hatch yet in case the water of the rough sea came in, flooding the interior.

She heard the hollow sound of something colliding with the figurehead from below. Sharks! They thought the drifting outline was a particularly fat victim. Jolly wasn't sure whether the wood could stand up to the heavy pressure of a shark's teeth if one of them really bit into it.

Something brushed across her face in the dark.

She screamed. For a moment she thought fingers had stroked her. But that was nonsense. The distance between the tip of her nose and the wooden wall of the hollow figurehead was less than twelve inches. She was alone. Of course she was.

Or perhaps not *entirely* alone.

One of the spiders was inside the figurehead with her! It must have crawled into the bag Jolly wore slung around her while she was still on board the galleon.

Now it was free and scuttling around on her.

Jolly began kicking and hitting out in the cramped space, hammering on the wood with her hands and feet, until she managed to get her panic under control well enough to think clearly again.

Lie perfectly still. Keep absolutely quiet.

And listen!

Jolly held her breath. Gooseflesh covered her body like icy armour, but it was no protection against the spider's poisonous fangs. She listened to her own heartbeat, not low and soft, but so loud that she thought it would break her ribcage apart.

There was another noise. Barely audible. Like fingertips drumming softly on something hollow.

The spider was scrabbling across the wood somewhere lower down.

Jolly bit her lower lip so as to make no sound. If she could only see something! A tiny glimmer of light would perhaps be enough. But she dared not raise a hand to open the hatch above her face, for fear of irritating the spider.

She must get rid of the brute somehow.

She breathed in and out very slowly, and then held her breath again, freezing rigid as if she were a piece of wood herself. She must lull the spider into a sense of security, must not on any account do anything to make it attack her.

And then, when she knew exactly where the horrible creature was —

Something nipped the back of her right hand.

Jolly let out a frantic cry and struck her hand against the

inside of the figurehead with all her might. The spider's body was harder than she had expected, its bristles pricked like pins, but all the same Jolly struck the wood again, over and over again. The twitching legs wrapped themselves around the back of her hand like fingers; she felt their pressure, and then sensed them going limp.

Nauseated, she shook her arm until the lifeless body of the spider slipped off.

It didn't matter now. It was too late.

The spider had stung her.

Jolly felt her senses failing. The darkness inside the drifting figurehead became deeper, took her breath away, seemed to be flowing into her nostrils, her eyes, her mouth, oily and cold.

I'm going to die, she thought with surprising calm.

Once again she raised her hand. Her fingers found the bolt above her face and pushed it back with the last of her strength.

The blue of the sky above was like steel blades piercing her eyes. Salty air streamed into the hollow space.

Breathe, she told herself.

Go on, for heaven's sake, breathe!

The sky paled, then the light and the whole world. Spider venom was coursing through her veins, and all thought evaporated through the pores of her skin.

Jolly's consciousness floated away like driftwood on an ocean black as night.

FLOTSAM

The boy was sitting on a cliff high above the bay, which spread out before him like a window opening on the sea. Whenever his father gave him time off from his duties on the farm he came up here to dream – of the sea, of a life on the great, stately ships he sometimes saw on the horizon.

Munk's hand rested on the rusty barrel of the cannon. A pair of birds had nested in its mouth last year. He had waited until the chicks flew away, and only then carefully cleared the nest out of the gun. He didn't know how you fired a cannon, but he thought it would be a good idea to keep it ready for use at any time. His parents, tobacco farmers and the only settlers on this tiny island, knew nothing about the old gun above the bay. The cannon was Munk's secret. Like this whole place: his refuge on the rocks with its view of the bay and the turquoise blue of the Caribbean Sea.

27

He had often hoped to see pirates from up here, the proud sloops and brigantines of the freebooters who brought more fear and terror to the Caribbean than any other sea or ocean in the world knew. He longed to see one of their black flags some day, with a skull above crossbones or crossed swords. And there'd be the gleam of gold shining through the vessel's cargo hatches, while its sails were bathed in the light of an eternal sunrise.

Dreams, said his mother. Crazy nonsense, said his father. They had both warned him more than once against attracting the attention of a passing ship to the island. He mustn't show smoke, or any other sign of life.

Munk smiled pityingly at his parents' anxieties. He might fantasise about pirates and daring raids, but he would never actually have lured a pirate ship here. After all, who was he? Only a boy with a couple of unusual talents. They'd never take a lad like him on board. He couldn't fight with a sword, but he could read; he couldn't shoot, but he did know a few useless magic tricks. If pirates ever really did appear on the island, he'd surely be the first to walk the plank.

Useless. It was a word he hated. His father had once called him useless when he lost his temper over one of the mistakes Munk made on the farm. And of course he was right. Munk would never be a good tobacco farmer, that was for sure. He spent too much time daydreaming for that, thinking of anything and everything except the harvest and how to tend the young plants. And he wasn't interested in the haggling that his father did so well when an occasional tobacco trader came to the island.

Munk sighed and squinted at the morning sun. The base on which the cannon stood was so rotten that he didn't sit on the gun itself for fear the wood below it might crumble. He had often wondered who left it here. Secretly, he felt sure that thirty or forty years ago, in the days of the first buccaneers and Henry Morgan's privateering expeditions, this island had been a pirates' hide-out. Perhaps they'd dug themselves in up here to escape the Spaniards – or even better, perhaps they'd hidden their treasure somewhere in the dense jungle.

Dreams, thought Munk. Just stupid dreams.

At noon today he'd thought he heard the rumble of cannon in the distance, and once or twice there had been a bright flash on the horizon, overshadowed by something that might be a plume of smoke. But the sun would soon be setting now, and there were no more signs of any sea battle.

Just another disappointment. Another vain hope that some day, something unusual might happen to relieve the boredom of life on this island.

He was about to get up and go back to the farm when he noticed something. Out where the water was deeper and darker, where the sandy yellow-green of the bay merged into the blue of the ocean, he saw something that ought not to have been there at all.

Feeling curious, Munk leaped to his feet. A narrow chain of reefs broke through the surface of the sea just there, acting as a breakwater against the surf and always surrounded by a wreath of spray and foam like a crown of flowers.

Something was drifting in the water between two of the rocky needles that lay furthest out. It was a little bigger than a man, and dark brown. Wet wood, of course. Perhaps part of a wreck. Or by Morgan's red beard, perhaps a sea-chest!

Munk felt the blood race through his veins. Excitement took hold of him. Pushing back a lock of fair hair from his forehead, he looked at the thing in the water and started towards it. He ran down the narrow path from the cliff that led to the beach by way of a small banana plantation, ignoring the leaves and branches that whipped into his face. Sand got into his sandals, rubbing the soles of his feet painfully, but he wasn't stopping for that.

He quickly reached the water, and only then did he come to a halt. He looked carefully around him — not out to sea but back at the land, where the white beach disappeared beneath the shade of palms, mahogany trees and tree ferns, a dark green wall of vegetation with parrots screaming beyond it.

No one in sight. His parents ought to be in the farmhouse at this time of day; his mother probably had supper ready. If his father saw him doing what he planned to do there'd be bad trouble. They had forbidden him to do it, first pleading, then threatening him, and even when he asked them for the hundredth time what was the matter with it they had said nothing, only exchanged dark glances. But how could they expect him to obey them – at a moment like this, when the great adventure might be no more than a stone's throw away?

Munk looked over his shoulder and back at the jungle one last time, and then put his left foot on the water. He had last done it over a year ago in secret, just to see if he still could. But his mother had been right when she said he would never lose the gift. He was the only person in the world, so she and his father said, to have that power. They couldn't walk on water themselves, anyway. He was sure of that.

He was a 'polliwiggle', they had said, adding that there were people who would envy him and hurt him if he let them know about his ability. That was all. No further explanations.

A polliwiggle, then. The last in the whole wide world. Did he believe it? He had never been off the island in his life, and neither the Ghost-Trader nor his parents had ever been able to give him a satisfactory answer to his questions.

Munk set off. It was always more difficult keeping his balance in the surf. There were hardly any waves in the bay itself; they broke against the reefs further out, so he made quite good progress. On the open sea he would probably have fallen over after two or three steps. Perhaps his gift was only good for running over quiet bays and calm seas. If it was good for anything at all.

The safer he felt, the faster he went. Not just out of high spirits but because he wanted to get back to land as quickly as possible. There'd be real trouble if his father saw him.

It didn't take him long to reach the reefs. As he ran past them Munk saw how thickly covered with shells they were. Perhaps he could come back later some time and pick a few of them off the rocks. But now he had more important things to do.

The long wooden thing was half wedged above the rocks, with foaming surf washing around it. Now he could see that it was a ship's figurehead. With a little luck he'd be able to catch hold of the trident carried by the wooden figure of Neptune without setting foot in the treacherous sea-spray. Yes, done it! He pulled the figurehead towards him without too much difficulty. There was a small opening in the middle of the sea-god's face. Munk suppressed his curiosity. He'd have plenty of time later to investigate the thing; it was too dangerous out here in the bay. Gripping the figure harder, he dragged it towards land until sand crunched under its wet wooden back, and he had firm ground under his own feet again.

Munk knelt down and bent over the figurehead. It was perfectly clean; nothing clung to its surface. On one side there were a few long indentations that looked like the marks of teeth. The wood there was very pale. The figurehead couldn't have been drifting in the sea for long. Was it part of the wreckage from the sea battle he'd heard at midday?

Munk looked at the opening in the figurehead's face. By now the sun had sunk even lower, hanging in the tops of the jungle trees like a glowing fruit. Deep shadows lay over the square opening in the wood, which was the size of a small plate. Munk had to roll the figurehead on its side to get a better look inside.

'By Morgan's red beard!' he exclaimed.

He said it again and again before he finally found how to open the back of the figurehead and pulled the unconscious girl out on the beach.

She had long black hair, and she wore loose brown cotton trousers and a man's white shirt pulled in around her slender waist with a belt. Four or five gold rings dangled from each of her ears. There were two tiny diamonds above her nose right between the eyes, one each side, held together by an invisible pin under her tanned skin.

Her eyes were closed, but the light of the setting sun broke on the cut facets of the two diamonds, and Munk felt as if the girl were looking up at him with sparkling insect eyes.

When Jolly came back to her senses the world was full of a golden glow. Reddish-yellow beams of light fanned through the gaps in a roof of palm thatch, and dust motes were dancing in the light like shoals of tiny fish.

'Good morning,' said a voice beside her. 'Can you understand me – I mean, do you understand my language?'

Jolly turned her head, surprised to find how easy and painless it was to do so. With every breath, part of her past seemed to come back to her. The first scraps of memory were returning even before her eyes fell on the blond boy's face.

'Where are the others?' she asked. 'And where am —'

'You're safe.' The boy's smile flickered; he was trying to hide his own uncertainty. 'No one will hurt you here.'

Jolly looked round the room. The furniture was simple and sparse. Her things were lying on a chair by the open window, neatly folded. Jolly saw her belt on top, with her dagger beside it.

Too far off for her to get at them from here. She slowly sat up. If the boy came closer to her she might be able to grab him by the throat, or even better disable him with a blow from the side of her hand, the trick that Captain Bannon had taught her.

'You don't trust me. I can feel it.' He shrugged. 'I'm usually right about that kind of thing.'

Jolly hesitated. There was something about his smile . . . he didn't look as if he were planning to trick her. Maybe he was telling the truth.

'Where is this?'

'One of the outer islands. The East Bahamas, if that means anything to you.'

Then she couldn't have drifted in the water for very long, a couple of hours at the most. 'I must get back to my crew.'

'We don't have a boat on the island.'

She didn't believe him. No one lived as cut off from the

world as that. But she didn't need a boat. If necessary she'd risk running over the sea on foot. Bannon and the other pirates were her family, she must –

Suddenly she thought of something else. 'The spider! It stung me!'

The boy nodded towards a small corked bottle beside the bed. 'My mother's all-purpose weapon. Cures athlete's foot, itchy scalp, toothache and most kinds of insect venom. Well, sometimes cures them, anyway. My father swears it's good for baldness too. They brought it from the mainland when we came here. It's very precious, Ma says, so she uses it only in emergencies.'

Jolly made a face. 'Like curing baldness?'

He grinned. 'You haven't seen Dad when he finds hairs in his brush.' Now he was laughing. 'Which luckily he uses only once a week.'

'What's your name?'

'Munk. And yours?'

'Jolly.'

'Are you . . . I mean, are you some kind of a pirate?'

'Well, yes,' she said, deliberately sounding casual, although in fact she was extremely proud of it. 'I'm Captain Bannon's second in command.' Something of an exaggeration, maybe, but what would a peasant like this boy know of such things?

Munk's eyes shone. '*The* Captain Bannon? The sea-devil of the West Indies? Bannon who hoodwinked Ossorio's armada in the Gulf of Campeche a few years ago? Bannon who kidnapped the Spanish viceroy's daughter from Maracaibo?'

Jolly wrinkled her nose. 'That cow! She treated me like her lady's maid. No one does that to me. I put a sleeping powder in her food and then tattooed a message on her behind – that shut her up.'

'*Kick me quick!* That was you?' Munk's enthusiasm knew no bounds. 'The whole Caribbean was laughing at it . . . or so the traders told us, anyway.' He shook his head incredulously. 'Was it really you? You can't have been more than six or seven at the time.'

'Six. Bannon taught me to read and write when I was four.' She saw that he still wasn't quite sure whether to believe her, but what did she care? She was alive, even though she'd been stung by one of the spiders. Didn't that mean there was still hope for Bannon and the others?

'Listen,' she said urgently. 'My crew . . . the spiders stung them all. It was a trap. We must get back to them as quickly as possible with this antidote and –'

He shook his head. His smile disappeared. 'No.'

Jolly's features hardened. 'Oh yes, we must! Whether you

like it or not.' She swung her legs over the side of the bed, snatching up the little bottle with the antidote in it at the same moment.

Munk didn't move. 'There's no point. You've slept for three days. The venom kills within a day. Even if you found your friends out at sea it would be much too late.'

Jolly froze.

'I'm sorry. Really.' He put out his hand to take the bottle from her, but Jolly was faster. Her left hand shot out, seized him by the throat and flung him backwards. Gasping, he fell off his stool, and as he tried to make out what had happened she was sitting on him, her knees pressed against his upper arms.

'Stop it,' he cried in pain. 'What's the idea?'

Everything was going round and round in her head. She herself wasn't quite sure what she was doing. Bannon dead? Like all the others? Her eyes were burning, but she'd rather fall to dust and ashes herself than burst into tears in front of Munk. To be honest, she knew she'd attacked him simply to take her mind off them, for something to do. She hated being helpless. Bannon had always dinned it into her: a pirate never gives up, he always finds some way out.

'That hurts!' Munk tried to throw her off, but didn't succeed. 'What's got into you all of a sudden?'

Jolly took a deep breath and then stood up. After a moment's hesitation she put out her hand to help him up. He rejected the offer and got to his feet unaided.

'That was a mean thing to do,' he said.

'Sorry.'

'Oh yes?' He just shook his head and rubbed his upper arms. 'Anyway, what kind of a name is that – Jolly?'

'Bannon bought me in Tortuga slave market when I was little. My parents were dead, and nobody knew what I was called, so Bannon gave me that name. Up to twenty or thirty years ago all the pirates here in the Caribbean flew red flags, and the French called the flag the *Jolie Rouge*, the Pretty Red. Later on the English turned it into the Jolly Roger, and that's what the black pirate flag we use now is still called.'

'Bannon called you after a pirate flag?' Munk grinned faintly. 'Terrific. I wish something like that would happen to me.'

'You wish someone would call you Jolly?'

'Adventures on the high seas. Pirates. Sea battles. Looking for treasure. All that. Nothing ever happens on this island.'

She looked at his upper arms. 'You're going to have bruises . . . I really am sorry. Honest.'

'That's all right. Now I can tell the Ghost-Trader I was badly wounded putting a band of fierce pirates to flight.'

'What on earth is a Ghost-Trader?'

He dismissed the question. 'Tell you later. First I'm going to introduce you to my mother. Pa is on the plantation, but Ma will be outside in the vegetable patch.'

Jolly put the little bottle back on the table beside the bed. Her fingers were trembling slightly. 'You really think they're all dead?'

'If no one gave them the antidote in time,' he said in a muted voice, 'they stood no chance.'

Munk's mother was an outspoken, kind-hearted woman who had no time at all for pirates. The lobes of her ears were split, and both her ring fingers were missing. Those were the scars left by a pirate raid many years ago; she and her parents had been among the victims. Captain Tyrone, leader of the attackers, was in a hurry to collect all the jewellery he could, and when the little girl didn't take off all her rings fast enough Tyrone did it for her with his sword.

Jolly was far from happy to hear Munk tell his mother about her so openly. Pirates were unwelcome visitors to the simple island farmers in general, not just to the Spaniards who lorded it over this part of the Caribbean and tried to send all corsairs packing.

On the other hand, it was her own fault. She ought not to have told Munk anything about Bannon. Now her chances of getting off the island were probably very slim.

For Jolly was determined to set out in search of Bannon and the others as quickly as possible, never mind what Munk said. Pictures of the events on the Spanish galleon went through her mind as she followed Munk over the plantation. His mother had suggested showing her the farm, but Jolly wasn't listening to what he told her. Bannon had fallen into a malicious trap planned by someone in advance. And if she really couldn't help him now, she'd do all she could to find out who was behind it. That was the least she owed him.

Munk, walking ahead of Jolly, had stopped talking, probably noticing that she wasn't attending. In silence, they walked through the dense rainforest under tall tree ferns with water dripping from their leaves even at midday, passing wild orchids and the largest hibiscus Jolly had ever seen. It must be nearly noon, and the air here in the jungle was sultry and oppressive, quite different from the air out at sea. Jolly found breathing difficult.

Munk turned to her and took a flat wooden box out

of a leather bag fastened to his belt.

'Here,' he said. 'Maybe this will come in useful.' He opened the box and held it so that Jolly could see inside.

It contained the body of a dead spider the size of a child's hand.

'I found it in the figurehead. See the pattern on its back? I've never seen a spider like that on this island. If you find out where it comes from maybe you'll discover who set the trap for you.'

Jolly looked from the spider to Munk. 'How did you know I . . .?'

Munk shrugged. 'How did I know that was what you were thinking?' He smiled faintly. 'I told you before, I can sense that kind of thing. And, to be honest, it really wasn't hard to guess, the furious way you were marching through the undergrowth just now.'

Against her will, Jolly had to laugh. Munk was obviously glad to have taken her mind off the pirates, but he soon turned serious again. 'Anyway, it's the best clue you have.'

'Not bad for a start,' said Jolly. 'Thanks.' She put her hand out for the box, but he closed the lid and put it back in his bag. Jolly frowned.

'Let me go with you,' he said. 'Or I'll die of boredom here some day.'

'It's not that simple.' She suppressed her annoyance and tried to be diplomatic. Of course she'd never take him with her. She was a pirate and he was only a farmer's boy. She could walk on the water and he didn't even have a boat.

'I want to go to sea too,' he insisted. 'I want to see pirates and get to know other islands. I'll never be a tobacco farmer like my father. I'd rather run away.' He had said it without thinking, and now gave a barely perceptible start. 'Sail away, I mean.'

Jolly sighed. 'I'll see what can be done.' She had only to find the right moment to get the spider away from him. She didn't want another fight, no need for that. This evening she'd creep into his room and steal the box.

Munk fastened the bag to his belt again. 'Come on, I'll show you the fields.'

She wasn't interested in tobacco-growing, but all the same she followed him through a patch of jungle. A clearing lay in the sunlight beyond its tangled undergrowth.

'Didn't you say you lived alone on the island, you and your parents?'

'So?'

'Well, your father can't possibly cultivate these fields without help.'

'No, he doesn't.'

'So there *are* other workers here?'

Munk gave her a broad grin. 'Oh, well,' he said, laughing. 'All those ghosts must be good for something, right?'

SHELL MAGIC

At first the sun dazzled her, and she could make out only the outlines of the nearest tobacco plants with a confused jumble of green and brown behind them, as if a painter had let the colours on his palette run into each other.

Then she saw something like wisps of mist drifting between the rows of plants. Wisps of mist which, on closer inspection, assumed human form.

Wisps of mist with *faces*.

'Good heavens!' Jolly stood there rooted to the spot. 'Are they . . . are they real?' What a stupid question! But it sprang to her lips of its own accord.

'Of course.'

She cautiously approached the front row of plants. A ghost was hurrying along it, picking the sticky, hairy leaves from bottom to top of each plant and throwing them into a cart that it was pulling along. It took no notice of the two visitors, as if it didn't even see them.

'Can you touch them?'

'You can try.'

She gave Munk an enquiring glance, then hesitantly put out one finger towards the ghost's misty body. The white mist quickly retreated from her fingertip, shrinking from contact. Jolly hastily withdrew her hand.

'I've never seen anything like it before.'

Munk looked bored. 'Oh, we have any number of them. They're expensive to buy, but they don't eat and they don't sleep and they don't waste time while they're working. They cost more than slaves, Pa says, but he doesn't want anything to do with slaves anyway. And in the long run the ghosts pay off.'

Real ghosts! Jolly didn't even try to hide her amazement.

'The Ghost-Trader says they're very popular on some of the islands. You ought to have seen them before if you've really been around as much as you say.'

She spun round. 'I *have* been around as much as I say. But this . . .' She fell silent, shaking her head.

The ghost went on with its work undisturbed. Jolly examined its face. She could clearly make out eyes, nose and mouth, yet the features had no individuality at all. It was as if someone had made a human being out of mist without giving him a trace of personality.

'Will we all be like them some day?' she asked uncertainly. 'I mean, will we all of us look so much the same?'

Munk shrugged. 'No idea. I've never been particularly interested in them. If you have them around the place every day . . . well, you know how it is. I just grew up with them.'

'How many do you have?'

'About fifty, I think. Now and then one of them disappears, just dissolves into thin air. Then Pa buys a couple of new ones, and they last for quite a time.' He made a face, showing his lack of interest. 'They're really nothing to get excited about. Honest.'

Jolly nervously threw her black hair back over her shoulders. She'd seen plantations worked by slaves, Africans, even Chinese – but ghosts?

Munk might think sailing the high seas and clambering around in a ship's rigging was a great adventure; she herself found this island entirely new and incomprehensible. Not that she'd have wanted to change places with him – heaven forbid! – but nothing like what she saw here had ever come her way before.

One thing, however, was certain: if this mysterious trader claimed that ghosts were working as labourers on many of the Caribbean islands, that was a downright lie.

'Munk!' A voice brought her back from her thoughts. 'Ah, and our young guest too!'

A man came striding down a path between the rows of tobacco plants towards her – walking straight through the ghost as he approached. The mute, misty creature frayed and fell apart for a split second, then came together again and continued its work unmoved.

'Pa, this is Jolly.'

The man offered her a large, horny paw, and shook her hand so hard that her shoulder hurt afterwards. Perhaps she was weaker than she'd thought after lying unconscious so long.

'Good morning, sir,' she said, looking him up and down. He had fair hair like his son's, falling to his broad shoulders. His bare torso was tanned by the sun and so muscular that he would have made a good seaman. The faint suggestion of a small paunch showed that the tobacco trade couldn't be doing too badly, even on such a remote island as this. He was very tall, and had a slight accent that betrayed Scottish origins.

'My Mary's been looking after you well, I'm sure. She knows about herbs and suchlike. Munk here just couldn't wait for you to open your eyes at last. So where do you come from, then?'

She was on the point of saying, 'Haiti', when she remembered that his wife already knew the truth. 'From a ship. The *Maid Maddy*.'

His expression darkened. 'Bannon's ship?'

Jolly cast Munk an uncertain glance, but he himself was looking at his father in surprise. 'Do you know it?' he asked.

The farmer nodded. 'Who hasn't heard of the *Maddy*? Yes, I thought you belonged with pirates, girl. My wife showed me the tattoo on your back.'

Munk's jaw dropped. 'You have a *tattoo*?'

Jolly felt uneasy, but she quickly recovered herself. 'It's not finished. One of the crew began it for me just before we saw the Spanish ship . . . the ship with the spiders on it.'

She had told Munk what had happened, but his father's brow wrinkled. 'You must tell me all about it at supper,' he said. 'I'm going back to work now. Munk, you can take the afternoon off.' He was about to leave them, but then turned back once more. 'And don't go putting silly ideas in my son's head, girl, will you? That lad's daydreaming the whole time as it is.'

'Don't worry, sir.'

When his father had gone, Munk grinned at her. 'So what silly ideas shall we begin with, then?' he said.

*

'My parents were map-makers,' Munk said as he led Jolly down to the bay where he had pulled her out of the water. 'They explored the routes between the islands and the reefs for one of the big trading companies. My father steered the boat and my mother drew the maps and sea-charts. She can draw really well, you know. She tried to teach me how, but I can never get it right. Though I think I can draw a bird . . . or a pirate ship.' He was obviously pleased to have made Jolly smile in spite of the loss she had suffered. 'Well, anyway, my parents had to tell the company all they found out about the routes between the reefs and sandbanks. That's what they were paid for. It usually took them some time to explore a route, but the company always wanted to be kept up to date. My father had warned their traders against sailing any route that hadn't been fully sounded out. One of them ignored his advice and set off along a particularly dangerous one before my mother had checked the sea-chart again to make sure all the details were accurate. He ran aground and his whole convoy of ships sank. He himself and many of the seamen drowned.'

'And he blamed your parents?'

There was a bitter expression in Munk's eyes. 'The trader's brother was Scarab, pirate emperor of the Caribbean. He put a price on my parents' heads. After that, all the pirates were after them and they went into hiding on this island. Our only contact with the outside world is a handful of traders they've known and trusted forever.'

'But why all the caution?' enquired Jolly. 'Scarab's been dead for years. Kendrick is pirate emperor on New Providence today. There's a rumour that he did away with Scarab to seize power for himself. Kendrick has reversed or ignored many of Scarab's decrees. I can't imagine why he or anyone else would still be after your parents now.'

Munk seemed to be thinking this over. But then, downcast, he shook his head. 'The fact is, I don't believe my parents are really afraid of Scarab or any other pirates. They like it here. They like the isolation, and the peace and quiet, and –'

'And everything that gets on your nerves.'

He smiled shyly. 'That's right.'

'And I bet your father wouldn't like you to go to sea. Even though he was at sea himself for years. Is that so?'

Munk nodded. 'He says he's seen too many ships sink and too many good men drown. These days he hates the sea. He can't understand why I want to go to sea myself.' He was looking really unhappy now. 'And I don't even get a chance to find out whether maybe I like the sea as little as he does.'

For the first time, Jolly felt sympathy. She loved the sea more than anything herself, and not just because she was a polliwiggle. She knew what Munk was missing if he stayed on this island, and she guessed how he must feel.

For a while they walked on side by side in silence, until they saw the white sand of the beach shining through the thick plants. Then Jolly thought of something. 'Why did you tell me all that? About your parents, and how they're scared of pirates? I'm a pirate myself.'

Munk smiled shyly, and then avoided her gaze. 'Because I trust you.' With that he ran off down the slope to the beach, leaving her behind. 'Come on!'

Jolly watched him in some surprise for a moment, then set off. Light-footed, she ran through the soft sand. When she saw the sea ahead all her strength suddenly returned to her. The sight of it overwhelmed her more than ever today: the yellow-green crescent of the bay, then the jagged chain of the reef, and beyond that the endless blue of the ocean. Gulls screamed in the air, and a warm wind carried the smell of the sea to her. It had an aromatic, salty flavour.

Munk didn't stop until they reached the empty figurehead that had been lying where he left it three days ago, in the damp sand just clear of the breaking waves. Jolly examined the wooden Neptune, shuddering when she saw the marks of the shark's teeth. At that moment her stomach contracted, and she felt ill.

'What's the matter?' asked Munk, concerned for her.

The pictures came back: the faces of Bannon and the others, scenes aboard the *Maid Maddy*, adventures, danger, but also the sense of being at home among the pirates. The laughter of her friends, the trouble most of them had taken to make a real pirate of the thin little girl whom Bannon treated like a daughter. And then of course the success she had brought them because she was a polliwiggle, their praise, their cheers, their encouragement.

And now she supposed all that was over. She had nothing left but memories that would fade more and more as time went on.

'No,' she whispered to herself, but Munk heard her.

'They're dead, Jolly. They must be.'

'But you said yourself, if someone had the antidote –'

'No one here does.'

'Your mother did.'

Munk took a deep breath. 'It comes from the mainland. That's over a thousand miles away. And you'd need twenty or thirty bottles of it to save a whole crew. We have only two.'

Jolly wasn't giving up. 'All the same, someone or other could have a lot more, right?'

'If so, why would he . . .' (he almost said *waste it*) '. . . why would he use it to save a pirate crew? And pirates he'd probably just lured into a trap himself? People like you aren't exactly popular on the islands.'

She had thought of that herself. Even so, not everything could be explained that way.

'If your parents had been on board,' she said, 'you wouldn't just give them up for lost, would you?'

Munk held her gaze for a couple of seconds, then shrugged. 'No.'

Jolly sat down in the sand beside the figurehead and stroked it for the last time, passing her fingertips over the wood. It was the only memento she had of the *Maid Maddy* and her friends. Then she pulled herself together and stood up, rather undecidedly.

'I'll show you something,' said Munk, still trying to cheer her up. 'What do you know about shell magic?'

'Only that some say it exists and others say it doesn't.' Her thoughts were still in the past; she hardly heard what he was saying, or even what she herself replied.

Munk was not to be deterred. 'Then get ready for a big surprise.'

She looked at him. 'Magic?' she asked, rather taken aback. The word brought her back from the misty world of her dreams.

'Magic,' he confirmed, beaming.

Munk emptied the contents of his leather bag out on the sand. Besides the box with the spider in it, it contained only shells, wrapped and packed away in leaves and straw: shells of all colours, shapes and sizes. Many were plain, the sort you can pick up on any beach, but there were others shimmering in hues and delicate colours such as Jolly had never seen before.

'Are they all from this island?' she asked, amazed.

Munk shook his head. 'Only a few, the plain ones. I was given the others by traders, specially the –'

'The Ghost-Trader,' she interrupted him.

'Yes.'

'It's about time you told me about him.'

'You'll meet him soon.'

The shells shone as if they had been polished. Jolly was more curious than she liked to admit. Shell magic was something she knew about from stories, like star dollars falling from the sky, or the giant squid that live in the ocean deeps. But she had never met anyone who had actually seen a shell magician.

Munk began arranging some of the shells in a circle in the sand. She didn't know why he reached for one particular shell and left others aside, and it was even more of a puzzle to work out why he kept moving his lips all the time, as if he were in silent conversation with the shells. She half expected some of them, empty as they were, to snap themselves open and shut in reply. But the shells just lay there, sorted apparently at random and yet in some secret, mysterious order.

'There,' he said after a while, when he had laid out a circle of twelve shells. 'Now, watch this.'

There was no need to tell her to watch. She was staring at him as if he'd lost his mind anyway.

'Not me,' he said. 'The shells.'

'Right.'

'What do you see?'

'Shells. Shells in a circle.'

'What else?'

'A silly idiot all puffed up with self-importance.'

He grinned again. 'Wait and see. Now – look!'

He swiftly moved the palm of his right hand through the air above the shells, closing his eyes and murmuring soundlessly again.

The sand in the middle of the circle formed a hollow. She

saw it clearly, although Munk's hand never touched the ground. A round depression appeared out of nowhere, a little larger than Jolly's hand and as deep as a wine-jug.

Something flashed in the middle of the hollow. At first she thought a piece of metal was buried in the sand there, perhaps a coin. But then she saw that the light hovering over the sand radiated from something that hadn't been there a split second before.

A pearl the size of a thumbnail was hovering in the centre of the hollow.

'You made a pearl appear?' She wrinkled her nose. 'I've seen better conjuring tricks than that.'

'We're not through yet.' His voice sounded tense, and his eyes were still closed, as they had been all along. 'What shall I do now?'

'Well, if *you* don't know . . .'

'Ask me to do something. Something magic.'

'I can't think of any ideas.'

He sighed. There were beads of sweat on his forehead. 'How about raising a gust of wind?'

Lifting her eyebrows in surprise, she nodded. 'All right, a gust of wind.'

Munk whispered something – and at the same moment a gust that would have done credit to any rising storm seized

Jolly. With a gasp, she felt herself lose her footing, was blown a couple of steps backwards and sat down suddenly on the sand.

A moment later all was perfectly calm and windless again.

Astonished, she stared at her footprints in the sand, then at the place where she was sitting now. 'Did *you* do that?'

Munk did not reply. He stretched his right hand out again, made the circular movement once more, and then pointed his forefinger at one of the shells. The floating pearl began to move and shot rapidly into the open shell, which closed over it with a sound like the snapping of bony jaws.

Munk opened his eyes, blinked, looked round for Jolly and found her still sitting in the sand. 'Oh,' he said, squatting down beside her. 'I didn't mean that to blow you over.'

'Are you seriously saying you did it?'

'Not me. The shell magic. It's only a matter of controlling and guiding them. There's nothing at all magic about me personally, but these . . .' He indicated the circle of shells with an almost affectionate gesture. '*They're* magic. Do you understand?'

'No, I don't.' Jolly got up, brushing sand off the seat of her trousers.

'The difficult part isn't setting the magic free,' he said,

'but catching it afterwards. At first I botched it a couple of times and couldn't shut the magic up again. It was left on the loose, and it did all kinds of disastrous things. Once the farmhouse roof went up in flames. I was only healing a goat's broken leg – but it was rather strong magic, I don't know if I'll ever get that one right. Another time when I didn't manage to get the pearl back inside the shell the leaves of all the palm trees round the farm had turned red next morning.' He packed the shells carefully back in their bag. Each one of them was individually wrapped and placed in protective padding. 'But since I realised that you can make anything you've conjured up go away again there've been no more problems.'

'So where does the pearl come from?'

'It's only a kind of embodiment of the real magic. The magic flows out of the shells when I want it to and makes the pearl in the middle of them. That means I can use their strength for the magic. Once the magic is over I have to move the pearl back into one of the shells, and that's it. When I open the shell next time the pearl's gone – it's turned back into invisible magic and I can conjure it up again. The bigger the pearl, the more magic there is available. It's quite simple really, if you have a talent for it.'

'Sure you're not having me on?'

'Word of honour.'

She grinned appreciatively. 'Not bad.'

Munk obviously felt flattered. 'Well, it's only a kind of game. Apart from the goat I cured, and a few other little things, nothing much useful has ever come of it. I once tried doubling the harvest, but that was a disaster. I'm not strong enough for that kind of thing.'

'So what happened?'

'Half the tobacco plants died. After that my father said I wasn't to work the shell magic.'

Jolly smiled. 'But you just did, all the same.'

'Only to cheer you up.'

She offered her hand to help him to his feet. This time he took it. 'That was nice of you,' she said.

Munk went red. 'You're not so much of a gun-woman as my father said.'

'A gun-woman? He said that?'

Munk nodded. 'He meant girls who go around with pirates.'

She gently removed her hand from his when she felt that he wasn't about to let go of it himself. 'Your father may not know everything. And as a matter of fact, he knows nothing at all about me.'

'Nor do I.'

She just nodded, avoided his eyes, and set off on the way back to the farm. Only some time later did she break the silence. 'I'll tell you something about me, though,' she said, making a face and grinning. 'I'm dying of hunger.'

THE EARTHQUAKE

Jolly abandoned any idea of trying to steal the box with the dead spider from Munk. By the time any trading vessel on which she could leave the island put in, there'd be no point in having the spider's corpse any more. In addition, she didn't want to provoke her hosts, particularly Munk. He was so different from the pirate boys she knew. He didn't strut and brag like them. He even seemed rather embarrassed to admit to his knowledge of shell magic. He was very kind and friendly, and he made sure she noticed it.

On the third day after she had regained consciousness, he took her through the banana plantation up to the cliff above the bay and showed her the old cannon. The rusty gun stood there alone, waiting for enemies who would never come. Jolly agreed with Munk that the island had probably once been a pirate base, now forgotten by everyone. Privately, she wondered whether Munk's father might be keeping something secret. Had he really been just the captain of a small vessel fitted out for map-making? Or were there other reasons why the former pirate emperor Scarab had been hunting for him?

Munk admitted that he had often dreamed of firing the cannon. However, he had no idea how to set about it. He was afraid he would blow himself up, so he had abandoned the idea. And the roar of the cannon would not be the only sound of fury to be heard on the island if his parents got wind of it – which could hardly be avoided if the cannon fired a shot.

Jolly thought it over, and then decided that she really had nothing to lose. They would simply say she had found the cannon in the undergrowth and wanted to show Munk how to fire it. She'd take all the blame herself. At the worst, Munk's father could send her away on the next ship to call in at the island, but that was what she wanted anyway.

'Do you have any gunpowder on the farm?'

'A small barrel full of it,' said Munk.

She told him how much she needed. While he went to fetch it she cleaned the barrel of the gun, wound leaves around a branch until she could use it as a ramrod, and searching the bushes under the cannon found an old copper ladle that must have been left behind by the old gunners.

When Munk came back, breathless with excitement and red in the face, she used the ladle to tip gunpowder into the breech of the gun until its weight was about a third that of a cannonball. Then she stuffed in leaves as a substitute for the rope yarn, followed by one of the old iron balls that they found stacked in a rusty pyramid beside the cannon. Finally Jolly filled the touch-hole with gunpowder and asked Munk to help her get the cannon in place, moving it carefully so that its crumbling base didn't disintegrate. She aimed it straight across the water to the tongue of land on the other side of the bay. Three huge palms grew from a thicket of ferns on its highest point, and Jolly told Munk she wanted to hit the middle tree.

She set fire to a branch with tinder and flint, and told Munk to take two steps back. Using the burning tip of the branch, she lit the gunpowder. Then they both covered their ears with their hands.

The cannon shot crashed out, seeming to tear the blue sky apart for a split second. At that moment the world consisted of nothing but smoke and splintered wood. The thunderous echo of the gun rolled across the bay and the entire island. The mounting of the cannon had burst when it fired the shot, and the base was shattered. The barrel of the gun itself hung askew in the ruins of the base, and a moment later broke away and rolled down the slope, crushing several shrubs and bushes before a mahogany trunk stopped it in its course. The impact shook a swarm of red insects out of the top of the tree.

'Wow!' said Munk, but his alarm had already given way to a broad, delighted grin. 'That was great!'

Jolly coughed, and waved the smoke away with her hand. When it dispersed they saw that there were only two palm trees still standing on the other side of the bay; the tree on the left had snapped like a blade of straw.

'You did it!' said Munk enthusiastically.

Jolly frowned. 'I really wanted to hit the one in the middle.'

'What does that matter? At this distance it makes no difference!'

'There's a difference between hitting the mainmast or the foresail of a sailing ship, though.'

But Munk wasn't listening. He was prancing around in delight. 'Crazy! A real cannon shot! Wait till I tell the Ghost-Trader.'

Jolly went up to the ruins of the gun, unimpressed. 'It could have gone wrong. If we'd been standing on the wrong side of the gun –'

'But we weren't!' Munk joined her and rubbed the back of his neck. 'Hm, do you think we could put it back together and try the whole thing again?'

'Most definitely not!'

At the same moment a third voice spoke behind them.

'That was a stupid thing to do,' said Munk's father. 'Just how stupid you have no idea.'

They were sitting under the palm thatch of the farmhouse veranda. Night was rapidly falling, but no stars showed yet in the dark blue sky. Only the moon had risen, and was casting its silver light on the tops of the jungle trees. The noises of the forest could be heard behind the jagged top of the palisade that surrounded the plain wooden house and its barn. This was the hour when some of the jungle creatures went to sleep and others woke to hunt by night. A couple of excited monkeys were chasing each other through the treetops, scaring up a flock of white butterflies with wings as big as Jolly's hands. A heady aroma rose from the rainforest, the warm air was humid, and every few moments came the sound of Jolly, Munk or one of the two adults hitting out at a mosquito.

'Perhaps we should have told you everything before now,' said Munk's father. 'But your mother didn't want to.'

'Don't let yourself off too easily,' said his wife. 'We both thought the same.'

The farmer sipped from his beaker of rum, then shrugged his shoulders. 'It began with the fall of Port Royal in 1692, fourteen years ago. Port Royal was once the worst pirates' lair on Jamaica – or no, in the whole Caribbean. But at the time of the disaster, that was already in the past; the pirates had gone in search of safer havens, Tortuga and later New Providence. In '92 Port Royal was a run-down city, but still a large one, and when the great earthquake struck over two thousand people died. The northern part of town with most of the docks slipped into the sea, and a gigantic tidal wave rolled over the rest of it. It was one of the worst catastrophes this part of the world has ever seen, at least since we Europeans have lived here.'

He interrupted his story to light a pipe. Jolly and Munk looked at each other uncertainly. The stern lecture they'd expected had not been delivered. Instead, Munk's father had sent them back to the farm and spent all afternoon standing on the highest point of the island himself, watching the sea. Only when he was sure that the roar of the cannon had brought no ships that way did he return to the house and join them on the veranda. He wasn't threatening or even scolding them, but he made it very clear that they had been luckier than they deserved.

After puffing a few clouds of smoke from his pipe, he went on with his tale. 'At that time everyone feared more tremors, and there was great relief when none came. No one could guess that the earthquake had released something else, something that might in the long run prove even worse than the death of all those people.' Gloomily, he rubbed his stubbly chin. 'I'm a simple man, I don't deny it. I've had all this explained to me by cleverer heads than mine.'

His wife put her hand on his and gave him a loving glance. Jolly realised for the first time how fond they were of each other.

'Well, anyway, the fact is that magic was released at that time in some way – the power of enchantment, hocus-pocus, call it what you like. And the result of that magic was the birth of what people were soon calling the polliwiggles.'

A sudden slap in the face couldn't have come as more of a surprise to Jolly. What did he know about polliwiggles? She was the last of them, Bannon had said. She hadn't set foot on the water since coming to the island, she hadn't even mentioned her gift to Munk.

Munk's mother looked at her and smiled. 'We know about it, child. You lay there delirious for two days, talking to yourself. It wasn't difficult to put two and two together. You kept saying you were running over the water, and talking about two ships . . . and the spiders.'

'And there had been rumours that Bannon had a polliwiggle on board his ship,' said her husband. 'We really knew what you were already, but when you told us about Bannon and the *Maid Maddy* it was all clear.'

Jolly looked enquiringly at Munk. He only nodded. Even he knew about it, and hadn't said a word these last few days. But now he leaned towards her. 'I'm one too, Jolly. I'm a polliwiggle like you.' An uncertain smile stole over his face. 'And until a few days ago I thought I was the last of them in the whole world.'

Jolly swallowed before her voice came back to her. 'That's what I thought as well.'

'Let me go on,' said Munk's father. 'The polliwiggles are children who were born immediately after the great earthquake in Port Royal. The magic that rose from the cracks in the earth's surface then . . . well, it somehow got into you children, into newborn babies. Only babies who were very close to its source. No polliwiggles were born on Haiti or Cuba or here in the Bahamas. Only on Jamaica, and only in Port Royal.

'It was two or three more years before it became known

that there were children who could walk on the water, and yet another few years before anyone was sure that the cause, for some reason or other, was the earthquake. The Spanish had the affair investigated. The English, the Dutch, every nation got its own groups of missionaries and military men and who knows what else to look into the whole thing.' His mouth twisted in derision. 'The first polliwiggles died in the course of the experiments they made, but that wasn't all. Those slave-drivers, curses on every one of them! Soon there were men hunting down all the polliwiggles, selling them to the highest bidder or using them for their own purposes. Many of the children were taken to safety, at least for a while, by their parents, so they were scattered all over the islands and the entire Caribbean Sea. There must have been about twenty or thirty of them in all, no more. After five or six years fewer than half of them were still alive. And today – well, I'm afraid you two are the very last.'

'No one's ever tried to harm me,' said Jolly doubtfully.

'You were under Bannon's protection. Few would have been bold enough to take on the sea-devil of the West Indies. Until a few days ago, anyway.'

'You mean . . .?' Jolly shook her head, unable to take it in.

Munk's father blew a smoke ring which immediately

dispersed in the air. 'I don't think that trap was for Bannon or his crew, Jolly – I think it was for you. Someone is hunting the last polliwiggles again, and presumably that someone is quite close.'

'But I'm . . . I mean, I'm only fourteen years old. I'm not *important*.'

'Perhaps you are. Just like Munk.'

The boy's mother spoke again. There was fear in her voice now. 'We were always afraid this might happen some time. No one can hide from the whole world forever.'

'So that's why you came to live here? To protect Munk?'

'That was one of the reasons, yes. It's true that Scarab put a price on my head,' said Munk's father. 'But the main reason for us to come here was Munk.' He looked his son straight in the eye, and now there was such concern in his glance that Jolly felt her throat tighten. 'No one was to know that Munk's a polliwiggle. That was what mattered most.'

Jolly cleared her throat, to get rid of the lump in it. 'You think I could lead those men here, don't you? You think they'll keep looking for me because I wasn't on board the ship, and they'll follow me to the island.'

'There's a danger of it. And after this silly business with the cannon today –'

'I'm sorry. I didn't know –'

'Of course not,' said Munk's mother. 'We ought to have talked to both of you before now. Once we realised who we were dealing with.'

'The cannon,' said Munk, 'it was my idea, not Jolly's. I've known it was up there for ages, and I always wanted . . . I wanted . . .'

'You wanted to play pirates,' said his father, but without a smile. 'What boy doesn't?'

Guiltily, Munk lowered his gaze.

His mother looked from him to Jolly. 'Perhaps we've been lucky. Perhaps the whole thing really was the Spaniards setting a trap for Bannon.'

'It was a Spanish ship,' said Jolly, and then she remembered the steersman's words. 'But the men weren't real sailors. They were prisoners, and someone had made them go on board and wait for us with their sails reefed in.'

'Which means someone knew for sure that the *Maid Maddy* would sail that way,' said Munk's father thoughtfully.

'We were on our way to New Providence.'

'That's about another two hundred miles from here. Why were you skirting the Bahamas so far to the east?'

'Bannon wanted to be extra sure. He'd had news of Kendrick the pirate emperor. It seems the Spanish are about to attack New Providence, and Bannon was planning to fight at Kendrick's side. He'd do all he could to avoid the Spanish armada, that's why we took the course we did.'

The farmer thought. 'Someone must have given you away. Did the whole crew know your route?'

'As far as I know, only Bannon, Cristobal the steersman and maybe one or two others. But I'm not sure.'

He sighed. 'I'm afraid all this is leading us nowhere. But one thing is certain: if someone really has set a crafty trap like this to get hold of you, he won't be happy with your disappearance. He knows you're a polliwiggle, and perhaps he thinks you've tried reaching one of the nearest islands on foot. In that case he'll turn up here sooner or later.'

Munk's mother propped her chin between the palms of her hands. 'We must leave. Find a new refuge somewhere else.'

Munk stared at her. 'Leave the farm? But you can't –'

'I'd a thousand times sooner lose the farm than you,' said his father.

Jolly slumped even further. 'I'm so sorry about all this. If I'd known – I mean, then I'd have . . .'

'You'd have let them capture you? Nonsense. How were you to guess you'd come to land here, of all places?' The farmer drew on his pipe, as if it helped him to think. 'Perhaps this is a sign from Fate. Maybe God wanted to show us we've been careless.'

'I thought you didn't believe in God,' said Munk, 'and certainly not in Fate.'

His father grunted, and laughed. 'You're right, my boy. We have to rely on ourselves. What your mother said is true: we must leave the island.'

Jolly turned to Munk. 'But you said you didn't have a boat.'

'We don't.'

'We can board one of the trading ships,' said Munk's mother. 'The next ought to be putting in here in about a week's time.'

'The Ghost-Trader's coming the day after tomorrow!' exclaimed Munk.

'How do we know who *he* may be in league with?' said his father grimly. 'He gives me the creeps, and I don't trust him an inch. Maybe he'd sell us off to the first pirate he met.'

'He's always been friendly to me.'

The farmer took his pipe out of his mouth and made a gesture clearly indicating that he would hear no objections to his plan. 'We'll leave next week with the Dutchman. He's always earned good money from us – we can trust him. Till then we must keep our eyes open and watch the sea.' He knocked his pipe out noisily. 'Time you two both went to sleep. Your mother and I have a few more things to discuss.'

Jolly and Munk obediently rose and went into the house, looking unsure of themselves.

Outside Jolly's room, Munk stopped. 'What my father said – about no one knowing I'm a polliwiggle – it wasn't quite true. Someone does know.'

She felt her heart miss a beat. 'Let me guess.'

He nodded guiltily. 'Yes . . . *he* does.'

THE GHOST-TRADER

The mysterious visitor arrived on the island two days later, as Munk had said he would. He was sailing alone in a tiny boat that didn't look as if it could cover the long distances between the islands. Jolly had only to glance at him to know what Munk's father meant: she would as soon have trusted a Tortuga gutter rat as this dark figure who came across the sea at dawn in his small sailing dinghy before the first ray of the sun fell on the land.

The Ghost-Trader wore a voluminous hooded cloak of coarse, dark fabric which fell to the ground, hiding his feet. In spite of the heat of the Caribbean once day dawned, his hood was up. Jolly could make out gaunt features and skin weathered by sun and wind below it. A black bandage ran over his forehead and cheek at a slant, covering his blind left eye. He had grey stubble on his chin and astonishingly white, almost shining teeth which didn't fit the rest of his shabby appearance.

Strangest of all, however, were the two coal-black parrots sitting on his shoulders. One had yellow eyes, the other's eyes were fiery red.

'Hugh and Moe,' whispered Munk, as he and Jolly went to meet the Ghost-Trader. 'He always has them with him. He talks to them.'

'Can they talk back?'

'He says so.'

Only now did the mysterious man come within earshot, but Jolly felt as if he had been listening to them all this time, for a knowing smile played around his thin, colourless lips.

'Good morning, Munk,' he said, sketching a bow which his parrots copied – a strange sight. 'Greetings to you and all who live on this island.' His sound eye, a bright sky-blue, was looking at Jolly. 'I see you have a visitor.'

'This is Jolly. She was shipwrecked.'

'Jolly. Well, well.' The Ghost-Trader nodded to her too. 'An unusual name for a girl. I thought it was the name pirates gave their flags.'

She could have denied that she had anything to do with pirates, but she was too proud for that. It just struck her as odd that he immediately connected her with them.

'And do you have a name?' she asked boldly.

The Ghost-Trader smiled. 'I've had various names.' But he told her none of them, merely turned back to Munk. 'I hope your family is well. Isn't your father here?'

'He went up the mountain this morning while it was still dark. But he must have seen you come ashore. I expect he'll be here soon.'

The Trader brought something out from under his fastened cloak which was another puzzle to Jolly: a silver metal circlet thinner than her little finger, though it had the diameter of a large plate. He let it dangle from his right hand as he walked over the beach with them and then through the jungle to the farm.

'How's the magic going?' he asked Munk halfway there. 'Made any progress?'

Munk sighed. 'Nothing worth mentioning.'

'It will come. Patience is the touchstone of all magic.'

Jolly didn't trouble to conceal her suspicion. 'You know shell magic too?'

'I can't work it myself, if that's what you mean, but yes, I know a few things about it.'

'He showed me how it's done,' said Munk proudly.

'No, that's not right,' the Trader contradicted him. 'I only told you what it does – I can't show you anything. I lack your talent.' He sounded perfectly serious, and said this without a trace of irony.

Munk's mother was waiting for them on the veranda. She had put several pottery beakers, a bottle of rum and a jug of water on the table, as well as a wooden board with bread and goat cheese. She greeted the Ghost-Trader with reserve, but in a not unfriendly manner. The two of them exchanged a few polite trivialities: what had his crossing been like, how was business, was there any news from the outside world?

'There are more and more signs that the Spanish are about to attack New Providence,' said the Ghost-Trader. 'The viceroy has sent out an armada, although no one's seen it yet. At least, no one I've talked to.'

Munk's father came down from the mountain, and soon they were all sitting at the table breakfasting together. In spite of his austere appearance, the Ghost-Trader ate twice as much as anyone else. Now and then he broke off a piece of bread or cheese and gave it to his parrots. Jolly's instinct told her that Hugh and Moe were no ordinary birds, just as the Ghost-Trader was certainly no ordinary man. Why did Munk trust him so much that he'd told him his greatest secret?

As if the Ghost-Trader guessed what was going through her mind, he suddenly put his hand under his cloak and brought out three polished shells, each more unusual than the last. 'I almost forgot these,' he said, with a twinkle in his one eye, and handed them to Munk. The boy beamed, thanked him, and put them carefully away in the bag at his belt. His father watched this with obvious displeasure, but said nothing.

During the rest of the meal they listened to the Ghost-Trader's stories, and one thing at least Jolly had to grant him: he could tell better tales than anyone she had ever heard. He was able to make a heroic saga out of the most ordinary event, yet you never felt that he was bending the truth, or inventing something to embellish his tale.

'You're as good a storyteller as ever,' said Munk's mother after a while. She had visibly thawed during the conversation, unlike her husband, who still preserved a cool distance.

The Ghost-Trader shrugged his shoulders. 'Long experience. And perhaps a disposition for it, who knows?'

Soon after that the men started talking business, which was confined on the whole to Munk's father saying that he wasn't interested in buying any more ghosts just now. He didn't add that they would soon be leaving the island.

'But I have some really outstanding new specimens,' said the Ghost-Trader, and he began singing the praises of his invisible wares. 'Princesses from the Far East, ghosts of

80

heroes from the frozen North, wise men from every point of the compass. Not forgetting good, capable workers from the –'

'To be sure, to be sure,' the farmer interrupted him. 'I believe you, but I still have plenty. We've lost only one since your last visit. What's more – as I tell you every time, my friend – I don't believe a word you say. I may be just a simple tobacco farmer –' and as he said this, Jolly felt as if his gaze was bent very forcefully on the trader's one eye – 'but I'm not stupid. Ghosts of princesses and heroes don't seem to be any different from all the rest, so those you offer might just as well be the souls of poor shipwrecked sailors.'

'Even princesses sometimes sink with ships,' said the Ghost-Trader, glancing sideways at Jolly in a way she found hard to interpret. 'It's been known.'

Munk's father dismissed the idea. 'You've always dealt honestly with me, but as for all your talk . . . I've heard of a ghost rebellion on Grand Caicos in which whole plantations were laid waste, for instance. What do you have to say about that?'

The Ghost-Trader smiled within the shadow of his hood. One of the two parrots, red-eyed Moe, uttered a shrill screech. 'Accidents happen, I'm afraid. And in that case, I assure you, it was entirely the foolish farmer's fault. He let a priest persuade him to have his ghosts blessed. Believe it or not, the idiot sprinkled them with holy water, and that's no way to treat a ghost. No wonder they went berserk.'

'However that may be, we don't need any more ghosts. Next time, maybe.' As if to send the Ghost-Trader quickly on his way, he added, 'Yes, I think next time I may be able to take two or three ghosts off your hands.'

The Trader nodded. 'A pity, but that's how business goes.' He turned to Munk. 'Tell me, do all the ghosts obey you now? Have any of them given you trouble?'

'No problems. It was all just like you said.' He glanced proudly at Jolly. 'When he was last here he told the ghosts to obey me too in future, not just my father.'

'At my request,' said his father. 'Out here you have to be prepared for anything. I could fall sick, or have an accident. Munk's old enough to run the farm alone if need be.'

The Ghost-Trader drank some water, and then rose. 'I won't keep you from your work any longer.'

'Aren't you staying the night as usual?' asked Munk's mother, surprised.

The Trader shook his head. 'I have to sail on as fast as possible. If the Spaniards really attack the pirates in New Providence I'd like to get as much business as possible done first. Who knows if the plantations will

82

find enough takers for what they grow afterwards?'

'Not everyone deals with the pirates,' said Munk's father, disapprovingly.

'I know, I know. You're an honest man.' The Ghost-Trader hid the mysterious silver circlet under his garments, and bowed to the two adults. Then he asked Munk, 'Will you and your friend here go down to my boat with me?'

'Of course.'

He and Jolly joined the Trader as he left the veranda, and they turned into the jungle track leading down to the beach.

'Safe journey!' the farmer called after them. 'And watch the weather. It looked as if a storm might come up just now. There were clouds on the horizon, and it's a long time since we had a cyclone out here.'

'Thank you, I'll take care,' replied the Trader.

They left the farmhouse with its roof of palm thatch and palisade fence behind the bushes and trees. Jolly, Munk and the Trader said nothing until they reached the beach. The little dinghy was bobbing up and down in the low water. A tarpaulin stretched taut over the deck offered the only shelter; there wasn't even a cabin. The slender mast would never stand up to a storm.

Jolly found all this more than strange. But most mysterious of all was the Ghost-Trader himself. Before he hitched up his robe and waded through the gentle surf to the boat, he shook hands with both young people.

'And take care, especially for the next few days.' Seeing Jolly's raised eyebrows, he added with a smile, 'The Spaniards will carry out their threat, and probably soon. You're a long way from New Providence, but who knows, perhaps the ripples of all this evil will be felt even out here.'

Jolly and Munk watched the man climb on board, hoist the sail, and manoeuvre the boat past the reefs and out into the open sea with astonishing speed.

Yet there wasn't a breath of wind on the beach.

'I thought you were going to ask him to take you with him,' said Munk. He added hopefully, 'Or have you changed your mind?'

Jolly shook her head. 'I have a better idea.'

'You have?'

'We'll follow him.'

Munk stared at her. 'We'll do what?'

'There's something not quite right about him. Don't tell me it's never struck you too. Do you seriously think he sails the whole Caribbean in that nutshell?'

'He doesn't lie to me. I'm sure of that.'

'But perhaps he doesn't tell the whole truth either.'

'If there was a larger ship out there somewhere, my

father would have seen it from the lookout point.'

Jolly tightened her lips and thought. 'Yes,' she said, at last. 'Probably. All the same, let's follow him for a little way.'

'He'll see us.'

'Not if we keep far enough behind.'

'If he does he'll be furious.'

'I thought he was your friend?'

'He won't be if I spy on him.'

Jolly sighed. 'Then I'll go alone. You'd probably only slow me down out there anyway.'

Anger flashed in Munk's eyes. 'I'm as much a polliwiggle as you!'

'But you're not experienced in running over the open sea. The waves will trip you up.'

'They won't!'

She was keeping the Ghost-Trader's boat in sight out of the corner of her eye. By now it was just a white dot on the endless blue. 'Then now's your chance to prove it.'

And so saying, she jumped over the surf, landed between two waves, and ran on.

Her fears had been right: Munk did slow her down. But she didn't complain. They mustn't go too fast anyway, or they would come too close to the boat and might be spotted.

Munk had difficulty keeping his balance on the rocking water beneath his feet. He stumbled several times, or made the mistake of running against the current and up the crest of a wave which almost sent him tumbling over on his back. However, it was obvious that he was trying very hard, and Jolly only once had to catch him when he looked like falling; the rest of the time he recovered by himself. As he went on he became a little more sure-footed, and soon Jolly was paying attention to the distant boat and not just to him.

'My father's sure to have seen us,' said Munk, glancing back at the lonely mountain that towered above the jungle canopy on the small island. Somewhere up there the farmer was keeping watch for foreign ships at this moment – and instead he'd see his son and the pirate girl defying his orders yet again.

Jolly, she told herself with amusement, you're a really bad influence on this boy.

All the same, she couldn't restrain her curiosity. She had a bad feeling about this Ghost-Trader. He was keeping something from them. Was she afraid of him? He made her uneasy, certainly, but she was a polliwiggle and could run away from him over the water if she had to.

But suppose he set his ghosts on her?

'Hey,' said Munk suddenly, after they had been running

over the waves for almost an hour. 'Look at that.'

'Yes, I can see it.'

A broad, swirling bank of mist had appeared on the horizon and was swiftly coming closer. White vapour like the shapes of arms hovered at its edges, seeming to reach for the seagulls in the sky. The Caribbean sun shone down on it, bright and dazzling. The Ghost-Trader's boat was making straight for the mist.

'Are those the clouds your father mentioned?' Jolly had seen more than one cyclone, but none of them had been preceded by mist.

'Probably not.'

'I knew it!' Triumphantly, Jolly quickened her pace. 'There's something wrong about that man.'

'And a pirate girl says so!'

'Listen, did he say anything to you about this mist?'

'Perhaps he didn't know about it in advance.' Munk's objection sounded half-hearted.

'So that's why he's sailing straight towards it? Any seaman with the faintest common sense, and in a boat like his, would steer right away from that bank of mist.'

Munk said no more. He didn't care for her suspicions of his friend, but even less did he seem to like what he saw before him. Jolly wasn't sure whether he shared her misgivings, but he was certainly wondering what was up.

The Ghost-Trader's boat was still steering straight for the mist. White fingers were already reaching out to the sail and the hull. They could see the Ghost-Trader himself, a tiny figure standing very upright at the stern.

Munk was keeping up with Jolly, if with difficulty. 'You're not going to follow him right in there, are you?'

'How else will we find out the truth?'

'Perhaps there isn't any truth. Perhaps it's perfectly ordinary mist ahead.'

She gave him a caustic glance and refrained from replying.

The boat had almost disappeared from sight now. Only a dark spot vaguely showed its position.

Jolly swore. 'We're going to lose him in there if we don't hurry up.'

Munk couldn't go any faster, she knew – he had too little experience of high seas, and the waves would toss him about like a toy. 'You go on ahead,' he said. 'I'll be all right.'

'No, we stay together,' she told him. 'Anything else is too dangerous.'

Munk tried increasing his speed again, with the result that he stumbled. At the last moment he caught himself, putting out both hands, jumped up again with a curse and ran on.

The mist had finally swallowed up the boat now. Jolly hoped the Ghost-Trader would hold the same course. That way they could keep on his trail simply by running straight ahead.

The wall of mist was a drifting mass lying on the sea, forty or fifty paces in width and as tall as the mast of a warship. Wisps at the front of it were wafting towards Jolly and Munk. After the hot sunlight of the last hour, they felt pleasantly cool on the skin.

Jolly instinctively held her breath as she plunged into the mist. An unnatural silence surrounded them. The white walls rising around her were strangely oppressive. Munk was running beside her, a grey outline, but she dared not speak to him, for fear the Ghost-Trader might be quite close and overhear her.

They hadn't gone fifteen paces through the mist when the view suddenly cleared. Soon she saw why: the wall of vapour was not a compact mass, but a ring hiding something at its centre.

Jolly caught her breath. She and Munk stopped at the same moment.

A galleon rose ahead of them.

With its masts and rigging creaking, the ship lay in the middle of a clearing in the mist. The water in its wake splashed with a clear, glassy sound, like the sound of water lapping in a harbour basin. Noises out here seemed strange and unearthly.

The hull of the galleon was made of dark wood. Seaweed and shells clung to it just above the waterline. The sails on the three tall masts were grey and ragged; not even the most easygoing captain would allow his ship to get into such a state. But Jolly doubted if there was any captain on board this ship. Or any crew.

'Is that what I think it is?' Munk's voice shook.

'Yes,' she said. 'Your Ghost-Trader has a ship that suits him perfectly.'

'And I thought there was no such thing as a ghost ship.'

She looked sideways at him. 'I thought there were no such things as ghosts.'

Reluctantly, they moved forward, finally emerging from the mist and coming out into the light with a blue sky above. But not even that could lift their gloom. All their attention was bent on the ghost ship.

'Careful! There are kobalins in the water!' called the Ghost-Trader's voice all of a sudden, before Jolly spotted him. Munk nodded in the direction of the superstructure at the prow of the galleon. The Trader had placed both hands on the rail and was looking their way with his cloak blowing in the wind. It was open, and Jolly could see the silver circle under it, hanging from his belt. His dark-clad body looked stronger than she had expected from his thin features. A black shirt covered his broad chest.

Only after a moment did she really take in his words. 'Kobalins?' she repeated in alarm.

Munk stood as if rooted to the spot.

'I'd keep moving if I were you,' said the Ghost-Trader. 'If you stand still like that it may encourage them to attack. Come on board. You'll be safe here.'

'He's right,' said Jolly grimly. She took Munk's hand and led him on.

'Did you see any yourself?' he whispered tonelessly. 'Kobalins, I mean.'

Her glance swept the water, but she could see nothing suspicious. 'No.'

'Nor did I. Do you think he's just trying to scare us?'

'Does he need to tell stories about kobalins to do that?'

They went the last part of the way in silence. A ghost that looked just like the insubstantial plantation workers threw them the end of a rope ladder. Jolly climbed it first, with Munk nimbly following her.

'Welcome aboard.' The Trader came to meet them as the ghost pulled the ladder in. 'I realised you wouldn't come with me if I asked you to.'

Munk turned even paler. 'Come with you? Where?'

'Away from the island.' There was sympathy in the man's voice now. 'And away from your parents, I'm afraid.'

'Never!'

'But that was what you always wanted,' said the Trader, and Jolly admitted to herself that the same thought had occurred to her.

'I'm certainly not leaving just like that.' Munk turned and went back to the rail. Jolly could see conflicting feelings of disappointment and anger in his eyes. 'The ladder!' he ordered the ghost, but it didn't move. More ghosts were moving about the ship now, some coming up from below decks, some down from the rigging, where it had been impossible to tell them from wisps of mist at a distance.

'Very well,' said Munk. 'No ladder, then.'

He was about to clamber over the rail, but Jolly was beside him in an instant, holding him back. 'Wait. Let's hear what he has to say first.'

The Ghost-Trader nodded to her and came closer. 'Munk, I mean the two of you no harm, and I certainly have no intention of abducting you against your will.'

Munk hesitated, cast a brief glance at Jolly and then swung his leg back on the deck. 'What do you want, then?'

'And what kind of ship is this?' asked Jolly.

'A former slave ship,' said the trader. 'Its crew let most of the men and women they were carrying in cramped quarters below decks starve to death. Those still living decided to revolt. The crew and the slaves fought until none of them were left alive. And the ship ran aground on a small island, where I found it twenty or thirty years later.'

Jolly gave him a contemptuous look. 'What you're doing with the ghosts is no better than what the slave-traders do with their prisoners.'

'Ah, but I haven't conjured them up. I only collect ghosts who would otherwise be wandering restlessly. They're glad of someone who'll look after them and give them a job to do.' He smiled, but there was anxiety in that smile, and a trace of sorrow. 'And we're not talking about the ghosts now, we're talking about you. You're both in great danger.' He glanced at Jolly. 'If I'd known you were a polliwiggle . . . I think I have made a mistake. I've been watching the farmers instead of you pirates.' He shook his head, and went on. 'I want to help you. But if you stay on the island they're going to find you. And quite soon, I'm afraid. There are more and more signs and portents. The winds carry disquiet with them, and there's something in the air that I don't like.'

'*Who* are going to find us?' asked Munk.

Jolly took a step towards the Ghost-Trader. 'The men who set that trap for the *Maddy*?'

'Worse than that, although they're on the same side,' said the one-eyed man. 'The Maelstrom is on the move again. And spewing out servants that are ready to obey it with every fibre of their being.'

Jolly and Munk exchanged a glance. Maelstrom? Servants? What was he talking about.

'There's a good deal you'll soon understand better if I can persuade you to come away with –'

A slapping sound interrupted him.

All three of them spun round. At first Jolly couldn't see what had made the noise. Then her eyes fell on something lying on the planks only a few feet away.

A dead fish.

'Where did that –'

The sound came again. And again. Jolly saw the body of a fish drop from above, passing through one of the ghosts and vaporising it. The ghost's body instantly formed again.

'Damn it!' swore the Ghost-Trader.

'What's that?' Jolly pushed the nearest fish with the tip of her toe.

More bodies were raining down on deck now. One

grazed her shoulder, and she was only just in time to avoid another before it hit her in the face. As if coming from nowhere, dead fish were positively hailing down out of the cloudless sky.

'The breath of the Maelstrom,' whispered the Ghost-Trader, staring intently at the wall of mist. 'There's something here.'

A dreadful scream sounded in the distance.

The trader narrowed his one eye. 'The Acherus. They've sent out the Acherus!'

Munk was agitated. 'Where did that sound come from?'

Jolly leaned over the rail as if that would help her to pinpoint the direction better. But the scream died away, and then rang out again.

'Did it come from the island?' Munk's voice rose and threatened to break. 'Is it . . . is it *on the island*?'

Jolly looked back at the Ghost-Trader. She was frightened to see how pale he had turned; he looked as ghostly as his own wares.

'It's with my parents, isn't it?' Munk's wide eyes were staring at the Trader, who did not need to reply. His expression was answer enough.

'Munk!' cried Jolly. 'Wait!'

But it was too late. With one bound he dived over the rail.

MESSENGER OF THE MAELSTROM

Jolly heard a muffled curse as Munk hit the water. He could think himself lucky if he hadn't broken both legs. But when she looked down she saw him running over the sea, straight towards the wall of mist.

'Munk!'

'Jolly!' called the Ghost-Trader in a tone of warning. 'Jolly, don't do it! The Acherus is not –'

She didn't hear the rest as she placed one hand on the rail, swung herself over and jumped to the depths below. She landed on her feet and one hand, swore out loud and much more distinctly than Munk at the pain in her joints, and raced straight off.

'Munk, wait for me! I'm coming too!'

She saw him ahead of her in the mist, but didn't catch up

until they had broken through the vapour again on the other side and were running as fast as they could go across the open sea, towards the distant island.

She caught Munk several times when, in his fear and panic, he lost his footing on the rolling waves, but he ran on in silence, never looking aside, just staring grimly at the island with the grey mountain peak above the dark green of the jungle.

Once, Jolly looked back over her shoulder, and had the impression that the mist was following them. But it didn't bother her. She thought she knew what Munk was feeling – she'd felt the same way when she had to leave Bannon and the others on board the galleon. It didn't seem right to get away scot-free yourself when those you loved were in mortal danger. Just as Munk wasn't going to give up at this point, she herself still couldn't accept Bannon's death.

By now they were close enough to the shore to see a brightly coloured flock of birds fluttering above the jungle trees. Hundreds and thousands of them, birds of every kind, as if all the birds on the island had risen in the air at once and were now circling above it, calling frantically.

Something flitted past beneath the waves at Jolly's feet, blurred and as if splintered by the multiple facets of light on the surface of the waves.

Kobalins!

But these were feeble, cowardly kobalins who didn't dare grab at their feet – most of them feared air and sunlight. Only the largest among them were brave enough to put their claws out of the water. The kobalin in the wreck of the *Maddy* must have been a chieftain, one of the leaders of the Deep Tribes.

No one had managed to find out much about the kobalins when they first appeared years ago. But they were as unlikely to attack people on land as an eagle was to hunt under water. And although they could scream and bellow horribly, the screeching just now had been something else: a hundred times louder than any kobalin's cry that Jolly had yet heard, and a thousand times angrier.

She was beginning to get breathless, while Munk still ran on with determination born of his fear for his parents. She was afraid too, but they'd soon both run out of strength if they kept this pace up.

'Munk . . . there's no point in it if . . . if we're exhausted when we reach the island . . . that won't help anyone.' Whatever had screeched like that would have no difficulty in dealing with two exhausted fourteen-year-olds.

But Munk didn't seem to have heard her.

'Munk, will you listen to me!' She grasped his shoulder as they ran.

Furiously, he swung round, so angry that she flinched away from him. This was not the Munk she had come to know over the last few days. Fear and rage distorted his features, and there was a determination in his eyes that sent a shudder down Jolly's back.

'They're my parents, Jolly! I must do what *I* think is right!' There was exhaustion in his voice, but he had himself under remarkably good control.

She was going to say something, but he was already running on, simply leaving her behind. Jolly swore quietly, bent over double with the stitch in her side, then clenched her teeth and followed him. Soon they were running level again.

The scream came for the second time, and this time the flock of birds above the island scattered in all directions like an iridescent fountain. Shots rang out, two in quick succession, and then, after a pause, a third.

Jolly looked at Munk, but his face was set like stone. Beads of sweat stood out on his forehead and cheeks, the back of his neck gleamed with it, but he ran forward like a ship under full sail that nothing and no one could stop.

They rounded the reefs, crossed the shallow semicircle of the bay, and finally stumbled ashore. When Munk's feet felt the ground he stood still for a moment. Dead fish lay all over the beach like seed corn scattered by a passing giant. They were already beginning to rot in the strong sunlight; the stench of them weighed down on the island.

The smell of death. In spite of the heat and her exhaustion, Jolly began to freeze. Her arms were covered with sweat and gooseflesh at the same time.

Munk closed his eyes for a couple of seconds.

'You can't help them if . . . if you kill yourself,' gasped Jolly. 'First we have to find out *what* it is . . .'

'Yes,' he said grimly. 'By taking a look at it.'

And he ran on again towards the outskirts of the jungle. Soon he was in the hot and humid shade under the trees. Jolly found herself wheezing as she caught up with him. She had drawn the narrow dagger she had been carrying during the attack on the supposed Spanish galleon; what her imagination conjured up from the sound of that screech made it seem a ridiculous weapon.

They stumbled through thick undergrowth – and were soon in a long, narrow clearing.

Munk uttered a stifled sound.

Something had flattened the jungle here. The trunks of mahogany trees as tall as houses were snapped or uprooted, giant ferns and hibiscus bushes were crushed. And over everything lay a carpet of dead fish.

The birds in the sky were screaming so loud that Jolly's ears hurt.

'They're all still in the air,' she said softly.

Munk looked at her. 'What do you mean?'

'The birds won't come down to the ground. Even to eat the fish. And they're screaming in alarm, which means that –'

Munk's lips were bloodless. 'That it's still here.'

They ran on, side by side this time, following the trail. Soon Jolly too knew where it was leading.

Something had broken through the palisade fence as if it were only a raffia screen. Tree trunks sharpened to points were scattered in all directions. Some had been flung aside with such violence that they were driven into the ground like outsize arrows, and now stood there like the pagan totems of many of the island tribes.

'Ma! Pa!' Munk jumped the ruined fence and ran towards the wreck of the house.

The veranda roof had been torn away in one piece, and was lying in the brown grass a few paces away. The table and chairs where they had sat that morning had been smashed as if by a mighty fist.

The farmhouse door was gone, and with it a large part of the front wall.

'Ma!'

Jolly raced through the ruins and saw Munk drop to his knees beside his mother's lifeless body. Tears were running down his face. Jolly stood helplessly beside him, wondering what to do and how she could help. Finally she knelt down on the woman's other side, took her hand and, with trembling fingers, felt for her pulse.

'She's alive!' she exclaimed a moment later. 'Munk, your mother's alive!'

He looked up at her through a mist of tears, then back at his mother's face, stroked her cheeks and dabbed at her scratches and wounds with his sleeve.

'I must find Pa!' Reluctantly, he leaped up and moved away from his mother. 'You stay with her.'

'Munk, it's too dangerous out there!'

'I have to look for him.'

'Then let me come with you.'

He shook his head and raced away. A moment later he had disappeared. She heard wood snapping as he jumped over tree trunks and smashed boards, and then the only sound was the endless screaming of the birds.

Shattered and at a loss she crouched there, still holding the unconscious woman's hand and trying to get her thoughts in order, make some kind of sense out of all this.

She failed. Instead, she rose to her feet, picked up a jug that was still intact, and hurried to fetch water from the barrel in the kitchen. She dabbed Munk's mother's face with it, washed away the dried blood from her features and neck as well as she could, and then opened her torn dress.

For reasons she didn't understand, the terrible wound on the woman's back had hardly bled at all – neither Munk nor Jolly had noticed it before. Yet a glance was enough to show that no one with a wound like that could survive.

Munk's mother would die. Whatever Jolly did, however she tried to treat the wounds, there was no point in it.

She began to weep uncontrollably, torn between the wish to stay with the dying woman and an urge to follow Munk and stand by him. She hated herself for her helplessness. Very gradually, she began to realise that none of this would have happened if she hadn't been washed up on the shore of this island, if she had stayed with Bannon and the other pirates, if the ruin and destruction that followed polliwiggles hadn't brought her here.

The screech sounded for the third time, and this time it was so loud that the ruins of the farmhouse shook, and several planks broke off and fell to the ground.

'Munk!'

She laid the woman's head gently on the ground,

gave her a last, sad look, and then she ran.

A broad trail of destruction behind the house led into the jungle, in a chaotic mess of broken palisades and splintered trees. Jolly leaped and stumbled over the shredded undergrowth, for the first time forgetting her exhaustion and the pain that tormented every part of her body.

The trail led through the rainforest to a tobacco field in a clearing a hundred paces beyond the farm.

And now she saw Munk again. She saw his father's lifeless body on the ground. And she witnessed a struggle that she could never have imagined even in her worst nightmares.

The plantation ghosts were clinging like ferocious dogs to something too large and terrible for Jolly to take it in at a single glance. Munk stood beside his dead father with outstretched arms, as if power were emanating from him, a power that forced the ghosts to obey his orders – and engage in a hopeless battle with the Acherus.

Jolly was still about twenty paces away when the creature uttered yet another long-drawn-out scream, struck out at the disintegrating ghosts with its claws, and howled again as the misty beings came together once more and continued their attack. Yet it was obvious that the attacking ghosts was merely getting in the monstrous figure's way, and couldn't really weaken it.

The Acherus might once, perhaps, have been human, or certainly human in form, although its body was made of ocean flotsam and jetsam: black silt, twisted and matted bladderwrack, mouldering tangles of seaweed with hundreds of sharp, bleached pinpoints sticking through them, the bones of dead sea creatures. Dull, oozing fishy eyes stared out all over the stinking body, but it was impossible to tell if the Acherus could actually see with them. It smelled of death, and when it turned once in its struggle with the ghosts Jolly saw the ribcages of dead, shipwrecked sailors pointing out of its back like pale fingers. The Acherus had sucked them all in, or else it had been made from their remains; perhaps it had never been just *one* being but many, made up of the bodies of dead fish, squids and sharks.

'Munk, get back!'

Jolly ran towards him when she realised that he hadn't seen the creature advancing on him – he was concentrating so hard that he still had his eyes closed. She jumped over his father's body, trying not to look, but even out of the corner of her eye she realised that the man must be dead; the Acherus had inflicted terrible wounds on him.

She just managed to seize Munk by the shoulders and pull him back as the corpse-like creature's claws shot out to grab him. One talon, long and sharp as a sword, thrust into the empty air and seized a ghost, cutting it in half, but the ghost immediately came together again.

'Get away from here!' yelled Jolly, but Munk twisted in her grip and tried to go back to face the monster. This was madness, not courage! Jolly shouted at him, shook him, and finally brought him to his senses.

Together, they ran for it. As she passed, Jolly snatched up Munk's father's double-barrelled pistol. One hammer was broken off, but the other barrel was still loaded.

They ran along the track and heard the Acherus rampaging after them. Jolly looked over her shoulder: the creature, tall as the trees and agile as a beast of prey, had taken up the pursuit on two disproportionately long legs. It was dragging the ghosts that still clung to its body behind it, like a train of mist. The ground quivered under every step it took, the birds were screeching in the sky, leaves fell from the trees all around them, shaken loose by its mighty impact as it trod on the earth. Again and again, the two young people leaped recklessly over twining plants and roots as they ran on.

'Not that way!' shouted Munk suddenly. 'Or we'll lead it back to Ma.'

Keeping beside him, Jolly turned left through the jungle

shrubs that were still intact. She and Munk were smaller than the creature and could move more easily through the tangled undergrowth — although the Acherus had shown that it could easily flatten the forest. All the same, Jolly hoped its breakneck speed might at least be slowed.

'Where to?' she uttered as she ran.

Munk did not answer.

'Back to the water, then,' she decided.

'But it comes from the water! You saw it!'

'*Out* of the water,' she said. 'But we can run *over* the water.' She was no more certain her plan would work than he was, but it was the only one to occur to her.

'I need time,' said Munk, gasping for air as they broke through a wall of ferns and fleshy leaves. 'Then I may be able to make the ghosts stronger.'

'Stronger?'

'I only set them on it. But they can't fight unless you tell them how. All they've ever had to do before is pick tobacco. If I'd had time to give them orders —'

They heard deafening noises behind them as the Acherus left the trail and smashed its way through the jungle after them by main force. The crash of falling tree trunks reminded Jolly of the sound of a sinking ship's hull breaking up. Once, in a sea battle, she had watched two galleons out of control ramming each other. That had been just as violent, had made the same kind of murderous noise, and was equally final and hopeless.

Munk gasped, with difficulty, 'If we can get far enough out on the water, that might give me enough time.'

With misgivings, Jolly thought of the kobalins below the waves, but she quickly nodded. After all, they had made it to the island without being attacked. And if they didn't escape this time – well, then it made no difference whether they fell into the clutches of the Deep Tribes or the Acherus.

Something fluttered in front of their faces – two black, winged silhouettes in the light of the sunbeams falling through the jungle canopy.

'Hugh!' cried Munk. 'And Moe!'

Jolly too recognised the Ghost-Trader's parrots. Had he followed them? Was he already close?

'Look – they're showing us the way!' Munk swerved to avoid the dead root of a giant jungle tree that might even be broad enough to withstand the Acherus.

What way? Jolly would have liked to ask, but she had no chance.

Directly behind them, the Acherus came breaking through the trees. Several trunks snapped and fell towards them, tearing up others and creating such chaos around the monster that it was invisible for another moment.

Jolly shouted a warning and tried to run even faster, although that was as good as impossible. It was hard enough anyway to avoid the creepers and roots without stumbling in the undergrowth or stepping into holes in the ground hidden under fern fronds.

She had exhausted her strength, and could hardly breathe, fearing that one of those sword-like talons might plunge into her back at any moment.

Hugh and Moe had fluttered up when the Acherus appeared, and now they turned and flew towards the corpse creature. What the birds intended to do Jolly had no idea, but she had no time to worry about them, for the undergrowth ahead of her and Munk was thinning out, the ground was becoming sandier, and soon they were running for their lives through a light palm grove. Beyond it, already within view, was a beach. The broad strip of sand shone golden in the afternoon sun.

Jolly glanced back over her shoulder. The parrots were flying on both sides of the Acherus, level with its deformed skull, made out of mud, seaweed and human bones by heaven knew what powers. The two birds screeched and chattered excitedly, and it seemed to Jolly as if something about them was slowing the Acherus down. It didn't stop, it was still coming on at incredible speed, but its body had lost some of that deadly power; it was even swerving to avoid some of the palm trees now instead of uprooting them.

Jolly spun round and raised the pistol. She aimed at the creature's skull, pressed the trigger – and hit her target. But it seemed to have no effect. The bullet was swallowed up in the dark mass, the Acherus kept on coming. Cursing, Jolly threw the useless weapon away.

Munk was coughing with exhaustion, gasping for air. 'Not far now.'

They left the dappled shade of the palm grove and stumbled out on the beach. The soft sand slowed them down, but all the same they somehow managed to reach the water. Jolly was looking out for kobalins – instead, her eyes fell on the bank of mist moving towards the island, just passing an outlying rock. So the Ghost-Trader hadn't reached land yet, but had only sent his parrots on ahead.

The water here was much deeper than in the shallow bay. They had left the jungle some way to the east, a good five minutes' walk from the bay. Jolly saw two tall palms on a hill rising in the distance; she had felled the third with that cannon shot a few days ago.

Taking long, unsteady strides, they raced across the

waves. They had soon put about fifty paces between themselves and the beach.

Jolly stopped. If they hadn't escaped the Acherus now, they weren't going to.

Munk came to a halt beside her. He put both hands on his hips and breathed in and out loud enough to drown even the sound of the angry monster as it emerged through the last of the palms. The swearing of the two parrots hadn't stopped it, but they had slowed it down considerably. Misty ghosts were still clinging to the creature's distorted body like burrs.

The exhaustion in Munk's eyes gave way to determination. 'Now we'll see who's stronger,' he whispered. He was obviously having difficulty in keeping on his feet, and if Jolly's own trembling knees were any indication of the way Munk felt, he wouldn't be able to stand upright much longer.

But he was holding out.

The Acherus stopped on the beach, staring at them with its hundreds of blind fish eyes, a dark figure as tall as four men, with gnarled limbs that had far too many joints in them. It looked as if it had been built where it stood of refuse and debris, a nauseating, distorted image of human life.

It seemed to be thinking. It took no more notice of the ghosts clinging to it. The parrots left it and flew back over the water towards Jolly and Munk.

'The brute!' whispered Munk, concentrating.

He closed his eyes again, spread his arms, and whispered his orders to the ghosts with trembling lips, although not a sound came from his throat. Jolly wondered whether anyone could do it, or whether you needed the Ghost-Trader's special magic to hand on the power of commanding ghosts to other people.

The Acherus put one foot in the water.

'It's coming!' Helplessly, Jolly clenched her fists and swayed back and forth on the waves. 'You must hurry.' More than likely it was a mistake to say so, but panic was rising in her again, overcoming reason.

Munk did not let her distract him. He went on giving silent orders. His eyelids flickered, his hair, wet with sweat, was clinging to his forehead. Jolly's own hair felt no better.

The Acherus was up to its knees in the sea now. But it couldn't walk over the water like the two polliwiggles. Would it swim out to them? Or rise from the sea-bed to attack?

The Acherus paused again. And now the mass of ghosts swarming over its shoulders, its breast and its back began to move. Jolly was too far away to make out details, but she thought she saw the misty beings thrust their arms into the rotting body of the Acherus like blades. They were no longer content with pulling at him, they had gone on the attack. Munk's orders were taking effect.

The screech of the Acherus pierced Jolly to the marrow. Even the waves of the sea rose higher, almost tipping Jolly and Munk off balance.

Munk opened his eyes. 'Ghosts can decide when and where they solidify so as to hold or carry something . . . I've told them to pass through the Acherus and become solid bodies as they do it.'

What was happening to the creature was not a pleasant sight. The ghosts disappeared into its massive body, which expanded further and further the more of them took physical shape. They were no longer wisps of mist, but bodies made of . . . made of what? Flesh and blood?

It was only a matter of minutes before the vast mass inside the monster made it explode.

Jolly didn't look as the creature's cries died away. When she did glance back at the shore, the ghosts were drifting away. A thick carpet of black silt and seaweed was floating on the waves, and a nauseating stench wafted over the sea, making Jolly's throat tighten.

The parrots flew away over their heads, out to sea again. Jolly turned as if numbed.

Misty arms reached out for her, but they couldn't keep her from falling forward. Then she got on all fours, exhausted, and threw up from sheer weakness. Out of the corner of her eye she saw Munk crouching there. He was in an even worse state than she was.

Hugh and Moe uttered shrill cries as they plunged into the mist.

And then there was nothing but milky whiteness around Jolly too, as if the air had suddenly frozen to ice.

'She will die.' The Ghost-Trader was sitting on the edge of the bed where they had laid Munk's mother. 'She's already forgotten that she is still alive.'

Munk did not collapse. He didn't even shed tears. His face was hard as glass. 'But there must be something we can do.'

Under his hood, the Trader shook his head.

Munk said nothing. Jolly put her hand over his. Its fingers were icy cold. She was so sorry for him; she felt tears come into her own eyes, and was not ashamed when they ran down over her cheeks.

'There's one thing I can do for her,' said the Trader.

Munk's expression became even more forbidding, and his voice could have cut steel. 'Are you planning to make her into one of your ghosts?'

'No, I mean something better. Something good.' He paused for a moment, and then added, 'Something she's earned.'

'What do you mean?' asked Jolly.

'I can give her another kind of life. One that never ends.' The Ghost-Trader lowered his voice to an intense whisper. 'Life as a story.'

'How does that work?' Jolly was still suspicious. Munk was simply looking at his mother in silence.

'She will live on, not as a human being, not in a body, but as a story that people will tell each other from generation to generation.' He leaned forward and stroked a strand of the dying woman's hair back from her face. 'I can make a legend of her, a beautiful fairy tale or a new myth.'

Jolly looked down at the floor, shaking her head, but said nothing out of compassion for Munk.

'Munk?' The Ghost-Trader touched his arm. 'I will do it only if you agree.'

The boy looked at his mother's face, holding her blood-less hands. They had bound up her wounds, but as they did it, they could see there was no hope for her. She was already deeply unconscious, and her breathing stopped for a moment more and more frequently.

'Munk,' said the Ghost-Trader urgently, 'I can do it only while there's still life in her.'

Jolly compressed her lips. She didn't know what advice she could give Munk, or whether he would even value it. She didn't trust the Ghost-Trader in spite of the help his two parrots had given them. Yet she couldn't rule out the possibility that he was telling the truth.

'Do what you can,' whispered Munk, without looking at anyone except his mother. Now his eyes did fill with tears, but his voice was so hard and determined that it made Jolly's flesh creep.

The Ghost-Trader nodded. 'You can hold her hand if you like.'

Munk leaned forward, embraced his mother for the last time and whispered something in her ear. When he sat up again her cheek was wet with his tears.

Something in the Ghost-Trader's features softened, as if an entirely different face were suddenly appearing under the one they knew. The many wrinkles around his eyes and lips smoothed out, yet it didn't make him look younger – only flawless, superhuman. His one eye shone as if it had turned to polished marble. Power radiated from his whole face.

'I make you into a story,' he said softly to the dying woman, as if she could hear his words. 'You will be a story where young girls meet mighty enchanters, where poor young men encounter bold princesses. A story in which Fate swings now this way and now that, deciding the way a whole world goes. A story where there are doors in unexpected places and windows everywhere. A story where the old gods walk the earth as they still sometimes do today.'

Munk's mother drew in her last breath. Then it escaped her with a soft sigh, her face relaxed, and Jolly suddenly felt as if they had all become a part of the story conjured up by the Ghost-Trader; as if they too were now legendary heroes of whom tales would be told for centuries to come; as if their own lives had a purpose of which they had never even dreamed, one that was waiting for them beyond the horizon.

'She will live on in a tale passed on from mouth to mouth,' said the Ghost-Trader, 'and perhaps one day someone will write it down and she will never be forgotten.'

He stroked the dead woman's hair one last time. 'Farewell, give comfort and happiness and sorrow. Farewell, and live forever.'

With these words, he rose and left the house.

Jolly looked from the dead woman to Munk. He was folding his mother's hands on her breast.

'We'll bury them together,' he said, rough-voiced. 'Both in the same grave. That's what they would have wanted.'

THE SEA OF DARKNESS

That night the Ghost-Trader asked Jolly and Munk to join him. They had all returned to the ghost ship several hours before, and had put straight out to sea. Now the mist and the ship were gliding through the darkness.

Jolly had dozens of questions that she was longing to ask, but she guessed it would be no good pressing the Ghost-Trader for answers. For the time being it was enough for her that he had agreed to take them away, back to her own world, where they could forget what had happened on the island, and she herself could begin trying to find out what had become of Bannon. New Providence had been his original destination. It was the headquarters of Kendrick the pirate emperor, and if anyone knew what was behind the trap set for the *Maddy* it would be Kendrick, leader of the freebooters and corsairs.

The Ghost-Trader had seated himself on one of the steps

leading up to the bridge, beside an oil lamp that swayed back and forth. At every movement the ship made it swung towards his face and then away again, bathing his angular features in glowing light for a few seconds. The eyes of the parrots perched on his shoulders shone like semi-precious gems.

There was impenetrable darkness on both sides of the rail. The ring of mist around the ship made the night even darker, wrapping it in deep, dense black. Only high above the masts could she see the stars in a circular section of the night sky, and even they seemed further away than usual.

Silence reigned except for the creak of the planks and the rigging. Even the gurgling of the ship's wake had died down. The mist seemed to carry the ship through the night as if on a cloud; they hardly felt as if they were moving at all.

Munk had scarcely spoken a word since they left the island. His tears had dried, but he only appeared to be in control of himself. His gaze was fixed on the dark night, and even when the Ghost-Trader began to speak Munk did not turn to him.

'The Acherus,' said the one-eyed man, 'is a creature of the Mare Tenebrosum. Few have ever seen its like, or if they did it was long, long ago, when the powers of the Maelstrom first tried to bring the world under their rule.'

'What does that mean – the Mare Tenebrosum?' Jolly asked.

'It means "Sea of Darkness", and sometimes it appears where no one expects it. Then storms rise where no storms ought to be, ships are wrecked although there are no reefs or sandbanks near, and human beings always die, swallowed up by something far deeper than the extinct volcanic craters on the sea-bed, and blacker than those places that no light ever reaches. The Mare Tenebrosum is a sea that knows no bounds, where there is no land, and the creatures that live in it cannot be compared with any we know here.'

Jolly and Munk exchanged a baffled glance. 'Any we know here?' said Jolly. 'So this sea you're talking about is somewhere else?'

The Ghost-Trader nodded. 'In a place that none of us can usually reach, in a world that lies beside our own. It is divided from ours by borders that ordinary mortals and even the gods cannot cross. Or at least, not the gods of *this* world.'

'What about the gods over there?' asked Munk in a brittle voice.

Jolly, who believed in neither one nor several gods, thought this a strange question. But perhaps Munk was just trying to take his mind off his grief. She thought he was being very brave. Whenever her mind dwelt on Bannon and the others she felt a sharp pang, followed by a moment of deep despair. Yet she still hoped to find them somewhere. Or at least to find the traitor who had lured them into that wicked trap. When her loss hurt too badly she could cling to that idea. But Munk had buried his parents with his own hands. There could be no reunion with them.

'I don't know if those who make their way here from the Mare Tenebrosum are gods or mortal beings,' said the Ghost-Trader. 'There have been times before, long ago and only very seldom, when breaches were made in the wall between the worlds. Then a little of the Mare Tenebrosum spilled over into our world, like water slopping out of a pan filled too full. Such things cause those disasters on the high seas we sometimes hear of, things that can't be explained, and I was speaking of them just now: shipwrecks, terrible hurricanes and stormy tides, black mists over the water from which no one ever returns. But usually such breaches close up so quickly that nothing living can get through them to reach us.'

'But the Acherus is a living thing. Or at least, something almost like a living thing,' said Jolly.

The Ghost-Trader nodded sadly. 'You're right. The

powers of the Mare Tenebrosum are no longer content with the water, they want to conquer land – and there is no land in their world. They have made a gateway to ours: a mighty Maelstrom, larger than any you can imagine, several miles across in diameter and as deep as the bed of the sea. A Maelstrom gifted with keen and dark intelligence.'

He paused, to let the image his words had conjured up sink in. 'If it opens up – and I pray we have not yet reached that point – it will mercilessly suck everything that comes within its orbit down into the abyss, into the darkness of its world. At the moment it has changed direction, and is spewing its advance guard up from the depths to us in the light of day, sometimes fish and sea monsters, sometimes creatures like –'

'Like the Acherus,' said Jolly in a neutral voice.

'Yes, indeed.'

'But why . . .' Munk began, and then hesitated and fell silent for a moment. Finally he got his feelings under control again. 'Why did it kill my parents?'

'It wasn't after them,' said the Ghost-Trader, putting Jolly's fears into words. 'It was after you two.'

'But why?'

'Can't you guess?'

'It's because we're polliwiggles,' Jolly realised.

The Ghost-Trader nodded.

Munk narrowed his eyes angrily. 'But what does it want from us? Why was it trying to kill us?'

For a while no one said a word. The oil lamp swung back and forth, casting light on the Ghost-Trader's face every time it swung forward before it disappeared into the dark again. Light, dark. Light, dark.

'I'm not sure that it was really trying to kill you,' he said in the end.

'Then what?' asked Jolly. 'Abduct us?'

'Possibly.'

This answer didn't satisfy her, sceptical as she was about most of what the Ghost-Trader said. Perhaps he was telling the truth. But was that really all he knew? She didn't for a moment think so. And did he really just want to protect them from this Maelstrom, or had he some other purpose in mind? His secretive attitude angered her, and she was even angrier because he made them feel it so clearly – as if he thought they were silly children who could be fobbed off with a few dark hints.

Looking at Munk, she saw that he was thinking exactly the same thing.

'That's not all,' she said, turning to the Trader. 'We have a right to –'

'To the truth?' the man interrupted her. 'The Mare Tenebrosum is the truth. Just like the Maelstrom and the Acherus.'

Munk narrowed his eyes again. 'Who are you, really?'

'Only one who sells the souls of others.' This sounded so weird that Jolly would have liked to seize him by the shoulders and shake him. Selling ghosts was one thing; selling the souls of the living would be another. Had they lost their own souls long ago just by getting involved with him?

'Tell us all about it,' she demanded. 'Everything you know.'

The Ghost-Trader looked away from her, straight into the light of the swaying lamp. As if obeying a silent order, the parrots too followed his movement.

Munk's voice broke the silence like a clap of thunder, even though he spoke very quietly, almost in a whisper. 'My parents are dead. What price did *you* pay for your knowledge, Trader?'

Jolly's stomach contracted. Not long ago Munk had called the Ghost-Trader his friend. But now he seemed to be blaming him for what had happened. The lively, cheerful boy Jolly had first met had changed. He was graver, more reserved, almost a little sinister.

'This knowledge is dangerous,' said the Trader, 'and all

who have it have paid a high price. Some with loss, some with responsibility, even a few with the guilt they had to take upon themselves. It is always painful to cross a threshold. New experiences seldom come as a gift.'

'New experiences?' Jolly's voice was cutting. 'I can think of a number of experiences during these last few hours I'd happily have turned down.'

Munk did not move.

'I'd be putting you in even greater danger if I told you everything.' The Ghost-Trader rose. 'The time will come when you'll understand it all. But not here, not tonight. The Mare Tenebrosum is closer than any of us guessed. The Maelstrom is turning. It's not good to speak about these things too long without knowing how far its senses may reach.' He stepped between the two of them, his black cloak brushing Jolly's cheek like an icy wind. 'Go and lie down in your cabins, rest while you can.'

Munk's eyes flashed, but he did not move from where he was sitting. Jolly, on the other hand, was so angry that she couldn't control herself. Leaping up, she seized the Ghost-Trader's arm. Her hand shot back at once, but all the same one of the parrots flapped its wings in agitation. The other uttered a shrill cry that hurt her ears.

'Hush,' said the Trader, soothing his birds. He stood there, but did not turn to Jolly and Munk again. His back towered up before them like the spire of some black cathedral.

'I'm sorry,' he said, 'and that's the truth. I am not the cause of what has happened, but I ought to have foreseen it.' Now he did turn round, but his voice dropped, as if losing itself in the shadow of his hood. 'Things have happened that might perhaps have been prevented. I shall not allow that again. The Maelstrom has woken. And the polliwiggles have grown in significance much sooner than any of us hoped.'

Hugh let out a sharp hiss at Jolly, but the Trader soothed him, stroking his black feathers.

'Loss, responsibility and guilt,' he repeated. 'We all pay in our own way, believe me.'

With that he left them and went below decks.

Jolly stared after him as if her glance alone would force him back into the open air. When she turned back to Munk, still furious, he surprised her by the improbably calm expression on his face.

'You don't know him,' he said. 'He's always like that.'

'Do *you* know him, then?'

He hesitated. 'Well, at least I've heard him talk like that before. It's his way.'

She snorted angrily, then sat down cross-legged on the

deck opposite Munk. 'I'm wondering why he agreed.'

'Agreed to what?'

'To take me . . . us . . . to New Providence. Certainly not just to do me a favour. He couldn't care less about Bannon.'

'Perhaps there's something in New Providence he's interested in himself.'

'He talks about not putting us in danger – and then he simply agrees to make for an island that could be attacked any day by the Spanish armada. And what's the idea of all that talk about gods and guilt and responsibility?'

Munk shrugged his shoulders, then put out an arm and took her hand. 'Whatever happens – we'll stick together, right?'

It sounded like a request, but wasn't there a note of demand in his voice?

'I want to go back to the pirates,' she said firmly. 'And I'll find Bannon and the others, I swear I will. All this nonsense about the Mare Tenebrosum and some Maelstrom or whatever it is . . . it's none of my business.'

'Jolly, listen! If the brute that killed my – if it was really sent by this Maelstrom, then I have to know more about it. I have to know *everything* about it.' His eyes flashed.

Impulsively, Jolly laid her hand on his. They had both suffered a loss, and were alone in their grief. Perhaps it would indeed be simpler if they joined forces. But did she really want any part in his revenge? Anyway, how realistic was it for a boy of fourteen to pit himself against powers like those of the Mare Tenebrosum?

And yes, good heavens, how realistic was it for her to think of finding Bannon and the others again?

On the spur of the moment, she pressed his hand more firmly. 'Look, if I can find anything out – about Captain Bannon, I mean – then after that I'll help you.'

Munk looked at her and nodded.

In silence, they sealed a pact which was to have consequences that neither of them could yet foresee. But it seemed the right thing to do.

They stayed on deck together, and curled up on the planks to sleep. Neither felt like exploring the interior of the old slave ship. Even out here the atmosphere was oppressive and sinister; below decks the cramped space and darkness would surely take their breath away.

A time came when Jolly fell asleep, although in the morning she felt she had scarcely slept a wink all night. She was worn out, as if nightmares had roused her from her rest, although she couldn't remember any of them. Nonetheless, the feeling remained: things she couldn't see and didn't

129

want to know about had haunted her in her sleep.

Rather as they did in waking life. She hadn't asked to be wrenched from her familiar surroundings and dumped in this nightmare.

Over and over again she heard the Ghost-Trader's voice saying, 'The polliwiggles have grown in significance much sooner than any of us hoped.' And each time it seemed to her more ominous.

Morning light filtered gradually through the ring of mist around the ghost ship. The depth of the shadows faded only when the blue sky of the Caribbean appeared in the opening in the mist high above them. Like the stars last night, the sun looked further away than usual. The outside world seemed to have been removed to some uncertain distance. Perhaps that was to do with the nature of the ghost ship, or perhaps it was the result of a whole series of events.

Grief weighed down on the ship like a miasma, and Jolly felt unable to do anything about it.

After they had woken and got up she left Munk alone, wondering whether to explore the ship on her own after all, but she decided against it. Instead, she clambered up on the bowsprit, straddled it as if it were a horse, and remembered sadly how often she had done the same on board the *Maid Maddy*, the ship now lying somewhere at the bottom of the sea.

Now and then she looked over her shoulder and saw Munk some way off, kneeling on deck with a frown on his face. He had spread all his shells out in front of him and was forming them into a variety of patterns. Several times he created a shining pearl above an empty half-shell, but immediately snapped the shell's hinge shut to make it complete again. Whatever he was trying to raise – perhaps a stronger wind for the sails, perhaps something to dispel his grief – he didn't seem to be having much luck.

The Ghost-Trader didn't show up until early in the afternoon. He placed one hand on the mainmast and closed his eyes. After a while Jolly realised that this was how he communicated with the ghost up in the crow's-nest.

Then he moved his lips, but only a cold gust of wind brought the words to Jolly's ears.

'We've arrived,' he said. 'The island ahead is New Providence.'

She strained her eyes to look out in front of them, but saw nothing except mist like cotton wool. Sometimes it seemed to her that, as it drifted, it formed wispy figures, faces, whole scenes.

New Providence, she thought in relief.

It was almost like coming home.

THE PIRATE CITY

The pirate emperor refused to see Jolly.

The place where he held court hardly merited the name of an inn. Taverns and low dives stood side by side in the narrow streets, but only two or three of them looked as if there was any hope that the food they served might be edible, the rum undiluted and the beds free of bugs.

The *Fat Hen* was in the centre of what grandly called itself a city, although the civilised sound of the word was deceptive when applied to a place like this. You wouldn't meet more rogues, murderers, card-sharps and folk with grandiose ideas of themselves anywhere than on New Providence. And here in Port Nassau, the only built-up harbour on the island, was the heart of the monstrous pirate empire, the pit where so many of the scum of humanity met that a white jacket would turn black merely approaching it.

Jolly felt wonderful.

She had grown up on the high seas, but it was at places like these that she had come ashore with Bannon now and then. To her, civilisation was the sight of stinking alleys, overcrowded taverns, and the occasional spectacle of a fist fight, a knifing, or a throat being cut in the dim light of lanterns burning low.

That was all she knew. The idea of perfumed palaces, powdered wigs and uniformed dandies nauseated her, just as many Spaniards, English and Dutch would have been sickened at the sight of this sink of murderous piratical iniquity.

Port Nassau was its capital, and Kendrick was its emperor.

She said so to the guard posted at the entrance to the *Fat Hen*, who didn't want to let her in. The man, a particularly dirty and unattractive specimen of humanity, was picking his teeth with the tip of a knife; he didn't take the blade out of his mouth even to shake his head. Only when he realised that Jolly wasn't giving up did he put the dagger back in his belt and lean forward.

'I know you, girlie.' His breath smelled of stale beer and old food. 'You're the littl'un from the *Maid Maddy*. A big-mouth, a know-all, a right pain in the neck, and all because the great Bannon was protecting you.' His grin revealed teeth the colour of sour milk. 'But the *Maddy*'s sunk, Bannon's gone to the devil, and so far as I can see you're just a pert little piece what deserves a good spanking. Only my opinion, know what I mean? Hey, give it a year or so, you could be not bad-looking if you survive! Then you can come back and say hello to me. But till then – off you go!'

With a confident smile, he straightened his back and yawned widely; in doing so he closed his eyes for a moment.

When he opened them again, his dagger was in Jolly's hand, pointing to a spot just below his belt buckle.

'Kendrick,' she said grimly. 'And now!'

'Jolly, don't,' whispered Munk, standing right behind her. 'You'll bring the whole pack of them down on us.'

'Did you or did you not want to meet pirates?'

'Not so *many*.'

'You should have thought of that before.'

Munk gave Jolly a pleading look. The two of them were on their own. As soon as they landed the Ghost-Trader had left them, without many words. But it had not been a goodbye, and Jolly felt sure that the Trader didn't intend to let them out of his sight even for a short time.

The pirate was staring at the tip of the dagger in Jolly's hand. It was prodding the flap of his breeches. A nervous grin flitted over his scarred features.

'You don't mean it, girlie. Not as crazy as they all say, are you?'

'And you're not as stupid as they all say, right?'

He blinked at her as if he still couldn't quite grasp what was happening: a girl of just fourteen had tricked him and was threatening him with his own dagger. Jolly saw his mind working it out. If anyone happened to see them, this awkward situation would be the talk of Port Nassau.

'What d'you want me to do?' he asked reluctantly. 'I s'pose I can go in and ask if Kendrick will come out to you.'

Jolly tried to ignore Munk, who was shifting nervously from one foot to the other. 'Is Kendrick spending the night at this inn?'

'You bet your life he is. He's hired all the rooms, bought up all the beer and rum and paid for all the girls. It's like his palace, the *Fat Hen* is.'

'And you're like his bodyguard, is that right?'

The pirate grinned. 'That's right. Me and a couple of others. One at each door, front and back. But it's obvious who's most important, eh?' He cackled. 'The man at the front door, for sure!'

Heavens above, how could Kendrick rely on such idiots? He seemed to feel very secure here in Port Nassau – and no wonder. He had killed or chased away all the pirates who

135

had openly been allies of his murdered predecessor Scarab.

'Right,' said Jolly, putting very slight pressure on the blade of the dagger, 'then if I let you go in to tell Kendrick I want to speak to him, will you give me your word not to try any dirty tricks? You'll come out again without a pistol or a sword or anything like that.'

'Word of honour, sure!' The pirate nodded, and managed a smile. 'Good idea of yours, that. Very good notion. You're a clever child. But yes, you can rely on me.'

Munk's voice faltered. 'You don't trust this fellow, do you?'

Jolly ignored him. 'Then get out and do as you've promised,' she told the pirate. She threw the dagger up in the air, caught it skilfully by its tip, and flung it across the alley. It stuck, quivering, in a window frame. Munk opened his eyes even wider.

Without another word the pirate disappeared inside the tavern. Noise and smells drifted out into the air as he pushed the door open and closed it after him again.

'Are you totally –' Munk began, but Jolly interrupted him by seizing his arm and dragging him away with her.

'Out of here! Quick!' she cried, and then they were running down the alley together among dirty men and scantily clad women, through several arches and down alleys

136

that were sometimes knee-deep in garbage. The stench of the whole place was revolting, yet Jolly hardly seemed to notice it.

After a few minutes she stopped. Breathless, Munk came to a halt beside her.

'What was the idea of all that?' he asked angrily. His breath was coming fast and short. 'Your little show could cost us our necks.'

'Maybe – if Kendrick catches up with us. But he won't. I'm sure he'll enjoy hearing the story that fool has to tell him. And suppose the guard and his lousy friends come looking for us – we're well out of it, right?'

'So what was the point?'

'I've found out what I wanted to know. Kendrick has hardly any guards on duty. He feels safe in the *Fat Hen*.' Her grin grew broader. 'Bad luck for him. Good luck for me.'

'You can't . . . no, you're not that crazy.'

Jolly laughed. 'I'm going to pay His Majesty a visit tonight. And then I'll find out if he knows anything about the trap that was set for the *Maddy*.'

'You're crazy!' Munk clapped his hand to his brow and turned round once on the spot in a circle. 'Completely crazy!'

She waved that away. 'I grew up with this riff-raff. Kendrick's rotten to the core and a murderer, but if he knows anything about it he'll tell me – always provided I come armed with the right arguments.'

'Your arguments wouldn't be knife-edged, would they?'

'Could be.'

Munk's suntanned face had turned white as chalk. 'You really and truly have lost your mind! It was all too much for you. The shipwreck, the ghosts, the Acherus . . .'

Jolly beamed at him. 'I haven't felt as good as this for ages.'

'That's what I was afraid of.'

'You wanted adventures, didn't you?' In high spirits, she dropped a kiss on his cheek. 'Well, here you are, right in the middle of them.'

The unnamed island where Munk had lived with his parents lay on the eastern outskirts of the Bahamas, a final outpost before sailors reached the huge, empty expanses of the Atlantic. By way of contrast, New Providence was at the centre of the island group. It was a small island, oval in shape from east to west, with just one harbour on its coast. Port Nassau was officially a British colony, but the governors sent out from Great Britain did well from granting asylum to pirates and receivers of stolen goods. It was said that an English governor of the island, paid a paltry thirty pounds a year by his government, could make forty thousand pounds if he did business with the freebooters and took part of their profits.

So the old fortress of the colonial British masters might dominate Port Nassau, and it was visible from afar, but it no longer impressed anyone. Kendrick was the real ruler of the island, not the English governor, who seldom showed his face outside the walls of the fortress and spent his days in good living, with wine and women supplied by the pirates.

Port Nassau had every advantage the freebooters could wish for. The harbour was deep enough for their sloops and brigantines, but too shallow for heavy naval warships. There was a good view of the sea from the surrounding mountains, and no attackers could approach unobserved. The dense forests on the island provided more than enough timber to build new ships, as well as tropical fruit and wild boar, not to mention the delicacies taken from the ocean in these latitudes: tasty fish, shellfish and turtles.

The settlement itself was a close-packed collection of hovels and wooden houses, most of them thatched with palm fronds, some merely covered with oilcloth. There were decrepit lean-tos and shacks everywhere, and pirates lived in them when they came ashore. The traders who bought the pirates' hard-won loot had settled in a large tented camp around Port Nassau. There were any number of gambling dens, taverns and houses of ill repute – along with the sale of stolen goods, these places were the islanders' only source of income.

Danger sometimes threatened from the cyclones which occasionally swept the Caribbean Sea, and could flatten places like Port Nassau to the ground within a few hours. But the pirates weren't about to let even a cyclone drive them from their warm nest – next day it would all be rebuilt in a great hurry, the dead buried, and soon they'd be celebrating again, enjoying the joys of a pirate's life and making merry.

Jolly told Munk all she knew about the island as they sat by the harbour waiting for twilight to fall. Munk had tried several times to persuade her not to carry out her plan, but she stuck to her guns. When he offered to go with her she vehemently refused. Even the prospect of a little helpful shell magic couldn't make her change her mind.

They hadn't seen the Ghost-Trader since morning. He had not thought it necessary to let them know what his business was in Port Nassau, but had just made them promise to keep an eye open for each other – whoever set that trap for Bannon on the high seas might well have spies and allies on New Providence too.

Although the ghost up in the crow's-nest of the ship had sighted the island on the afternoon of the previous day, the Trader had preferred to spend the night on board, as far from the mountains on the island as possible while still keeping them in view. Only at dawn had the three of them climbed into the little dinghy that the ghost ship towed along, and crossed to the island in it.

The boat was now in the harbour basin of Port Nassau, among countless rowing boats and yawls which brought the freebooters ashore from their sloops lying at anchor further out – or from any galleon they might have taken as a prize.

Jolly and Munk were sitting on some empty barrels and crates close to the water's edge.

This was not a built-up harbour of the kind to be found in the big cities of Haiti or Jamaica, only a fortified shoreline. The line of taverns and shacks running along the sea-front mingled with the traders' tents. The wind always blowing off the sea drove the smells of food and stale beer inland. In fact the beach was one of the few places in the whole of Port Nassau where the stench of a pirates' den didn't turn your stomach.

Munk's face was gradually regaining some colour. In spite of the prospect of Jolly's nocturnal expedition and his grief for his parents, a smile occasionally crossed his face, and sometimes he was even fascinated. Most of the pirates stumbling around dead drunk outside the taverns might be scum, devoid of dignity or any idea of decent conduct, but just a few of them matched Munk's ideal of the noble corsair: men in expensive clothing with tall boots, shining swords and ornate plumes on their hats.

'Can I see your tattoo?' he suddenly asked Jolly after they had been sitting in silence for some time, watching the tipsy cavorting outside the taverns.

She laughed, making her earrings clink. 'You want me to undress? Right here?'

Munk went red as a turkey. 'I didn't mean it like that. I was only thinking . . .' He fell silent. 'Sorry. 'Scuse me.'

'Oh, come on.' Jolly made a dismissive gesture and swung round, still sitting, to turn her back to him. 'Push up my shirt and waistcoat, and then you can see it.'

'You mean I –'

'Don't make such a fuss about it, just do as I say.'

She felt him place both hands on her waist. Was he actually trembling? Good heavens, she'd grown up among pirates, a crew of seventy men. There'd never been any insinuating remarks or suggestive looks – every man jack of them knew he'd have had to account for himself to Bannon in person.

142

Hesitantly, Munk pushed up her white linen shirt and her waistcoat. She held both garments in place in front of her, arms folded, but her back was soon bare.

'What is it?'

'It was going to be a coral reef. Our cook, Trevino, had just begun it when the lookout saw the Spanish galleon. I'm afraid it didn't get further than a few lines and curlicues.'

'Are you going to leave it like that?'

'Maybe I'll find someone with enough talent to finish it some day.' She turned. He quickly withdrew his hands, and her shirt and waistcoat dropped into place again. 'But at this moment, to be honest, I'm not bothered.'

'No, of course not.' He was still red in the face, which made him look healthy again for the first time since the events on the island. A little excitement suited him better than all his gloomy brooding on board the ghost ship. She'd have to put other ideas into his head, and this was the perfect opportunity: no Ghost-Trader in sight to spread doom and gloom with his ominous stories.

'Come on,' she said, standing up. 'Let's go and have a drink.'

'You mean . . . alcohol?'

Jolly gave him her most winning smile. 'Well, you want to be a pirate.'

'Not a *sozzled* pirate.'

'Come on, that's all part of it. Better learn to deal with it early on.' Jolly herself didn't like rum, and beer was too bitter for her, but she'd drunk a glass of wine with the pirates now and then. She didn't know if Munk had any experience of drink, so if not it was high time he did. This was the Caribbean, after all! Nowhere else were so many commandments broken!

Munk's surprise gave way to suspicion. 'You just want to put me out of action so I'll let you go tonight.'

'You'll do that anyway, great magician!' She took his hand and led him over the beach to the nearest taverns.

'I don't know if this is a good idea,' said Munk.

'Don't be so faint-hearted.'

Jolly was making for the nearest taproom when the door of the place crashed off its hinges, and several intertwined bodies flew through the air and fell on the sand. The pirates moaned and groaned. One of them was swearing about a sprained ankle.

Munk would rather have turned back, but Jolly, delighted, stood her ground. 'Great, a brawl!'

'Can't we watch from a distance?'

Jolly sighed as if he had said something amazingly childish. 'But then we won't see anything!'

'But then again we won't be *hit* by anything – like fists or heavy flying objects.'

'You're such a scaredy-cat!'

He did not reply to this, and stood beside her while the heap of human bodies on the ground disentangled itself. The men, cursing and swearing, were about to get to their feet when another figure sailed through the open doorway, landed on top of them, and knocked them all flat again.

There was a lot of shouting, then the sound of furniture crashing about inside the tavern, and a chair followed the latest arrival out into the open air – one of the heavy objects that Munk had mentioned. The chair missed the group on the ground and landed a short way from Jolly with its back buried in the sand.

'Seen enough?' Munk turned to walk away.

Jolly stayed where she was, staring wide-eyed at the boy who had been the last to fly through the doorway. '*Griffin?* Well, blow me if it isn't Griffin!'

Munk pulled a face. 'Who?'

Jolly kicked the chair aside and went closer to the men, who were rapidly getting to their feet again. The first of them were about to run for safety when a huge man stepped through the tavern door and into the sunlight. He was taller than any of the others, and so broad-shouldered that he had to turn his upper body sideways to get through the door frame. He wore black breeches and boots, but instead of a waistcoat he had a metal breastplate over his shirt, the kind that pirates sometimes found in fortresses abandoned by the Spaniards. Strangest of all, however, was the iron helmet covering his head. The visor was closed, and hid his face. Knights in the Old World had worn helmets like that, as Jolly knew from stories: people like St George or Sir Lancelot. But a pirate, in the humid heat of the Caribbean? That was more than unusual.

The group on the ground had broken up by now; only two figures were still sitting in the sand, the man with the sprained ankle and the boy Jolly had recognised.

'Griffin, good heavens . . .!'

Munk crossed his arms. 'Are you going to tell me who this is?'

'Griffin,' she repeated. 'About your age and mine. He grew up on a number of pirate ships – and was thrown off as many again. Claims he could play cards when he was six or seven better than all the other pirates put together.' She smiled. 'He's shockingly boastful. I can't stand him.'

Munk looked quizzically at her. 'Doesn't look like it to me.'

Her smile grew broader. 'Appearances can be deceptive.'

146

Munk snorted derisively, but turned his attention, with new interest, to what was going on.

The giant in the knight's helmet strode forward in silence. He swept the injured man aside with a single blow. The man landed in the sand a few paces further off, struggled to his feet with difficulty and limped away, muttering angrily.

Griffin, dazed, was holding his head. He was fair like Munk, but wore his hair shoulder-length and plaited into dozens of small braids which coiled around his head like little snakes when he moved. Slaves from Africa had brought this hairstyle to the Caribbean with them, but Griffin was the only white person Jolly knew to do his hair like that. His clothes were the usual pirate gear: breeches, boots, shirt, and instead of a waistcoat a blue velvet frock-coat, mended in several places.

'Look, he has a knife,' whispered Munk. 'Why doesn't he defend himself with it?'

'This is a fight between men of honour.'

'Oh, of course.'

'I expect Griffin tried to cheat the others at cards. In fact I'm sure he did.'

'So now he's going to let this man murder him?'

Jolly was beginning to fear that herself. The giant in the

helmet didn't seem to have any friendly agreement in mind. His fists were as big as buckets, the backs of his hands were covered with dark, bristly hairs.

Griffin was coming back to his senses. He hadn't seen Jolly yet; his eyes were fixed on the giant standing over him, legs planted wide apart.

'Er, Buenaventure . . . that was just an oversight. Honest. A little bit of bad luck. You can understand that, can't you?' A broad grin appeared on his brown, sunburnt face. His blue eyes shone like the ocean in the sunlight. 'Come on, you wouldn't hurt your old mate Griffin. We're friends. It was a fair game, right? Maybe except for that tiny little incident at the end, but such things are easily forgotten, don't you think?'

Buenaventure said nothing, just looked down at the boy through the slits of his helmet.

Griffin shrugged. 'Oh, very well, then.' Without warning, he raised his right leg and kicked the giant's lower abdomen as hard as he could.

Sympathetic groans ran through the crowd, and many hands instinctively moved to the flaps of the spectators' own breeches.

Buenaventure did not move. Not a sound emerged from the helmet. His fists were still clenched.

Struggling up out of the sand, Griffin got to his feet. He was about to swing round and run for it when a mighty hand fell on his shoulder. Another closed around his throat.

Jolly gasped. Munk, transfixed, stared at what was going on, and was unable to say anything.

A noise that didn't sound like words came from under the helmet. Buenaventure was growling like a fighting dog.

Jolly wondered whether there was any way of helping Griffin. He had no chance at all against this man Buenaventure on his own, that was obvious. But she wasn't sure that she wanted to run the risk. What she had said was true: she didn't particularly like Griffin. Or at least, sometimes she didn't. Now and then.

But then the giant dug his hand into both pockets of Griffin's frock-coat, tore them away from their seams and took out the gold pieces he found in them. Then he dropped the boy, turned and strode away. The crowd immediately divided, leaving a pathway for him. Moments later the giant had disappeared into a gap among the shacks.

Griffin jumped up, grinned awkwardly at the crowd, muttered something like, 'Still in one piece! No damage done! I sent him packing!' and hurried away as fast as he could – just in time too. For now the other men who had flown out through the door with him had joined the chase.

They too were demanding the money he had won from them under false pretences. Amidst the shouts and bellowing of the pirates standing around, Griffin ran along the beach, braids flying, and turned down an alley. The others chased after him. Soon the pack had disappeared from the spectators' view. After a while the angry shouts of Griffin's pursuers died away too. The crowd dispersed.

Jolly shook her head. 'He'll never learn.'

Munk was looking sceptically at her. 'You like him.'

'No, I don't!'

'I can see you do.'

'Nonsense.'

'How long have you known each other?'

She sighed dismissively. 'Oh, for ever. He was once cabin boy on one of Bannon's ships – but the steersman threw him overboard for cheating at cards.'

'What, just like that? On the high seas?'

Jolly grinned. 'Griffin's a good swimmer – he's had to be.' She shook her head, dismissing the memory. 'Come on, let's have that drink.'

Munk breathed sharply in and then, resigned to his fate, stepped over the broken door and followed her into the tavern.

PRINCESS SOLEDAD

Nights on New Providence were bright with the light of lanterns and open camp fires. There were shadows only in the narrowest alleys, the most remote nooks and crannies — and the back yard of the *Fat Hen*.

Jolly was making her way precariously over one of the few tiled roofs in Port Nassau. The buildings around the inn lay below the British governor's fortress, and unlike those in other parts of town they were stone houses, some of them on two or three floors. This stone-built quarter rose from the sea of palm-thatched roofs and single-storey hovels like a castle, taller and more massive than the rest of the town. If anyone attacked, the roads passing through it and the gates could be closed, making the whole quarter into a little fortress where Kendrick and his men could take cover.

The tavern yard lay about eighteen feet below Jolly, a black rectangle where there must be a back door leading into the *Fat Hen*. But it was too dark down there for her to see either the door itself or the guard who was presumably posted in front of it.

She tried to find out where he was by listening, but it was no good. All the sounds she could hear came from inside the tavern: merrymakers bawling and singing, and now and then a crash or a scream mingled with shrieks from the serving maids.

Jolly had no choice but to keep her eye on the shadows and inch her way towards one of the windows on the upper floor of the inn. At least the pirate at the entrance seemed to have been right when he said there was only one man on guard down below. She'd have been bound to hear two or more talking, or at least whispering.

All the same, she didn't like climbing over the slope of the roof in the open while unseen eyes might be watching her from below. How long would it be before the guard raised the alarm? Would he wait until she was in the middle of the roof and at her most vulnerable?

Just do it, she told herself. Come on!

She inched forward, fingers and toes seeking a foothold or handhold among the brittle tiles of the roof, and doing her best to make no noise. The black abyss below pulled at her, whispering to her to let go. You won't do it, a voice said in her ear, you haven't got a chance!

She was already halfway when a tile cracked under her right foot. Jolly froze. Faltering, she looked down, and saw that the terracotta tile had broken in half. The lower part had worked loose and looked like sliding off the roof the moment Jolly raised her foot.

Now what? She was stuck, unless she was going to risk attracting the attention of the guard down below.

If there was a guard there at all.

Still, she couldn't wait here to be spotted. One way or another she had to go on.

She was about to move when she heard a creaking sound down in the yard. A strip of light fell through the darkness; the noise from the inn immediately grew louder.

Someone had opened the back door. Now Jolly could see it for the first time; it was in the right-hand wall of the yard as seen from her perch on the roof. A man came out into the open air, swaying slightly and holding a beer tankard. He stopped, raised the tankard, cursed in Italian when he realised that there was no beer left in it, and took aim, about to fling it against a wall.

'Hey there!' shouted a voice from the shadows before the man could throw the tankard. 'Kendrick wants this door to stay closed. I'm not standing here all night for nothing! You go back inside! No one has any business out here!'

The pirate in the doorway swore again, called the invisible guard names – and furiously flung the empty tankard against the opposite wall.

Jolly raised her foot. The half-tile slipped, scraping as it slid over the edge of the roof, and fell. The noise when it crashed to the ground came a split second later than the breaking of the pottery tankard. She clenched her teeth and narrowed her eyes. And held her breath.

Down in the yard the door slammed shut behind the drunken pirate.

The other man, who had been standing in the darkness all this time, was quiet again – he might just as well have been gone too. He must have heard the tile crashing to the ground, but he obviously connected it with the broken tankard – just as Jolly had planned. Her heart raced with relief.

But she still had half the roof to cross. However, she now knew for certain that there really was a man in the yard. She hadn't been able to see him in the light falling through the open doorway, so he must be on her side of the yard, directly below her. At least that meant that she was outside his field of vision.

She shivered. She'd been lucky that the tile hadn't fallen on his head.

154

Keep going!

Her hands and feet groped for support on the crumbling slope of the pitched roof even more cautiously than before. Somewhere in the distance, in the tangled alleyways east of the stone-built quarter, she could hear the clash of sword blades, wild cries and then a scream. Someone roared with laughter, others joined in. Welcome to Port Nassau.

Jolly reached the other end of the slope. Here the roof of the tavern annexe met the wall of a higher storey, the upper floor of the main building. Kendrick's rooms, she suspected, would be somewhere here.

A final glance at the black abyss below, and then she was close to a window. It was bolted on the inside. She drew her dagger, thrust it into the crack of the frame, and easily levered the catch open. Without a sound, the window swung inward.

Jolly slipped through it. She found herself in a small bedroom. The bed was dirty and unmade, clothes were scattered all over the floor. Beside the stained wash-basin stood a small iron-bound chest which was fastened to one of the beams in the ceiling with a chain. Two padlocks prevented anyone from getting at the loot of the pirate who owned it. Jolly suspected that one of Kendrick's close friends was staying in this room.

The only door had no lock and was easily opened. Peering round it, Jolly saw a narrow passage. There wasn't a soul in sight.

She darted out, closed the door behind her, and listened. There were footsteps down in the stairway, and the voices of a man and a woman. Both footsteps and voices were coming closer.

Jolly let out her breath sharply, went to the end of the corridor and tried another door. It opened into a larger room, dominated by a four-poster bed with a velvet canopy and adorned with a coat of arms in gold and silver, probably looted from the ship of some Spanish or English nobleman. A great many trunks and chests stood around the room, and its floor was covered with several layers of oriental rugs. There were half a dozen chandeliers and several cupboards, some stuffed so full of expensive fabrics and garments that their doors wouldn't close.

Jolly wondered why the pirate emperor bothered with all this stuff. He could have sold it to the traders for a pretty penny in the tented camp on the outskirts of Port Nassau. But no doubt he had more than enough gold already, and Kendrick was known as a fashionable dandy who liked fine clothes, cleanliness and an attractive appearance – not at all like his disreputable followers.

There was a persistent rumour that his hair was naturally ginger, but he dyed it black.

She had no time to take a closer look, for the loud footsteps and the voices were approaching. They'd reach the top of the stairs any moment now.

Quietly, she closed the door behind her, went to the window and looked out. A daring leap and a little luck might take her to one of the slopes of the annexe roof – but she would be in full view of the man on watch in the yard. She couldn't hope to escape that way without being noticed.

The voices came closer: a rough male voice and the softer tones of a young woman.

Jolly didn't have much time to look for a hiding-place. She ran to one of the wardrobes and pushed her way into the soft, musty warmth of mountains of silken clothing. A mingled smell of perfumed toilet water, male sweat and damp fabric surrounded her, taking her breath away. Dagger in hand, she pulled the wardrobe door almost shut, leaving only a crack open through which she could see the bed. Now she just had to wait for the right moment.

The door of the room flew open, hitting the wall.

'And suppose the Spaniards really do attack?' the woman was asking. She was the first to come into Jolly's field of vision. She must have been in her early twenties, and she was very slender and pretty as a picture, although she wore too much garish make-up. Long, dark red hair flowed over her shoulders. The dress she was wearing seemed to consist mainly of ribbons and thin strips of fabric, and revealed a good deal more of her than it covered.

There were hundreds of trollops like this on New Providence, women who used their looks and skills to fleece the pirates. Jolly didn't have much time for them, but nor did she despise them – like all the lawless folk of the Caribbean, they worked hard for their living.

The girl sat down on the edge of the bed with an affected sigh.

'The Spaniards?' Kendrick uttered a derisive sound. He too was now just outside the gap through which Jolly was looking. 'They haven't a hope of getting close enough to the island. I've posted men on all the mountains to keep watch for any armada, and as soon as more than three ships at once approach they'll raise the alarm.'

Kendrick was tall and powerful. He wore a richly embroidered frock-coat, breeches of a fabric shot with gold thread, and immaculately polished boots. His curly hair was long and slightly tousled. A gold earring dangled from his left ear. His right ear was missing – it had been shot off during a skirmish, leaving only a scar, which he was usually vain enough to cover with his profuse locks. But now Jolly could clearly see the pink remains of the ear.

'You seem to trust your men a lot,' said the young woman, stretching. 'Aren't you afraid they may be bribed by Spanish spies?'

'My followers are men of honour.' Kendrick clumsily tugged off his coat and flung it over a chest. 'I can count on every one of them as I'd count on a brother.'

Only now did Jolly notice that Kendrick's voice was slurred. He must be drunk, although it was said that, unusually for a pirate, he hardly ever touched alcohol. But his movements now were nervous and his tread unsteady.

'Aren't you feeling well?' murmured the girl, baring a knee as if by chance.

Oh no, thought Jolly, this is too much. Do I really have to watch? How nauseating!

Kendrick approached the bed with a lopsided grin. 'Just a trifle . . . a trifle dizzy. Can't think why. Didn't take a drop of rum.' He paused before stationing himself four-square in front of the girl. 'If I didn't know better I'd say someone had put something in my food.'

The young woman raised her eyebrows. 'Who'd dare to do a thing like that?'

The pirate emperor laughed unpleasantly. 'Ha! No one! I

only have to give those lily-livered cowards a look for their hearts to drop into their boots!'

'Oh, no wonder, with muscles like yours!'

Jolly rolled her eyes.

Kendrick grinned. 'Come along, pull my boots off.'

He put one foot on the edge of the bed beside the girl. For a moment it looked as if she were hesitating. Then she took hold of the boot and pulled.

Kendrick was still laughing, but then he suddenly lost his balance and fell backwards to the floor, where he sat dazed.

Now! thought Jolly.

She pushed the wardrobe door open, jumped Kendrick from behind and put the blade of her dagger to his throat.

'You keep quiet!' She gave the young woman on the bed a menacing glare. 'Don't move, and nothing will happen to you.'

She was well aware how crazy this situation was. A girl of fourteen threatening the king of the Caribbean pirates, and at the same time trying to keep a grown woman at bay.

Kendrick tried to get to his feet, but Jolly pressed the blade even closer to his throat until he stopped resisting.

'Who are you?' asked the pirate. 'Do I know you?'

'I'm Jolly,' she said. 'Yes, we've met a couple of times. I belong to Bannon's crew.'

160

'Jolly . . . of course. The little polliwiggle. For the Lord's sake, girl, stop this nonsense or I'll throw you to my dogs.'

'The four-legged or two-legged kind?'

'What do you want?'

'I want you to listen. This is for your ears alone . . . well, your ear.' That had slipped out before she could stop it. She hadn't come to crack jokes at Kendrick's expense.

The young woman sitting on the edge of the bed hadn't moved. She did not look at all alarmed, more surprised.

'I'd let you go,' Jolly told her, 'if I could be sure you wouldn't raise the alarm in that pigsty down there.'

A smile stole over the woman's face. She really was extremely beautiful, in spite of the narrow scar down her left cheek. But then her expression became suddenly grave, almost angry. She still said nothing; she was watching and listening.

'Put that damn knife away!' said Kendrick. 'I'll have you strung up from the tallest gallows in town. I'll skin you with my own hands and feed you to the beasts. I'll slice your innards open and –'

'Yes, I'm sure you would,' said Jolly, although she was secretly terrified. 'Let's get down to business, shall we?'

'What business?'

'I need your help.'

His voice sounded steadier now, as if the shock had brought him back to his senses. 'And you think this is the best way to get it?'

'Your life in exchange for your help, Kendrick. That's the bargain. I want your word of honour.' She wasn't sure what Kendrick's word of honour was worth, but she had to start somewhere. 'You know what happened to Bannon?'

'The *Maddy* sank,' he said. 'Everyone's talking about it. The Spaniards have butchered him and his crew, or taken them prisoner, no one knows which for sure. Why weren't you with him?'

'They weren't Spaniards,' said Jolly, ignoring his question. 'You're powerful enough to find out the truth. You have ships you can send in search of Bannon.'

He smiled grimly. 'You're asking me to do that? Send men looking for Bannon?'

'That's why I'm here.'

'You could have saved yourself the trouble, girl. No one's found either shipwrecked sailors or bodies.'

Jolly remembered the venomous spiders, but immediately dismissed the thought from her mind. She mustn't weaken now. After all, as Kendrick himself had just said, no one had found any corpses.

162

'Then you and your men can look for evidence.'

'We'll do no such thing.'

The edge of the blade scratched his skin. A drop of blood trickled over the steel. Kendrick tried to shake Jolly off again – in vain.

'Oh, for God's sake!' sighed the young woman suddenly. 'Let me show you how to do this kind of thing properly.' She clenched her right hand, examined the white knuckles of her fist for a moment – and then jumped up swiftly and punched Kendrick in the face with all her might.

She grinned as he collapsed with a groan. '*That's* the way to do it!' Blood shot from his broken nose. She made a face and imitated Jolly's voice. 'Let's get down to business . . . I need your help . . .' She laughed derisively. 'Good God in heaven! *This* is what that toad understands!' And so saying she swung her foot and kicked the pirate emperor between the legs. Kendrick gasped, suddenly turned pale and almost lost consciousness.

Jolly looked up at the young woman in surprise. 'You're not an ordinary trollop at all, are you?'

'Hm . . . seems my disguise wasn't quite as good as I thought.' She looked down at Kendrick with extreme distaste. 'Good enough for this scum, anyway. I think you can take your knife away now. He won't be defending himself again in a hurry.'

'Hey, this is my business! I decide what happens next.'

'It was *my* business until you turned up!'

'So what do *you* want from him?'

The woman made a dismissive gesture. 'Not his help, for sure.' She was about to strike the pirate again, but Jolly cried, 'Wait! He's no use to me if he's unconscious.'

'Why should I care? I want to see the swine die for what he did to my father. If you hadn't interfered . . .' She broke off, looked around and picked up a sword from an open chest. 'You'd better get out now. This isn't going to be a sight for children.'

Jolly clenched her hand around the dagger. 'How about *you* getting out? Without Kendrick I can't . . . Just a moment. Your father, did you say?'

'Scarab, the rightful pirate emperor – murdered by this devil.'

'You're Scarab's daughter?' Jolly thought for a moment, and then remembered the name. 'You're Soledad?'

The young woman nodded, but not for a moment did she take her fierce gaze off the half-unconscious Kendrick. 'I've been planning this for months. It wasn't easy to get close to him. The landlord down there is very choosy about the girls he hires.'

Jolly wrinkled her nose. 'I climbed in through the window – that worked all right.'

Soledad stared at her angrily. 'You don't mean one of the windows looking out on the yard?'

'Why not?'

'Dear heavens above!' Soledad stepped over Kendrick, flung the door to the corridor open, and listened. 'Oh, well done! Absolutely brilliant! They're already on their way!'

Sure enough, the tramp of many boots could be heard on the stairs, and a loud, confused noise in which heavy footsteps mingled with cries and the clash of steel.

Soledad closed the door and pushed a chest in front of it. 'All the windows are secured by strings. If one of them's opened a bell rings down in the kitchen. Kendrick's idea. If anyone breaks in he won't know he's been found out until he's surrounded.'

Jolly felt the blood rise to her face. 'I wasn't to know that.'

'You think I'm wearing this appalling garment for fun?' Soledad indicated her revealing dress. 'I've been haunting the place for weeks just to find out how to get in. It's not as easy as you think to fool Kendrick.'

'And that's a fact,' groaned the pirate emperor, who was coming back to his senses. Jolly's knife went straight to his throat again. 'You're done for,' he added. 'The pair of you.'

Soledad gave him a mocking grin. 'So what do you suggest? You want us to surrender?'

'No,' he said, unmoved. 'You'll die anyway.'

The pirate princess snorted scornfully, and then began reinforcing the barricade in front of the door. Showing a strength that Jolly wouldn't have expected of her slender frame, she heaved a second chest on top of the first, and then started moving a cupboard.

Suddenly Kendrick's fist flew up. It was aiming for Jolly's chin, despite the blade of her dagger – perhaps he thought she wouldn't use it anyway. But it wasn't so easy to dupe Jolly. She moved like lightning to avoid the blow, and it missed her by a hair's breadth. Instinctively, her own hand shot out, grabbed Kendrick's hair and bent his head back. He screamed. His throat was exposed now. She could have used the dagger, and any other pirate would have done it, but she hesitated.

Kendrick was her only chance. If anyone could find out about the trap that had been set for Bannon, it was the pirate emperor.

'You owe me something. I've saved your life,' she whispered to him.

'Huh!' was all he replied.

166

'You heard her, didn't you?' Jolly pointed to Soledad. 'She'd have killed you tonight if I hadn't intervened.'

Soledad's eyes flashed. 'Don't get any ideas about that, my girl. I haven't finished with him yet.'

Jolly ignored her. She stared intently into Kendrick's brown eyes. 'I *did* save you from her, didn't I?'

'No,' he said coolly. 'My men are doing that at this very moment!'

Something crashed against the door. There was a lot of excitement out in the passage. A number of voices were shouting in confusion, boots clumped over the tiled floor. Then a shot rang out, and the barricade shook. The bullet must have buried itself in one of the chests or the cupboard.

'How long do you think you can hold out against them?' Kendrick grinned triumphantly. 'You're both dead already.'

Soledad snatched up the sword and made for her father's murderer with it. 'You'll die first!'

Once again Jolly came between them. Sparks flew as she parried Soledad's sword-thrust with her dagger, just an inch or so away from Kendrick's chest.

The man froze rigid as a silent trial of strength went on above him. Jolly resisted as best she could, but very slowly Soledad succeeded in forcing the dagger further and further down with her sword.

'Stop it!' Jolly managed to say. 'He's no use to us dead.'

'He's no use to me anyway.' The pressure of the blade did not lessen. The look in Soledad's eyes was pure venom. 'I want to see him die.'

Jolly's left leg shot out. She kicked the pirate princess on the shin with all her might. Soledad cried out in surprise and then fell to her knees.

'You stupid cow!'

'We have to get out of here! And I know how, too.'

'Oh yes? Tell me.'

'Only if he stays alive.'

'It's a funny thing, I thought you'd say that.'

Jolly sighed. 'You must help me.'

Soledad was clutching her painful shin. 'First he has to help you, now I do – can't you do anything at all for yourself?' But she didn't wait for an answer. Instead, she got to her feet again and looked at the door, which was now shaking under a series of rhythmic blows. The pirates in the passage outside were ramming something against it. The fact that they hadn't broken the barricade down yet was due solely to the narrow width of the corridor: only two men could get near the door at once.

Jolly pointed her dagger at Kendrick. He was still white in the face, but he tried to struggle up. 'You stay where you are!' she snapped. 'Soledad, let's tie him up. But he has to stay conscious.'

Some impatient pirate or other fired another shot at the door. This time the bullet passed through the back of the chest of drawers, whistled past Soledad and smashed a glass carafe beside Kendrick's four-poster.

The princess didn't let it distract her. With Jolly's help, she tied up the pirate emperor with a gold cord she had torn off the canopy over the bed. He was cursing the whole time, but he had given up trying to defend himself. Perhaps he had realised that he would stay alive as long as the younger girl was in charge.

'Now then,' said Jolly, 'we must get him up on top of the chests.'

Soledad's eyebrows drew together. She said, 'Hmph!' as she saw what Jolly's plan was. But then she murmured, 'Could work.' She took Kendrick by the shoulders while Jolly raised his feet.

He protested, but they took no notice. Moments later they had heaved him up on top of the two chests. He was now lying lengthwise right across the barricade, close to the door, with his hands and feet bound.

An axe chopped through the wood just a hand's breadth away from Kendrick's head.

'*You idiots!*' His voice cracked. 'Stop that, you brainless apes! I'm right behind the door! You stupid riff-raff – stop it, I tell you!'

Jolly smiled, pleased. 'That ought to give us a little time.' She hurried over to the window and pushed it open. Light fell through the open back door of the inn. The yard was empty. The guard down there must have run upstairs with the others.

Soledad stood in the middle of the room, evidently torn two ways. On the one hand, she wanted to escape; on the other, she still felt a burning desire to be avenged on Kendrick.

He himself was shouting to his men not to touch the door, certainly not to shoot at it.

'But Cap'n,' said a faint voice through the wood, 'how else do we get it open?'

If Kendrick's hands hadn't been bound behind his back he would surely have been tearing his hair.

'Come on!' cried Jolly, clambering on to the window-sill.

Soledad realised that Kendrick would only be any help in their escape as long as he was shouting at his men and keeping them from breaking down the door. With a regretful shrug of her shoulders, she turned away from him and joined Jolly.

170

Jolly was already taking off from a crouching position and diving for the nearest slope of the pitched roof outside. She landed on the tiles with a clatter, got a grip on them and made her way quickly up to the roof ridge.

Soledad was a head taller than Jolly, and had much more difficulty in launching herself from the little window while crouching down. But she too made a safe landing, and sought frantically for support with her hands and feet. For a moment she was in danger of falling, but Jolly, quick as lightning, seized her by the arm.

Moments later, bending low as they ran, they were on their way along the roof ridge.

Kendrick's shouts pursued them out into the open air. 'They're through the window, you stinking sea-snails! Get down and catch them! . . . Dear Lord, am I entirely surrounded by soft-boiled jellyfish brains?'

The noise of boots running downstairs immediately followed – some of his men at least were on the way down. Shadows were already showing on the strip of light in the yard.

'Along here!' Jolly pointed to the back part of the inn, the building that linked the two annexes at the sides. 'The rope I used to climb to the roof is hanging from the back wall.'

They reached it just as a great deal of shouting rose from

the yard below. One of Kendrick's men had seen them on the roof ridge just before they slid down the slope behind it. Pistols were cocked, and the first bullets whistled through the dark.

'Quick!' Jolly's hands burned like fire as she slid down the coarse hempen rope. She reached the ground, swearing, and swerved aside to avoid Soledad.

Side by side, they ran for it. The pirate princess knew the nooks and crannies of the stone-built quarter better than Jolly, and soon she took the lead. They ran through arched gateways and under the makeshift bridges that linked some of the taller buildings; they crossed small squares as busy as oriental bazaars even after midnight; they made their way along alleys almost too narrow even for their slim shoulders, and climbed over mountains of rubbish, once even over a bunch of protesting drunks thrown out of a tavern by the landlord.

Then, after endless minutes, Soledad stopped.

'They've lost our trail,' she said, gasping for breath, 'or they'd have caught up with us by now.'

Jolly pressed both hands to her sides. Her throat was sore with exhaustion. 'How far from here to the harbour?'

The princess tried to straighten her flimsy dress, not very successfully, and then pointed left. 'Go along there, then it's only a stone's throw away. But steer clear of any open spaces.'

Jolly thought for a moment. 'You could come too. I have friends down by the harbour, and a boat. Maybe you can –'

'No.' There was finality in Soledad's tone. 'I don't need anyone's help to get what I want.'

'Kendrick's head?' Jolly gave her a tight-lipped smile. 'Looks like neither of us got what we wanted.'

'Because you stopped me.'

'And *you* stopped *me*.'

They looked at each other for a moment in silence, and then Soledad shrugged her shoulders. With a quick gesture, she pushed strands of red hair back from her face. 'Another time Kendrick won't escape me.' She hesitated, and then added, 'You saved my life up there on the roof. Thanks.'

Jolly smiled. 'What are you going to do now? He'll have mounted a search for us.'

'First I must get out of these ghastly rags.' She tugged in vain at the tangled straps and ribbons of her dress once more. 'After that I'll see.'

'You're still planning to avenge your father?'

'Of course.'

Jolly sighed, and finally nodded. 'Well, good luck, then.'

'If you want my advice I'd say get out of New Providence. At once, if you can.'

'I'm not afraid of Kendrick.'

Soledad smiled, and for the first time it was an almost friendly smile. 'No, I can see that. All the same, the Spaniards are going to attack, maybe as soon as tonight.'

'Tonight? But Kendrick said —'

'Kendrick's a fool. Another reason why he didn't deserve to lead the pirates. He really believes his men are so afraid of him they'd turn down bribes offered by Spanish spies. Whereas the whole place is teeming with traitors.'

Jolly remembered what Soledad had said at the inn. 'You think the men on watch in the mountains have been bribed? By the Spanish?'

'I'm sure they have. If Kendrick listened more to what's going on around him he'd have realised that long ago. Half Port Nassau and the whole Caribbean are talking about the armada's forthcoming attack. More ships have put to sea these last few days than in four weeks before that. The men still here are as blind as Kendrick — they're like children closing their eyes and thinking no one can see them. But the Spaniards are somewhere out there at this very moment, and they're not far off now. I was going to settle accounts with Kendrick tonight — too late now.'

'What will you do?'

'Go inland. There are a few ships whose captains were

loyal to my father anchored on the other side of the island – one of them will take me aboard.'

'Why not come with me?'

'Kendrick knows who I am now. If he survives the Spanish attack he'll hunt me down with everything he has. There are still a good many who despise him and would rather see Scarab's daughter on the pirate throne. He has good reason to fear me, and not just because of tonight. I'd be doing you no favours by bringing half the pirate fleet down on you.'

Jolly realised that she wasn't going to change Soledad's mind. The princess shook hands as they parted.

'And another thing,' said Soledad. 'About Captain Bannon . . .'

'Yes?'

'You might stop to wonder whether Kendrick had something to do with it himself.'

Jolly wrinkled her brow. She would have asked more questions, but Soledad's red mane of hair was already merging with the shadows of an alley. Her footsteps died away in the dark.

GIDEON'S GRAVE

One of the two parrots was waiting for her on the little sailing dinghy in the harbour. It was Hugh; she knew him by his bright yellow eyes. He was sitting on a piece of paper covered with elegantly ornate handwriting.

Too dangerous to spend the night in the open, said the letter. *I've rented a room at an inn called* Gideon's Grave. *Munk and I will wait for you there. Follow Hugh. He'll lead you to us.*

The note was signed with the initials *GT*, which Jolly thought slightly silly. And there was a postscript under them: *What the devil did you pour down Munk's throat? He cast a spell to turn poor Moe purple!*

Jolly chuckled to herself. Munk had drunk two large glasses of wine in the tavern, and had suddenly been so tipsy that she'd had trouble getting him back to the boat. Once there, she had left him to sleep it off under the tarpaulin in the bows, where he couldn't prevent her carrying out her plan.

She imagined the Ghost-Trader's face when he came back to the harbour and found his protégé in such a state. She couldn't help laughing, in spite of the fear she still felt in her bones after the flight from the inn.

Only the thought of Soledad's words abruptly sobered her up again. She didn't just have the pirate emperor and his entire pack on her heels; the threat of the Spanish attack was even more alarming. She had to find Munk and the Ghost-Trader and persuade them to set off at once. Perhaps they could get back aboard the ghost ship before the armada reached New Providence.

Flapping his wings, Hugh rose in the air and flew ahead of her. As she ran, Jolly crumpled up the Ghost-Trader's letter. She hoped it wasn't too far to the tavern where he and Munk were waiting for her. Who on earth, she thought, would put up at an inn called *Gideon's Grave*?

The place was at the far end of the harbour, a two-storey wooden building with all the noise and dubious aromas of an overcrowded tavern wafting out of it. The upper windows were dark.

'Jolly! There you are at last!' The voice came down to her from one of those pitch-black rectangles. Only when she looked again did she recognise the figure keeping watch for her up there, almost invisible, as if he himself had no more substance than the shadows.

She waved to the Ghost-Trader.

'Wait!' he cried. 'I'll come down and fetch you.'

She shook her head. 'Don't bother.' And with that she stepped through the door into the tavern and made her way fast through the crowd, before anyone could get more than a fleeting glimpse of her. It did the Trader credit that he was concerned about her, but she'd been in worse dens of cutthroats than this with Bannon. She knew how to avoid drunks, and how to defend herself if necessary.

Not even the landlady or any of the maids serving customers noticed her. It was long past midnight. Rum, gin and beer were flowing freely. The room was hot and stuffy, and the smoke of innumerable pipes restricted the view ahead to a couple of yards or so.

Jolly saw a staircase leading up to the guest-rooms, and quickly climbed it. The triangular shape of a dark, hooded cloak abruptly appeared at the top of the stairs. The Ghost-Trader pointed to an open door.

'In here!'

Munk was lying on one of the three beds in the room, snoring loudly enough to wake the dead. The Ghost-Trader closed the door behind them and put the back of a chair under the handle. There was no lock.

Hugh landed beside Moe on the window-sill. The Ghost-Trader had told the truth: the red-eyed parrot's feathers shone bright purple in the candlelight. Munk's shells were set out on a small table.

'It's passing off,' said the Trader. 'His feathers will be black again in a few hours' time.'

'The Spaniards are going to attack!' Jolly came straight out with her news. 'This very night!'

The Ghost-Trader raised his left eyebrow very slightly. 'Who says so?'

'Princess Soledad. Scarab's daughter!'

The eyebrow rose higher until it almost disappeared under the edge of his hood. '*Princess* Soledad? Since when did pirates have royal titles?'

'I think she was telling the truth.'

'Well, before we do anything hasty, you'd better tell me all about it.'

'But we have to get away from here!'

'Later . . . perhaps. First I want to hear your story.'

She sighed impatiently, glanced with a slightly guilty conscience at the sleeping Munk, and started telling her tale in full. The Ghost-Trader listened attentively without sitting down. He stood there, kneading his chin between thumb and forefinger, and looking intently at Jolly, as if he could read more in her eyes than her words told him.

'Hmm,' said the Ghost-Trader finally, and after a pause he repeated it: 'Hmm, hmm.'

'What's that supposed to mean?' Jolly's heartbeat was racing fast enough to pump out the hull of a holed ship.

'Scarab's daughter is a clever girl. She certainly doesn't issue such warnings lightly.'

'Then what are we waiting for?'

'Well, to be honest, for a ship. And her captain.'

Jolly shifted from foot to foot. What was this nonsense he was talking? They had a ship! She might not be the most inviting vessel in the Caribbean, but who cared about that just now?

The Ghost-Trader looked at her and answered her question before she had to put it.

'We must leave the ghost ship. We need a fast, easily manoeuvred vessel now. And an experienced captain.'

'I can sail a ship if I have to,' she said.

The Trader smiled understandingly. 'I don't doubt it. But what we need now is an old hand. A skipper who's up to every trick – and can still be trusted.'

She frowned sceptically. 'And you think you've found one? Here?'

'Captain Walker. He's sitting down in the tavern gambling. As soon as the game's over he'll need money. And then he'll talk to me.'

'Walker?' Jolly covered her face with her hands and uttered a cry of desperation. '*The* Walker? The man who personally cheated Scarab out of a whole cargo of Jamaican rum? The man who changed sides in battles between the Spaniards and the English faster than their cannonballs?'

The Ghost-Trader nodded. 'He commands one of the fastest ships in the Caribbean. And he's a cut-throat, but with a certain sense of honour. We won't find anyone better here, I'm afraid.'

'Honour!' she cried scornfully. 'Maybe he's anxious to have the honour of handing me over to Kendrick.' Exhausted, she dropped on the side of Munk's bed. An idea suddenly occurred to her, and she stared suspiciously at the Trader. 'So why do you really want to get away from the island in such a hurry? Until a minute or so ago you didn't even know the Spaniards were going to attack.'

The Ghost-Trader's face darkened. 'There'll be neither Spaniards nor pirates here soon if we can't put an end to what the Maelstrom is doing. Believe me, the Acherus was only a harmless bogeyman compared to what the Maelstrom will spew out if its power grows. And it *is* growing, with every day and every hour.'

Jolly understood only about half of what he was saying, but at these words she began to feel cold. 'So what are you planning?'

The Ghost-Trader did not answer. He seemed to be uneasy. He took a few steps towards the window and looked out. Only then did he turn back to her. 'Much still lies in darkness, and matters are moving faster than we feared.'

Jolly thought of what had happened on the island and said nothing.

Suddenly Munk stretched in his sleep and laid a hand on Jolly's thigh.

'Oh, for goodness' sake!' She pushed his fingers away in annoyance and jumped up. 'A fieldmouse could hold its liquor better than this . . . this . . .' She broke off. Munk looked very peaceful lying there, as if he had been able to forget his grief for his parents at least for a few hours.

'Don't blame him,' said the Ghost-Trader. 'He can't help what's happened any more than you can.'

She looked at the floor. 'I lured the Acherus to his island,' she said, despondently. 'I can never put that right.'

'Oh yes, you can, and sooner than you think.'

'But what must I do?'

The Trader came closer to her and took her hand, smiling. 'You'll understand it all in time, little polliwiggle.'

Jolly sat on her bed, her knees drawn up, and stared out through the open window at the night. She couldn't sleep, although the Ghost-Trader had advised her to rest. The starry sky above the Caribbean seemed to her too bright today, the roar of the breakers too loud. Many thoughts were going through her mind. She felt a vague, unfocused sense of responsibility weighing on her shoulders, a commitment that she had taken upon herself against her will. What plans did the Ghost-Trader really have for the polliwiggles? And what would become of her search for Bannon with all this going on? She wasn't going to give up looking for him, with or without help. Kendrick, the Ghost-Trader, this Maelstrom – what did she care for any of them?

She jumped when the sound of a terrifying crash came up through the floorboards. Something had been flung against the ceiling of the taproom down below with great force. Something – or someone!

She swung her feet down on the floor – and swung them back again as the crash came again, more violently this time. Then she heard the sound of window panes breaking, and loud voices outside the tavern. Obviously there was a fierce fight in progress down there.

The door flew open. The Ghost-Trader, who had gone downstairs only a few minutes ago, stood four-square in the doorway, one side of his cloak thrown back. His left hand was resting on the silver circlet at his belt.

'Come on, we're off!'

'Has Walker really agreed to help us?'

'Not yet. But once he comes to his senses again he'll see he has no other choice. We'll just pick him up outside the window – that's where he's lying at the moment.'

Jolly looked hard at him. 'Something tells me you had a hand in this.'

'Who knows?'

'But you're not a magician, you said. Just someone who conjures up ghosts.'

The Ghost-Trader laughed suddenly, a sound that made Jolly jump. Even Munk grimaced in his sleep.

'I don't conjure them up, I only trade in them. I collect the ghosts of the dead, I don't raise them. But I can't expect you to understand the difference . . . not yet. And as for the good Captain Walker: this inn is haunted more than any other by the ghosts of men who drank themselves to death or lost their lives in a brawl. Not for nothing is it called

Gideon's Grave. All I did was get a few of those poor souls to upset the captain a little while he played cards.'

'That was a mean thing to do!' said Jolly, but the Ghost-Trader had already turned on his heel and was going back to the stairs. 'Bring the baggage with you!' he called over his shoulder.

Jolly looked after him, feeling cross. 'Yes, sir. Certainly, sir. Your obedient servant, sir.'

Swearing, she stood up, packed Munk's shells in his leather pouch, fixed it to her own belt, and set about waking the boy on the bed. He muttered and grumbled, but finally and unsteadily sat up.

A little later they were both making their way along the taproom wall, avoiding flying tankards and staggering men, ducking as an empty barrel broke apart against the wall above them, and doing their best to avoid the blows, kicks and punches of the brawling pirates.

In the middle of all the bodies chaotically milling around, a gigantic man was running amok. Jolly recognised him by his huge helmet – Buenaventure, the giant from the tavern the day before. He was smashing chairs and tables, not with his fists but with bodies that he sent flying around him like weapons, clearing broad swathes through the crowd of scuffling men. Since everyone was keeping an eye open for him instead of paying Jolly and Munk any attention, the two of them had soon left this scene of carnage behind them.

The Ghost-Trader was standing out in the open air beside a man who sat in the sand, looking dazed and holding his head in his hands.

Walker hadn't changed since Jolly last met him at Bannon's side – apart from the bleeding wound on his forehead. He was of middle height, and lean. His dark hair fell to his shoulders, and just now it wasn't a pretty sight, for strands of it stuck to his face as if the shadows of all the bars behind which he had ever been imprisoned were imprinted on his features.

Bannon had liked Walker, although Jolly didn't; on their rare encounters he had always treated her like a small child. That in itself she couldn't forgive him – let alone the fact that she thought it was silly for a man to wear a gold ring in his nose just because he found it convenient to rest the heavy Cuban cigars that he liked to smoke on it.

Walker was getting to his feet, with difficulty, just as Jolly and Munk arrived.

He looked up and saw her for the first time. 'Good God, if it's not the little toad!'

'Polliwiggle,' the Ghost-Trader corrected him.

'Toad or polliwiggle or newt – comes to the same thing.'

Munk, now reasonably coherent again, looked doubtfully at Walker. 'Who's this wreck, then?'

'He's the best sea captain in the Caribbean,' said the Ghost-Trader. 'Or at least he was before he nearly got his skull smashed in just now.'

Jolly pulled herself together. 'We'd better get moving before that man Buenaventure follows us.'

'Buenaventure?' Walker laughed. In view of his wound, it looked a painful process. 'Oh, him! He was keeping those devils away from me.'

Jolly pursed her lips. 'A friend of yours, is he?'

'My steersman,' Walker told her. 'The best in the business.' He turned to the Ghost-Trader. 'Is the toad coming on board with us, then?'

Jolly gave him a look of scorn. 'I just can't wait to see the *Carfax* again.'

'You always were a horrible child. Loud-mouthed and opinionated and –'

'We can discuss all that on board,' the Ghost-Trader interrupted him, making his way between the two of them as they sniped at each other. 'It probably won't be long before –'

He fell silent.

They all did.

Suddenly there was complete silence over Port Nassau, as if some mysterious power had sucked up all sound. Behind them in *Gideon's Grave* a final crash was heard, and then all was still even there. Buenaventure came out of the doorway and stopped, staring motionless at the nocturnal sea like all the others.

The unreal moment lasted barely long enough for anyone to draw breath, but to Jolly it seemed like an eternity.

Then a flash like lightning flared up on the other side of the bay. It was followed by a second flash, a third and a fourth, until they came so thick and fast that no one could count them. They lit up angular outlines rocking on the sea as if someone had built a whole town on the waves. Deafening thunder sounded as broadside after broadside was fired at Port Nassau.

Screams rang out. Roofs were shattered. Fire immediately flickered up from the maze of hovels and houses.

Jolly and the others threw themselves flat on the sand.

Gideon's Grave exploded, blown apart in millions of splinters of wood sweeping past overhead like swarms of bad-tempered mosquitoes.

Something heavy fell beside Jolly. At first she thought it was a cannonball, but when the dust died down she saw

Buenaventure. He was already scrambling up again; his massive frame filled her whole field of vision.

His helmet lay in the sand in front of her.

Amidst the inferno of explosions and gunfire, she looked up and saw his face.

Buenaventure was no ordinary man. He had the head of a pit bull terrier.

FIRESTORM

'Run!' roared the Ghost-Trader. 'Run for your lives!'

At first Jolly thought he was warning them against the pit bull man. Buenaventure bent over her and took hold of her arms. As she screamed in protest, he set her on her feet, growled something like, 'Move!' and turned to help Munk up too.

Then they were running, all of them racing over the beach together, Walker and Buenaventure in the lead, followed by Jolly, Munk and the Ghost-Trader. The two parrots fluttered through the air above them, screeching.

The foremost row of houses in Port Nassau was in flames. It was impossible to see what was going on behind them because of the smoke and fire. People were breaking through the blaze and the drifting black smoke to escape. The cannonballs of the Spanish armada were shredding palm-thatch roofs and wooden walls, and wherever candles, torches or lamps had been burning indoors fire spread like the wind. Muzzle flashes could be seen on the battlements of the governor's fortress, west of the harbour and the stone-built quarter, but the defenders had nothing to set against the superior force of an entire fleet. Kendrick's ignorance and incompetence had brought the pirate city to ruin.

'Where's the *Carfax* lying?' called the Ghost-Trader.

Jolly saw Walker look over his shoulder in the flickering light of the fire. 'There's just one little problem there,' he said.

'What problem?'

'The *Carfax* isn't mine any more.'

'*What?*' cried Jolly, Munk and the Ghost-Trader in chorus.

Three cannonballs landed close to them in rapid succession. Clouds of sand blew through the air above the beach. Screams rose into the air in all directions. More and more people were breaking through the ruins and the walls of flame to reach the harbour.

'I lost it,' shouted Walker, not slowing down. 'Two days ago, playing dice with a trader.'

This was the first time Jolly had seen the one-eyed Ghost-Trader really angry. He had been sad, disappointed and downcast when Munk's parents died, but now rage almost as fierce as the firelight of the burning city blazed in his face.

'You must have forgotten to mention that in our conversation, Captain.'

Walker grinned, which in view of the circumstances seemed doubly outlandish. 'The situation was different then.'

'Does this mean you don't have a crew either?'

'Well, yes. Unfortunately.'

Jolly looked from Walker to Buenaventure. The dog-headed giant looked grim. His teeth were bared and his ears pricked. The fall of Port Nassau, an inferno of red and yellow flames, was reflected in his round brown eyes.

The Ghost-Trader pointed to the bay, where most of the pirate ships lay at anchor. Some had lost their masts, two or three were already sinking. Surprisingly, however, most of them were intact – the Spaniards were obviously concentrating on attacking the pirate city and its people first, before destroying the fleet.

Jolly furiously imagined the pirates on their lookout posts above the town counting the gold they had earned for their treachery. Gold gleaming and sparkling in the light of the distant fires. Blood money.

The companions were among the first to reach the rowing boats.

'Now where?' asked Jolly, while Buenaventure, whirling like a dervish, laid into a group of pirates trying to dispute possession of a boat with them. Men flew through the air to right and left, their screams dying away in the booming thunder of the cannon.

'Where's the *Carfax*?' asked the Ghost-Trader urgently.

Walker pointed to where the ships lay crowded together. 'In front there. As far as I know she was to put out to sea tomorrow with a new cargo.'

'Good,' said the Trader. 'Then kindly do what you do best – steal her!'

Walker grinned. 'Think of my good reputation . . . I'll suffer financial loss for this in the long run.'

'And we'll pay for it,' replied the Trader grimly.

Munk clenched his fists. 'How can this fellow haggle over a few ducats while the world's ending?'

Jolly was about to say something when her eyes fell on a solitary figure in a billowing hooded cloak coming their way.

'Soledad?'

The pirate princess's hood slipped back. Buenaventure, growling angrily, was going to bar her way, but Jolly kicked his shin from behind. 'Leave her alone! She's with me.'

Munk stared at her. 'She is?'

Buenaventure gave Jolly a dark look from his dog's eyes, but allowed Soledad to join them. She was out of breath, her cloak charred. She smelled as if she'd just been rolling in soot.

'Does your offer still stand?' she gasped, looking Jolly's way and ignoring the others.

Jolly nodded, and was about to say something when Walker pushed her aside and, with a beaming smile on his face, made the princess a gallant bow. 'An offer for you to come with us, pretty lady? By all means!'

Buenaventure growled and rolled his eyes. This looked so strangely human in his dog's face that it made his whole bizarre appearance more extraordinary than ever.

Soledad made a face as if someone had just shown her a particularly unpleasant insect. Shaking her head, she put Walker aside and looked at Jolly again. 'Charming friends you have.'

Jolly snorted angrily. 'That's not a friend of –'

'Oh yes, a good friend.' Walker grinned even more broadly. 'The best, you might say.'

The Ghost-Trader came between them. 'Over there about a hundred men are making for us, undoubtedly anxious to save their lives in this boat. We'd better put this argument off until later.'

While Buenaventure planted himself in front of them all as protection, Walker, Munk and the Ghost-Trader pushed the boat into the water. Jolly and Soledad jumped in with them. The pit bull man brought up the rear. Soledad gave him a suspicious sideways glance, but said nothing.

The four adults took the oars, while Jolly looked frantically around. She and Munk could have run over the water, but the waves were so churned up by the shots fired into them that she doubted whether the inexperienced Munk could have kept going.

A large troop of pirates with some women among them were just reaching the place where the rowing boats had been tied up. Too late. All the boats were already in the water, rowing out to the ships at anchor as fast as they possibly could. Cannonballs hissed above their heads. The Spaniards kept up their bombardment of the town. More and more explosions were heard, mingled with the terrible sound of countless dying screams. Suddenly one of the leading boats was hit. The impact sent bodies flying out of it in all directions, and seconds later the boat had disappeared. Only a few planks and a boot still drifted on the water.

'There's the *Carfax* ahead!' Walker pointed into the darkness, where a slender sloop lay on the water amidst swathes of smoke. She and a couple of other ships were anchored a little way from the rest, so none of the parties in the other rowing boats were trying to reach her. Walker frowned. 'We'd better take one of the ships which still have enough crew to make her ready to put out to sea.'

The Ghost-Trader shook his head. 'No, it has to be the *Carfax*. You'll get the crew you need, Captain, don't worry.'

Sure enough, most of the fugitives were trying to climb aboard the two nearest ships, a brigantine and a dilapidated galleon.

'Oh, how could I possibly worry?' Walker's voice was full of sarcasm. 'The six of us will simply set all sails, raise the anchor and –'

'There'll be a crew waiting for us on board the *Carfax*, Captain. Trust me.'

The pirate was going to protest again when a cannonball brought down the mainmast of the galleon close to them. It collapsed with a crunching sound, burying dozens of fugitives under it, and fell full length over the deck of the second ship.

'Very well,' growled Walker.

They brought the rowing boat alongside the hull of the *Carfax*. The ship could have done with a lick of paint, but apart from that she was in excellent shape. She was like the

Maid Maddy in size and construction, with a plain rail and a simple superstructure at the stern. The sails on all three masts were reefed, and there wasn't a soul on the long, narrow deck.

The Ghost-Trader went on board the ship first. He immediately stepped to one side, took the silver circlet from his belt, and slowly ran his fingers over it.

'There!' cried Walker, unable to decide between triumph and despair. 'So where's your –' All at once his eyes widened and his voice faltered. 'Where's your . . .' he repeated, and then his mouth dropped open, but not another word passed his lips.

Misty figures were rising from between the planks everywhere on board the *Carfax*. Ghosts obeying the Trader's summons. Many of them immediately floated up into the rigging and set to work on the furled sails. Others manned the guns.

'Jolly!' called the Ghost-Trader. 'Come over here, will you?'

She did as he said, while the others stared at the apparitions. Only Munk was unimpressed. He was more concerned about the Spanish cannon fire, which was shifting further in the direction of the ships riding at anchor now.

'Put your fingertips on the circlet,' the Trader told her.

A strange tingling went through her hand as she

touched the silver circlet. However, she did not withdraw her fingers.

The Ghost-Trader murmured words and syllables that she didn't understand.

Jolly felt a brief, twitching pain in her fingertips, and then the Trader said, 'That's all right. You can let go now.' And in a louder voice, so that everyone but more particularly Walker could hear him, he added, 'The ghosts on board this ship are under this girl's command from now on. They will obey you, Captain Walker, in matters of seamanship. But if you should try anything to harm your passengers, Jolly will set the ghosts on you and your pit bull friend, and nothing and no one will be able to save you then.'

Walker made a face, threw back his long hair, and looked darkly at Buenaventure. 'This is all your fault! You persuaded me to accept that lousy offer!'

The pit bull man shook his head morosely, and dismissed this reproach with a gesture.

'Don't worry,' said the Ghost-Trader. 'You'll both be adequately rewarded for this voyage. Take Jolly and Munk to Tortuga. You'll find out the rest once you get there.'

Tortuga, Jolly thought in surprise. Why Tortuga?

Soledad touched her shoulder. 'If you'd told me before

what interesting people you know, I might have considered your offer earlier.'

Munk cleared his throat. 'Don't you all think it's about time we set sail?'

'I don't like this kind of thing. I don't like it at all.' Walker turned to the ghostly crew with visible discomfort. 'Men!' he called. 'Raise the anchor! We're putting out!' He couldn't have been more astonished when the misty beings swarmed over the ship to obey his orders.

'I must leave you for a while,' said the Ghost-Trader. Several cannonballs hit the turbulent water in the background.

'Leave us?' faltered Jolly, bewildered. 'But why – how –'

'We'll meet again on Tortuga. If I happen to be late, you can pass the time looking for Bannon if you like.'

'But how?'

'Munk,' said the Trader, 'have you still got Jolly's spider?'

Munk's hand went to his belt, where his leather bag used to hang. Grey sailcloth unfurled behind him, mercifully hiding the view of the fall of Port Nassau.

'Here, I have it,' said Jolly. She took the bag off her own belt and handed it to Munk. The boy opened it, rummaged around briefly, and brought out the little wooden box. He snapped the catch open. Inside lay the corpse of the venomous spider that had been hiding in the figurehead when Jolly escaped from the *Maid Maddy*.

'Good,' said the Ghost-Trader, satisfied. 'There's an old flag-maker by the name of Silverhand on Tortuga. Show him the spider. Perhaps he'll be able to tell you where it comes from. It's possible that you may find a trail leading to whoever lured Bannon into the trap.' Quietly, he added, 'But don't forget that there's far more at stake just now.'

'The Maelstrom?'

The Ghost-Trader clapped Jolly on the shoulder, smiling. 'It's good that there are two of you. That doubles our chances.' He turned to Munk, who was putting the spider and its box back in the bag at his belt. 'And Munk, you must promise me to keep working at your magical skills. You have great talent. Some day you may yet save us all.'

Munk's eyes shone with pride, despite the destruction all around them, despite his fear. But then anxiety cast a shadow over him. 'Can't you stay with us? New Providence is going to fall.'

'The pirates will fall, maybe, but not the island. Nothing will happen to me.' And with that he wrapped his robe around him, its fabric fluttered, and a gust of wind blew in their faces and made them close their eyes for a split second.

When they looked again, the Ghost-Trader was gone. After a brief search, Jolly spotted him on another ship fifty feet away. But seconds later he had left that ship too in a swirl of black fabric, to appear again on yet another ship further away, and dissolve into thin air once more.

Creaking and grinding, the *Carfax* began to move. When Jolly looked up she saw the pit bull man at the wheel, while Walker stood four-square on the bridge, shouting orders at his undead crew.

The thunder of the cannon grew louder as the three-master glided with gathering speed towards the exit from the bay – straight towards the rampart that was the Spanish ships of war.

The armada had taken up position in a semicircle around Port Nassau. Cannon fire thundered incessantly over the bay, cutting huge swathes through the tangled alleys of the town.

Only a handful of Spanish ships to starboard of the *Carfax* had been ordered to keep the anchored pirate fleet under fire instead of the houses. Most of the armada was devoting its attention to the town and the governor's fortress. The English gunners on the battlements had managed to land a few hits, although they had far fewer guns; three Spanish ships were so badly damaged that their crews had to transfer to nearby galleons in rowing boats.

Walker made two decisions. First, he ordered the *Carfax* to turn to port as she left the bay, away from the ships aiming to destroy the pirate fleet. Second, he told Buenaventure to set a course straight for the Spaniards in their lifeboats. As long as the *Carfax* was among the shipwrecked sailors, he hoped, none of their captains would turn all their guns on the sloop.

'At least he knows what he's doing,' muttered Munk, ducking as a couple of isolated gunshots whistled above the deck.

Jolly snarled disparagingly. 'Even a repulsive creature like that must have *one* good quality.'

'He's a good captain,' Soledad agreed. She was crouching beside the two of them among crates and barrels, part of the cargo with which the new owner of the *Carfax* had been planning to put to sea next morning. Now they made good cover from gunfire and ricochets.

'You can always marry him,' Jolly snapped.

'Who knows?'

Wide-eyed, Jolly stared at her.

Soledad laughed. 'Don't worry.' She looked up at the bridge, where Walker was standing unmoved among the crossfire of rifle bullets, giving orders, while Buenaventure expertly steered the ship past the lifeboats and warships. Jolly reassured herself by thinking that Soledad surely admired only that cut-throat Walker's skill as a seaman, not his dubious qualities as a human being.

The Spaniards had fanned their fleet out in a wide arc to take the pirates' headquarters under fire from as many angles as possible. Tactically it was a clever move, so long as not too many of the freebooters' ships succeeded in leaving harbour. The attackers were relying on the surprise factor that had made the lookouts' treachery possible – they were trying to shoot down any opponents in their huts and tents, and incidentally to leave the English governor's fortress in ruins at the same time.

The Spaniards and the English had been at odds in the waters of the Caribbean for many decades. Each nation hoped to expand its overseas colonies, conquer new and fertile islands, and bring the goldmines and spice planta-tions on the mainland into its power. On the surface, the attack on Port Nassau might look like an act of retribution by the Spanish crown for the countless attacks the pirates had mounted on their merchant ships, but it also concealed a desire to send the governors appointed by the British Empire packing.

The loose formation of the warships allowed Walker to break through the ring of besiegers without much difficulty. The ghosts at the guns of the *Carfax* didn't fire a single shot. They successfully got away without having to put up any resistance. Protected by the lifeboats rowing frantically around them, they reached the rear of the Spanish fleet and were soon out in the open sea. One Spanish captain fired a broadside after them, but didn't venture to use his guns until they had left the shipwrecked sailors well behind – and by that time it was too late for him to do any damage. Not one ball hit its mark.

'Why aren't they giving chase?' asked Munk in surprise as he looked back over the ship's rail to the inferno off the coast of the island. Gun-smoke drifted like yellow mist over the sea. As long as the muzzles of the guns weren't pointing their way, the dull crash of the cannon sounded strangely unreal – like a thunderstorm passing by a long way off.

'They're not after every single ship,' said Soledad. 'Port Nassau, being the pirates' headquarters, is a thorn in their flesh. They cleansed Tortuga of freebooters first – or at least most of them – and now it's the turn of New Providence. Although I'm not sure whether they'll really succeed there unless they've left a permanent garrison in place.'

'Which again they won't dare to try,' added Jolly, nodding, 'because New Providence is a British colony, and if the Spaniards openly conquer the island it could lead to war.'

Munk shook his head, baffled. 'But they're attacking the island. That's not so far from a conquest.'

Soledad yawned, and smiled forbearingly. 'They'll make out that they were mounting a punitive expedition against the pirates, not an attack on the British Empire. If the British object, they'd look as if they were favouring piracy, which certainly wouldn't be in their own interests.'

'That means,' said Munk, 'that the Spanish will raze Port Nassau to the ground and then move out and disappear again.'

'Exactly.'

Jolly kept looking back at the narrow ring of smoke and fire lighting up the nocturnal horizon under the starry sky. By now there must be almost ten miles between the ship and the island, but the stink of burning and gunpowder still hung in the air; the *Carfax* dragged it after her like the train of a dress. 'The British will send out a new governor,' she said, 'the fortress will be rebuilt on the ruins, and in six months' time it will all be the way it was before.'

Soledad looked grim. 'I hope they at least got Kendrick.'

'We're not the only ship that broke through the ring of

the Spaniards,' said Munk. 'I saw two others. One was just behind us, but then she turned away.'

'If that devil was on board I'll find him.'

Jolly looked up at the mast where the ghosts, on Walker's orders, were hoisting a British flag. The sloop, like every pirate ship, carried a wide range of flags of all the nations, including, of course, the flag after which Jolly herself had been named, the Jolly Roger, the black skull-and-crossbones emblem of the freebooters. It was usual for the pirate flag to be hoisted only just before an attack, when their opponents had no chance of escaping by flight.

Soledad leaned back against a sea-chest, drew her knees up and closed her eyes for a moment. Under her hooded cloak she no longer wore the dress in which Jolly had met her at the *Fat Hen*, but trousers, shirt, and a broad belt with half a dozen throwing-knives stuck in it. She did not carry a sword, although Jolly would have wagered that she could handle any kind of blade skilfully. If only half of what was said of Scarab's daughter in the islands was true, she was a better fighter than most men among the pirates, and was blessed with a calculating mind and beauty into the bargain. It didn't escape Jolly's notice that not only Walker but also Munk kept glancing surreptitiously at her.

Soledad yawned again, picked her nose, rolled the result

between her fingers and flicked it into the shadows.

Jolly giggled when she saw Munk make a face.

The pirate princess folded the cloak under the back of her head to make a pillow. 'Wake me up if anything important happens.' And within a few moments she was asleep.

Jolly signed to Munk to follow her. She led him over to the ship's rail, out of earshot of Soledad. They both leaned their elbows on the rail and looked into the night, deep in thought. Jolly told Munk what had happened at the *Fat Hen*, and listened patiently as he gave her a piece of his mind for putting him out of action so cunningly. After he had given vent to his annoyance, they both fell into a brooding silence.

After a while, Jolly asked, 'Why didn't he come with us?'

'The Ghost-Trader? No idea.'

'What can be important enough to make him go back for it?'

'Did he tell you about the sea eagle he sent off?'

Jolly shook her head, and felt a sudden pang of jealousy. Why had the Ghost-Trader taken Munk into his confidence and not her?

'He visited an old friend on New Providence, the only man in the Caribbean who can train sea eagles.'

Jolly had never before heard of one of those proud

creatures letting itself be tamed, but she waited curiously without interrupting Munk.

'They sent one of the trained eagles out to spread news that the Maelstrom has woken.'

'So that's why he agreed to take us to Port Nassau.'

Munk nodded briefly. 'I suppose so.' After a short pause he added, 'Perhaps he's stayed behind on the island to wait for an answer.'

'And that's worth dying for?'

'He seemed to take the whole thing very seriously. The Maelstrom, the Mare Tenebrosum, all that.' He fell silent for a moment as the shadow of dark memories touched him. Jolly put her hand over his on the rail. She knew there was nothing that could comfort Munk, yet she longed to say something that might help him in his grief.

'Hey, you two,' a voice suddenly said behind them. 'Sorry to interrupt your cosy get-together, but I have to talk to you.'

Jolly turned round, sighing. 'What do you want, Walker?'

'Your gloomy friend with the fowls made me a lot of promises, but apart from a few coins I haven't seen much sign yet of all the riches supposed to be waiting for me.'

She held his penetrating gaze with ease. She had learned

years ago not to let any pirate in the world intimidate her. Nose in the air, eyes straight ahead, an austere expression – she had come out on top in thousands of moments like this. 'That's not our problem.'

'Oh yes, I'm afraid it is. You're passengers, and you haven't paid your fare yet.'

'Have you forgotten what he said about the ghosts?' She tried to give her voice a menacing undertone.

He scrutinised her. 'Who's talking about such . . . well, unpleasantness? Buenaventure up there is a veteran of the mines of Antigua, and he'd be capable of just about anything. But do I threaten you with him? I'd never dream of it.'

'You're such a noble soul, Walker.'

He grinned, showing his white teeth. 'Business, that's all I'm interested in. No quarrels, no silly argument about who's the stronger. Just . . . purchasing power, understand?'

Munk stared at him without a word, but his dark look spoke volumes.

Jolly thought for a moment, and then took a deep breath. 'So what you want is a guarantee that you'll really get your gold, right?'

'It'd be a nice gesture.'

'Agreed.' Munk was looking at her askance, but she

ignored that. 'I'm looking for Bannon. You've probably heard what happened.'

'The *Maddy* was sunk, the whole crew disappeared without trace. It's rumoured that they're dead.' He looked at her keenly. 'Come to think of it, how did you get away safe and sound yourself?'

'None of your business. You only have to know that I want to find Bannon – or at least some clue to what happened to him.'

Walker nodded. 'I'm with you so far.'

'If we succeed in finding Bannon again, dead or alive, there's a huge reward waiting for anyone who helps me.'

'Fine words,' said Walker, unimpressed.

Jolly sighed, then turned her back to him and lifted her shirt. 'See that tattoo?'

'Ugly. What's it supposed to be?'

She let the shirt drop back into place and turned to face him. 'It's half of a map. The way to Bannon's treasure. The other half is tattooed on his back. If we find Bannon, the treasure is yours.'

Walker thought about it. 'He won't like that.'

'You have my word.'

'Well, you know how it is in business . . .'

'I can't give you any proof. Only my word of honour. If

we find Bannon I personally will make sure that you get the opportunity to copy his half of the map from Bannon's back – and my half from mine.'

Walker thought again. He took his time. Presumably he was weighing up the pros and cons of the deal. The cons were many, the pros were few.

'Agreed,' he said at last. 'On your word of honour?'

'On my word of honour.' She offered her hand. He took it and shook it vigorously.

'Good girl,' he said, before he turned and climbed the steps to the bridge again. 'Bannon would be proud of you.'

Munk came closer to her. 'You told me the tattoo on your back was supposed to be a coral.'

'So it is.'

'But –'

'I was lying to him.'

'Oh, great.'

Furiously, she darted an angry glance at him. 'Well, did you have a better idea?'

Walker's voice made them jump and fall silent. 'Jolly!'

Heart thudding, she looked up at the bridge. 'Yes?'

'These ghosts of yours may be all very well,' he called down to her, 'but they're rather too taciturn for my liking.'

'What do you mean?'

'I need someone to go below decks and tell me what things are like down there. The *Carfax* is lying lower in the water than usual. Go and see what's up, will you? I don't want any unpleasant surprises.'

'I can do that,' said Munk.

Jolly shook her head. 'I'll go.'

She moved away from the ship's rail and went to the cargo hatch. With both hands, she put it back and climbed down steep steps into the hold of the ship.

Munk saw her disappear, then glanced at the sleeping pirate princess, shook his head slowly, and looked out at the calm sea again. The light of countless stars sparkled on the waves, silvery, almost white, like the shards of millions of broken mirrors.

'Er, Walker?' Jolly had clambered back up from the belly of the sloop and was standing on the top step.

The Captain interrupted a conversation with Buenaventure. 'What is it?'

'Bad news.'

'How bad?'

'We have stowaways on board.'

Walker thumped his fist on the rail. 'I'll come down. Stowaways? Several of them?'

A grim smile flitted over Jolly's face. 'At least fifty, I'd say.'

'Fifty?' With one bound, Walker leaped down the steps to the main deck.

Jolly nodded. 'And they smell – well, they don't smell good, I'm afraid. Not good at all.'

MAKING GOLD

Munk and Walker came to a halt beside Jolly at the same moment, and looked down through the cargo hatch.

'Upon my soul!' said the captain.

'Ugh!' said Munk, turning away. 'Are those –'

'Jean-Pauls,' said Walker.

Jolly's eyes were wide with surprise. 'Jean who?'

Munk held his nose. 'Do all Frenchmen smell so bad?'

'They're not Frenchmen,' said Walker impatiently. 'That's just the name they were given.'

'Pigs,' said Jolly. 'The entire hold is full of pigs.'

The grunting and snorting of the animals were clearly audible on the steps down to the hold, even drowning out the sound of the sea and the sails flapping in the wind above them.

Walker started down the steps, although the pigs' broad backs could be seen from above. 'A particularly fat, heavy breed,' he said. 'The French were the first to breed them, on Haiti, so someone or other called them Jean-Pauls. The trader I lost the *Carfax* to must have been going to ship them somewhere.'

Jolly left the top of the steps and joined Munk as Walker climbed down, cursing and groaning. But he was back only a little while later.

'Disgusting. Pigs on my ship! It'll take months to get the hold aired again.'

'Will their weight hold us up much?'

Walker shrugged. 'We'd be faster without them.' He thought for a moment. 'We could drive them overboard.'

Jolly flared up, horrified. 'Certainly not!'

Walker rubbed his chin. 'Sooner them than us, I'd say.'

Munk came to Jolly's aid. 'No one's chasing us. The pigs won't hold us up.'

'Not yet,' said Walker.

The idea that the pirate might drive the defenceless animals into the water shocked Jolly to the core. What was more, it confirmed all her prejudices against him. 'Those pigs stay on board!' she said firmly.

Walker scratched the back of his head. 'Hm. That makes them passengers, right?'

Jolly took a deep breath. She felt she was about to explode.

215

'If you insist, they stay,' Walker went on, 'but you'll have to pay their passage as well as your own, like it or not.'

'You can't mean that seriously!' Jolly had to restrain herself from going for his throat.

'Rubbish! There are rules on board ship. One of them says passengers must pay for their transport. And if you want those pigs to come with us, you'll have to pay for them.'

'I've promised you a whole *treasure*!'

He considered that. 'It'll have to be a really big treasure.'

'It is, I tell you!'

'How big?'

'It . . . it . . .' Jolly was too angry to get a coherent sentence out.

At that moment Soledad came to her aid. 'Walker!'

The pirate turned to her.

'You know who I am, don't you?'

He nodded. 'Your father was a good . . . er, business acquaintance of mine.'

'You cheated him.'

'Oh, *that* . . . just a minor misunderstanding.'

'A whole cargo of rum. He swore to have your head for it.'

'God rest his soul. He was a just man, in spite of everything.'

'You owed him a debt. And now that he's dead you owe

it to me. How many ducats were all those barrels of rum worth, Walker? A hundred? Five hundred?'

He heaved a deep sigh. 'I take your point . . . very well, the pigs can stay. But then we're quits.'

Soledad did something that seemed completely unthinkable to Jolly, but its effect was breathtaking: she stepped forward, dropped a light kiss on Walker's cheek, winked at him and whispered, 'Honour among pirates, right?'

Walker was beaming from ear to ear. He scratched the back of his neck, embarrassed, cleared his throat, muttered, 'No offence meant!' to Jolly, and strode back up to the bridge.

Jolly blew her top. 'The revolting, rotten, underhand –'

'Do you think he'd kiss a girl nicely?' Soledad was looking up at Walker.

'*What?*'

Soledad laughed, and this time Munk joined in. Jolly looked darkly from one to the other. 'Doesn't anyone here take me seriously?'

Soledad and Munk just laughed even louder.

Next morning they held a discussion in the captain's cabin.

Walker had seated himself at a broad table. The light of the morning sun came in through the porthole behind him. Soledad had taken possession of the only other chair. Jolly and Munk leaned against the walls with their arms folded.

'It'll take us about four days to reach Tortuga,' said Walker. 'That's if we have a favouring wind and no Spaniard or anyone else crosses our path. We'll sail around the Bahamas to the north-east. We'll find slightly rougher weather in the open Atlantic, but that may help us to make faster progress. Then we go south through the Caicos Passage and straight to Tortuga.'

Several sea-charts, faded and cracked from many years of intensive use, lay open or half unrolled on the broad desk. Some of them were weighted down at the corners with all kinds of different objects: a pistol, filigree navigational instruments, a handful of pewter figures, a shrunken head (too wrinkled for anyone to know for sure if it had once belonged to a European or a native of the islands), a golden statuette of the Madonna with a third eye on her forehead, a dried-up, dark brown banana, and an ornately decorated pipe. The cabin smelled pleasantly aromatic, of good tobacco and polished wood; neither fitted easily into the idea that Jolly had formed of Walker as a wild, uncouth pirate.

'Any objections?' asked the captain, looking round at them.

The two polliwiggles shook their heads, but Soledad

frowned. 'Isn't it rather risky to entrust ourselves to the Atlantic winds in our situation?'

'No riskier than breaking through the Spanish armada. And those ghosts your friend left us are pretty good seamen. D'you think I can keep them when all this is over? A friendly gesture because I so unselfishly volunteered to help you out of your little difficulty?'

Munk smiled gleefully. 'They're the ghosts of all the men who died aboard this ship. It's just possible they may not be too well disposed towards you, Walker.'

'Ah.' The pirate swallowed. 'Well, perhaps that wasn't such a good idea.' He quickly turned to Soledad. 'As for the storms, they usually go another way at this time of the year. I don't think we'll have any problems.'

The princess shrugged. 'It's your decision, Walker. You're the captain. What does Buenaventure say?'

The pit bull man was the only one who had stayed on deck. Since they put to sea he had stuck to his post at the wheel, never taking a rest. Jolly wondered how much dog there really was in him. All the dogs she knew spent the whole day snoring in some corner on board.

'He agrees,' said Walker, passing the flat of his hand over the top sea-chart. 'To be honest, it's not the weather that bothers me. There've been reports recently . . . or let's call them rumours . . . anyway, folk are saying the man in the whale has been seen around here.'

Jolly and Munk exchanged a brief glance.

'The man in the whale?' asked Munk. 'Who's he?'

'Someone the seamen in these latitudes talk about,' explained Jolly. 'There's a huge whale and a man who lives in its belly. They say the whale obeys all his orders. It appears out of nowhere, rams ships and drags them down into the depths. Any survivors of the shipwreck are devoured by the huge beast.'

Munk smiled. 'How could a man live inside a whale? That's only a sailor's yarn.' He looked from Jolly to Soledad and then Walker. None of the three returned his smile. 'Isn't it?' he asked uncertainly.

'The man in the whale is one of the great threats to shipping here,' said Walker gloomily. 'Worse than the Deep Tribes, worse even than the giant kraken.'

'Have you seen him?' asked Munk.

'If I had I wouldn't be standing before you now, boy. No one who sees the man in the whale with his own eyes survives it.'

Jolly and Soledad nodded in agreement.

Munk said nothing. Perhaps he was imagining the horizon of the Caribbean Sea suddenly torn apart as a mighty creature rose from the depths, a humpbacked body with a human figure standing in its open mouth, pointing to the *Carfax* and urging the furious monster on with wild cries.

'Munk?'

He jumped. 'Yes?'

'Everything all right?' asked Jolly.

'Yes, of course. Why?'

Walker's grin was almost painful. 'You were quite pale around the tip of your nose, boy.'

Munk just shook his head in silence. Jolly spoke instead, flashing her eyes angrily at the pirate. 'Munk lost his parents only a few days ago. Satisfied now, *Captain* Walker?'

The captain stared at her, taken aback by her angry outburst. Then he gave Munk an almost sympathetic look.

'Drop it,' Munk told Jolly. 'That's no one's business but mine.'

She looked at him, feeling downcast. He was shutting her out too, like everyone else.

Walker turned to Soledad. 'Can you steer a ship? Buenaventure must get a few hours of rest. This seems a good moment for it; the sea is calm, everything's going to plan.'

'Of course,' she said.

'What about us?' asked Jolly. 'Is there something we can do?'

Walker rose from his chair and nodded. 'See to your friends in the hold. They'll be getting hungry. There's plenty of sacks down there. I just hope they have pig-feed in them.'

'Aye, aye,' said Jolly. 'Coming?' she asked Munk.

'Sure.'

The galley and the ship's arsenal opened off the narrow gangway outside the captain's cabin. A few steps at the end of it led up to the deck. Outside again, Jolly took a deep breath. The Caribbean Sea lay bright blue under a cloudless sky. A warm wind blew over the waves and was caught by the sails. The air tasted salty. A bird screeched from one of the masts, but when Jolly and Munk looked up it wasn't one of the Ghost-Trader's parrots sitting there, only an albatross, returning their gaze from its beady eyes. The ghosts were almost invisible in the bright sunlight, just phantoms with the light falling straight through them.

While Soledad took over from Buenaventure at the wheel, the two polliwiggles climbed down into the hold. The stench was almost unbearable. The pigs stood crammed close together on a thick bed of straw. There were several troughs there, a few containing dirty water. But most of them were empty. That was where the feed from the sacks had to go.

Jolly held her nose. 'It's disgusting.'

'Oh, I don't know.' Munk dismissed her comment and felt the back of one of the front pigs. 'We had a few pigs on the farm. Feeding them twice a day won't be enough. Their hearts stop if they get too hot.'

'Meaning?'

'Well, really they ought to wallow in mud. But for this voyage maybe pouring water over them now and then will do.'

'Pouring water over all fifty pigs?'

He nodded. 'It's going to be a hard slog.'

'Walker will be just thrilled if we flood his ship below decks.'

'Then we'd better start right after feeding them, while he and Buenaventure are asleep.'

It was indeed a hard grind, tipping feed out of the sacks into the troughs, then bringing bucket after bucket full of sea-water up on a rope, taking the buckets down the steps to the hold and pouring water over the pigs. Soledad was by no means happy about the amount of water the two of them were taking below decks, but Munk assured her that most

223

of it would quickly evaporate among the overheated pigs' bodies. And he was right, although the whole process made the stink even worse. It now seemed to be rising through the planks and filling the whole ship.

They had sluiced down almost all the pigs when there was a disturbance in the far corner of the hold. Suddenly a dark figure rose to its feet among the animals.

Jolly was alarmed, but her fears were calmed when she recognised a boy under the encrusted dirt. 'What kind of pig are you, then?'

Munk's expression was even less welcoming. 'Isn't that –'

'Griffin?' Jolly pushed her way past the pigs and towards the boy. 'Good heavens, what are *you* doing here?'

Griffin smiled. His countless braids were stiff with all the dirt covering him. 'I was on the brigantine when the mast of the other ship fell on its deck. I jumped overboard and swam after your boat. Then I climbed aboard on the other side of the ship and hid down here.' He patted a bristly pig. 'Charming company, really. We're too pre-judiced against these poor creatures. They can be very thoughtful of other people, and their conversation –'

'You could have come out right away,' said Jolly reproachfully. She wasn't quite sure what she felt at the sight of Griffin. A little malicious glee. Dislike, and a touch of anger, but also . . . well, a certain relief to find that he'd come through the attack on Port Nassau safe and sound. She had been wondering whether he might have escaped from that fiery inferno.

'Come out? And have that monster up there wring my neck?' He dismissed the idea with a gesture. 'I'd had a little . . . incident, you might call it, with Buenaventure.'

'You cheated him at play,' said Munk morosely.

'We saw it all.' Jolly backed him up.

'You mean you were at the harbour when . . . oh, heavens, that was really bad. I thought I was as good as dead. Did you see what he did to us? I never saw anyone wade in like that before.' Griffin pushed past the pigs. 'Do you think he'll throw me overboard?'

Jolly shook her head, sighing. 'Not so long as we pay for your passage.'

Munk cast her a warning glance.

'Would you do that?' asked Griffin doubtfully. 'Do you have so much money?'

Munk's expression was even darker. 'All the treasure in the world.'

Jolly's laugh had no humour in it. 'We found a way of paying Walker *without* paying him.'

'Sounds good,' said Griffin. 'So I can stay with you, then?'

225

'I don't know,' said Munk. 'Jolly tells me you're a good swimmer.'

'Munk!'

Griffin frowned.

Munk grinned. 'I saw some seagulls. It can't be far to the nearest island.'

'*Of course* you can stay.' Angrily, Jolly intervened. 'And first of all you can help us.'

'Help you carry water, right?'

'We could appoint him swineherd,' suggested Munk. 'Then he can work for his passage.'

Griffin's mouth twisted. 'At least the company down here is no worse than yours up on deck.'

'Oh, it's you, is it?'

A throbbing vein stood out on Walker's forehead when he recognised Griffin. Jolly got in front of the pirate boy to protect him, while Munk, a smile of amusement on his face, watched the show from a suitable distance. Jolly suspected he was still secretly hoping that Buenaventure would simply throw Griffin over the ship's rail. There seemed to be mutual dislike between the two boys, which annoyed Jolly. They didn't even know each other, yet there had been obvious tension between them from the first.

'You little devil!' cried Walker, storming out on deck from the gangway leading to the cabin. 'You louse! You useless horse-thief! You miserable son of a –'

'Oh, come on, Walker,' said Jolly. 'Calm down.'

'I wasn't thinking of calming down.'

'Then think of something else – the treasure, for instance.'

Walker stopped. 'That rat stole five ducats from my pocket! If Buenaventure sees him here, then . . .'

At that very moment the gigantic shape of the pit bull man appeared in the cabin doorway. For a moment he stood there as if rooted to the spot. Then they all heard an ominous cracking sound as he clenched his fists.

'Oh, heavens!' Griffin whispered. But he wasn't going to let Jolly protect him. He pushed her aside and stepped forward bravely to face Buenaventure and Walker. 'Listen, could we maybe settle this like gentlemen?'

Walker smiled unpleasantly. 'I'll have you dangling from the mast by your braids.'

Jolly knew that Griffin was an excellent fencer, but she wasn't sure if he had a chance against the more experienced pirate captain. Quite apart from the fact that Buenaventure would chop him into pieces with a single blow.

The pit bull man marched towards Griffin, his footsteps echoing.

'Stop!'

Soledad's voice made them spin round. She had seen it all where she stood at the wheel.

'That will do!' she cried. 'No one's going for anyone else's throat on this ship!'

'I didn't know you'd already taken over your father's command, Pirate Empress,' said Walker mockingly.

'Hold your tongue, Walker. And you, Buenaventure, stay where you are.'

'I'm the captain of this ship,' Walker insisted. 'And I say he goes overboard.'

'How many barrels of rum would you say his life's worth, Walker?'

'Rum?' asked Griffin, annoyed.

Munk rolled his eyes.

Walker put his hands on his hips. 'You can't keep doing business with nothing but hot air. It's not . . . not right.'

'Your debts to my father were high enough to have a dozen bounty-hunters set on you. A dozen paid murderers, Walker. That's a dozen human lives. Which ought to be enough to balance out a few pigs and this boy, don't you agree?'

Walker let out his breath sharply. 'That's not a fair bargain.'

'You're a pirate, Walker. You've never made a fair bargain in your life.'

'Then why don't we begin now?'

Munk sat down cross-legged on the deck, took out his shells and arranged them in a pattern on the planks. As the adults went on quarrelling, and Jolly and Griffin looked from one to the other of them in surprise at the course events were taking, Munk made a magic pearl rise in the air above the shells. It hovered, shimmering, in the middle of his pattern.

Jolly noticed it first. Then Griffin looked, finally Soledad and the two men.

'What the devil . . .!' exclaimed Walker.

Munk closed his eyes. Murmured something. Completed a complicated movement of his hand.

Gold pieces rained down on deck from inside the glowing pearl. Twenty, thirty doubloons fell on top of each other, ringing, and rolled around without leaving the circle of shells.

Sweat was running down Munk's face as he silently ordered the pearl to go back into one of the shells. The bright little globe floated into a small, nondescript mussel-shell. Munk snapped it quickly shut, took a deep breath and looked at Walker.

'Do you think that . . . will be enough . . . for him?' he asked, his voice unsteady.

'Munk!' Jolly caught him before his upper body could fall forward, exhausted. She held him firmly, dabbing at his forehead with her sleeve. He raised his face, looked silently into her eyes, and smiled.

'Oh, Munk!' she whispered, hugging him. 'That . . . that was terrific!'

'Give them the gold . . . quick, before they think better of it.'

She nodded, made sure that he could sit upright unaided, then picked up the coins with both hands and took them over to Walker. He was still staring at Munk, wide-eyed.

'He . . . he can make gold?'

'That's very much what it looks like,' she replied coolly, and let the doubloons fall on Walker's boots. 'Enough gold for Griffin's passage, anyway. And for us and the pigs too.' She grinned maliciously. 'Looks as if your debts to Scarab and Soledad are still outstanding.' With relish, she stood on tiptoe and put her mouth close to his ear. 'If I were you, I'd be getting worried about those bounty-hunters.'

Walker just stood there with his mouth open. Then he abruptly swung round to Buenaventure. 'Did you see that? The boy can actually make gold! We're rich!'

Buenaventure just growled; it was impossible to tell if he was agreeing with Walker. Jolly had already heard him speak, but for some reason or other he seemed to content himself with animal sounds most of the time.

Soledad spoke up from the bridge. 'Take your gold, Walker, and leave Munk alone. I'm warning you, don't get any stupid ideas!'

The pirate picked up the coins, bit one to test it, and nodded approvingly. Then he looked at Jolly. 'I still get the treasure, all right?'

She didn't deign to reply, and hurried back to Munk. Griffin was crouching beside him, supporting the back of his head and trickling water from a leather skin over his lips.

'Hey,' he whispered. 'I owe you.'

Jolly bent close to Munk. 'How long will it last?'

'The gold?' A fleeting smile played around the corners of Munk's mouth. 'A week. Maybe ten days.'

'And then?'

'Air,' Munk managed to say, with difficulty, and coughed. 'As Walker said before: nothing but hot air.'

'That'll have to do.' Jolly looked back over her shoulder at Walker and Buenaventure, who were whispering confidentially to each other. 'We'll be in Tortuga well before then.'

A little colour was coming back into Munk's face. He was just preparing to rise to his feet when something splashed down on the planks beside them.

They all spun round.

On the wood, not far from the shells, lay a dead fish.

Walker dismissed it. 'Dropped by some bird, that's all. Nothing to –'

He stopped short, for at the same moment it began to rain.

And what rained down from the sky wasn't water.

THE DEEP TRIBES

Within a few minutes the deck was covered with dead fish. The whole ship's company flailed their arms around to fend off the damp, stinking bodies that came raining down on them with considerable force. A barracuda hit Walker on the head, and Jolly was only just in time to avoid the limp tentacles of a cuttlefish. Soledad came off worst; a dead spider crab caught in her red hair and clung to the back of her head like a particularly tasteless ornament.

The disgusting rain ended as unexpectedly as it had begun. All of a sudden no more corpses fell from the sky. It was as if the *Carfax* had suddenly sailed out of a storm – or else had sailed into the eye of the storm, and the worst was still ahead of them.

Walker vented his disgust and surprise in no uncertain terms, while Jolly and Munk just looked at each other, silent and anxious.

Griffin shook a dead fish off the toe of his boot and looked incredulously out at the sea. 'Can anyone here explain that to me?'

By now Soledad had succeeded in disentangling the spider crab's horny legs from her hair. Furiously, she flung the horrible thing over the ship's rail.

Walker interrupted himself in the middle of a string of curses. 'This happened because of you two, right? Of course – it was *you*!'

'Nonsense!' cried Soledad. 'How could they –'

'He's right.' At first Jolly's voice was quiet, almost as if she felt guilty, but then she spoke with all the determination she could muster. 'Munk and I have seen something like this before. But –'

'I guessed as much!' Walker cursed again. 'I knew you two would only bring trouble.'

'*But*,' said Jolly emphatically, 'there's worse to come.'

Walker fell silent and looked at her darkly.

'The same thing happened just before Munk's parents were murdered. I think this rain of fish is a kind of warning.'

'A warning of what?'

Jolly looked around, searching for any sign, but the sea still lay there calm. An idea immediately came to her: whatever was approaching under cover of the rain of fish was not coming *over* the sea.

'From below!' she cried. 'It's coming from below!'

'What is?' Walker drew his sword from its sheath, though presumably even he didn't know whom he was hoping to threaten with it. 'By all the kobalins in the sea, what's going on here?'

'Kobalins, exactly,' whispered Munk, who had realised what Jolly meant at once. 'When the Acherus came up there were kobalins in the water too.'

Griffin laid a soothing hand on his forearm. 'I've fought kobalins before. Can't be helped if a person . . . er, *falls* overboard now and then.' But his wry grin was half-hearted, and fooled no one. He was just as uneasy as all the rest of them.

'Wait!' cried Soledad from the bridge. 'Do you feel that?'

They all fell silent. Buenaventure's nose was raised, sniffing the air; only his jowls quivered slightly at every breath. Walker's gaze frantically searched the deck, while Munk kept his eyes closed as if he were concentrating on more magic. But the shells had been back in the pouch at his belt for some time.

A shudder ran through the hull of the *Carfax*. It had nothing in common with the usual swaying and rocking of a ship in the swell of the sea. This was a slighter, almost delicate trembling that crept up from the deck and into the crew's feet and legs.

'Footsteps,' said Walker tonelessly. 'Those are footsteps!'

But none of them moved. And the ghosts, going about their work undeterred, hovered weightlessly without touching the deck at all.

'It comes from underneath the ship,' said Buenaventure – the first complete sentence that Jolly had heard from his dog's mouth. His voice was deep and rumbling, with an almost imperceptible speech defect that she would have taken for a slight accent in anyone else. But in Buenaventure's case it was because his jaws weren't really meant for talking. He couldn't say the sharp 's' at the end of 'comes' properly; in his voice it sounded strangely soft, almost like a quiet humming.

Walker cast a glance at Munk. 'You were right, boy. Kobalins they are. But since when has it rained dead fish anywhere when kobalins turned up?'

'There must be something else with them.' Jolly's voice was so husky she was afraid no one but herself would be able to make out what she said.

'Acherus,' murmured Munk.

'What?' asked Walker. 'What did you say?'

'My parents . . . they were killed by an Acherus.'

Soledad had lashed the wheel in place with a rope and ran down the steps to the main deck. She had drawn two of her throwing-knives. 'What kind of thing is this –'

'Acherus,' Munk repeated.

'A huge, horrible monster,' said Jolly, coming to the point. This was not the time for pointless explanations of the Maelstrom and the rest of what the Ghost-Trader had told them.

'I have a really nasty feeling about this business,' said Walker.

The pit bull man growled his agreement.

'A weapon.' Griffin looked around. 'I need a weapon!'

Walker pointed to a chest screwed to the planks of the deck beside the entrance to the cabins. 'Look in there!'

Griffin hurried over, lifted the lid, snatched up a sword and weighed it in his hand, testing it, then chose another. 'Jolly? Munk?'

Munk exchanged a glance with Jolly, and then shrugged. 'A pistol wouldn't be a bad idea.' He went over to Griffin, found what he was looking for, and immediately began stuffing powder and a bullet in the muzzle. 'I've never learned to fence, but I'm a passable shot. At least, I think so.'

Jolly picked up a sword too, while Buenaventure drew a blade from his belt that was twice as broad as the others, much longer, and with both edges serrated like a saw. Jolly shuddered at the sight of it.

'There's something wrong,' said Munk, as they all took up their positions in a close circle, back to back.

Soledad, standing beside him, cast him an enquiring glance.

'If it were really an Acherus,' he said, 'then it would have attacked long ago. Jolly and I have fought one, and it just couldn't wait to tear our heads off.' He nervously moved his loaded pistol from his right to his left hand and back again. 'An Acherus wouldn't wait so long to attack.'

It occurred to Jolly that the creatures of the Maelstrom might be as different from each other as human beings, and were certainly not as predictable as Munk obviously assumed. Moreover, the Ghost-Trader had spoken of *the* Acherus, not *an* Acherus. Perhaps there had only ever been one. All the same, she would almost rather think that Munk was right – with an Acherus, they would at least know what they were dealing with. Whatever was down there, however, might be a thousand times larger. And a thousand times more murderous.

'Perhaps it's waiting for reinforcements,' said Walker.

Jolly shook her head. 'Such a being doesn't need any reinforcements. And the Deep Tribes are on its side. But these vibrations are –'

'Kobalin footsteps.' Walker nodded. 'They're swarming up the hull under water and now they'll cling to us like ticks. But that doesn't mean they'll actually attack. Sometimes they just cling on for a few miles and then suddenly disappear as if they'd never been around at all. Most kobalins would never dare attack anything larger than themselves – certainly not a ship.'

'But there have been attacks on merchant vessels,' Jolly objected.

Walker shrugged. 'I've heard such stories too. But it could always have been a case of pirates making it look as if the attackers were kobalins.'

Soledad wiped sweat from her brow with the back of her hand. 'My father would have known about it.'

'Your father didn't know everything, sweetheart.'

Soledad was about to flare up, but Munk calmed her with a touch of his hand, shaking his head slightly. Drop it, said his glance. There'll be time for that later.

Jolly admired Munk for his self-control even in a situation like this. They both knew what a creature of the Maelstrom could do. Jolly could hardly feel her legs, she was so frightened, hard as she tried not to let it show.

The waiting was almost unbearable.

Jolly glanced up at the lonely albatross looking down at

them from the side of the crow's-nest. She imagined what it was seeing: six figures formed into a close circle, faces and weapons on the outside, standing there in rigid, tense expectation, and around them an empty ship's deck with misty beings moving busily over it like strange clouds of pipe smoke.

No sign of any attackers. No indication of danger.

And yet . . .

'Jolly,' said Munk suddenly. 'The Trader left you in command of the ghosts. They could help us now.'

'I thought of that too.' She made a face. 'Unfortunately he forgot to explain how to give them orders.'

'That's really good to know.' Walker looked as if he had bitten a rotten banana.

'Just tell them to get into a circle round us and fight off anything coming too close.'

Jolly nodded half-heartedly, and was trying to find the right words when Munk added, 'You don't have to give the order out loud. Just think it.'

'But back on the island you used words of some kind . . . in a foreign language.'

'The Ghost-Trader explained it all to me. But now you'll just have to do without him.'

All very well for you to talk, thought Jolly. 'Very well,

you say the words, then.'

'It's you these ghosts obey, not me.'

'But I don't know the wretched spell!'

Munk sighed. 'It's not that simple. It has to come from yourself; you must put your thoughts and your concentration into words deep inside you and –'

Walker rolled his eyes. 'Could you two just keep your mouths shut? All this drivel! It's like being in church.'

Jolly looked daggers at him. 'As if you'd ever seen the inside of a church in your life.'

'Well, I looted a church once.'

'There!' cried Soledad. 'It's stopped!'

No one dared to breathe. They all listened.

The pirate princess was right. The scrabbling and scraping on the hull of the *Carfax* had fallen silent. Only the sound of the waves, the foam breaking at the ship's bows and the creaking of the planks and the shrouds could be heard.

'Have they gone?' whispered Griffin.

Walker took two rapid strides to the ship's rail, looked down at the water and held up his hand imperiously. 'Hush!'

They fell silent again. Listened. And waited.

Soledad was the first to relax. 'No kobalin can keep still for so long.'

Buenaventure nodded, but Walker waved them all back to their places.

Munk was staring at his pistol as if he suddenly had no idea how it came to be in his hand. 'I'm going over to the rail.'

'No!' Walker's tone would allow no contradiction. 'There's nothing to be seen. Kobalins always stay below the surface of the water. If they do attack, they'll come through the hull. But we'd notice if we'd sprung a leak already.' He grinned wryly. 'What's more, the squealing of your friends in the hold would warn us.'

But rumour suggested otherwise. Every attack on a ship by the Deep Tribes – if they ventured on one – began with their chieftains climbing over the rail. The first rule in the case of a kobalin attack, therefore, was always to keep the deck in view. As long as no particularly large and ugly kobalin appeared on deck, the hull was considered safe.

Walker must know that. So why was he trying to keep Munk from looking over the rail? Jolly couldn't make sense of it.

Unless Walker had seen something – and wanted to prevent panic breaking out!

An icy hand seemed to pass down her back. Her knees, almost numb just now, began trembling again.

She broke out of their circle and ran to the rail.

'You little toad!' roared Walker. 'Don't do it!'

She wasn't listening any more. Her fingers clutched the wood as if she was about to tear it from its fixings.

The water of the Caribbean Sea is said to be clearer than any other in the Seven Seas. At that moment Jolly wished it had been the murkiest water in the world.

She could see about twenty or twenty-five feet down, and what she saw turned her stomach.

Kobalins were moving through the water. The sea was full of them, just below the surface as well as down in the darker, colder depths. And Jolly had no doubt that there were more kobalins swimming outside her range of vision. Thousands of them.

It was an army. A hundred armies.

The Deep Tribes were gathering and moving in a south-westerly direction – on the same course as the *Carfax* herself was steering.

'Why don't they attack?' asked Griffin.

Jolly still felt dazed. She hadn't noticed him come up beside her. Now Griffin was standing on her left and Munk on her right, and the adults too were leaning over the rail.

'It would have been better if none of you had seen that,' whispered Walker. 'It's quite enough for only one of us to be unable to close his eyes for the next few days.'

Jolly had too much else on her mind to wonder about Walker's consideration for them just now. Perhaps she'd misjudged him after all. Well, not *entirely* misjudged him, but a little anyway.

The kobalin army poured out in an unbroken torrent. As far and as deep as Jolly could see, the underwater troops swam on. It was a mustering of the Deep Tribes such as no one had ever seen before.

The Ghost-Trader was right: events had started moving, and none of them could yet assess their extent.

'They're not attacking because that's not their orders,' Jolly answered Griffin's question. 'Just now, when the dead fish fell out of the sky, one of their commanders must have passed the *Carfax*. The kobalins themselves aren't creatures of the Maelstrom, so the rain has stopped. But whatever is leading them comes from the Mare Tenebrosum. Just like the Acherus.'

Walker, Soledad and Griffin exchanged blank looks. Only Munk nodded thoughtfully.

And still the shoals of kobalins moved on under the *Carfax* as if the ship wasn't even there.

'They must have picked up the scent of the pigs just now,' said Munk. 'That'll be why a few of them left the others. You can be sure their chieftains called them off again before they could start working on the hull.'

'There must be tens of thousands of them,' said Soledad. Her voice was hoarse.

Walker was staring at the surface of the water as if spellbound. 'Perhaps even more. I've never seen anything like this in my life.'

They were all fascinated by the unimaginable spectacle beneath their feet. Fear lay in the air like a bad smell, yet none of them could tear their eyes from the sight. Only after what seemed to Jolly half an eternity did the shoals of kobalins thin out, until at last they dispersed entirely. Soon after that the depths of the sea were azure blue and shining again.

Walker took Jolly roughly by the shoulder and pulled her away from the rail. 'Looks as if you owe us a few explanations. What's this Maelstrom you were talking about? And that other thing – the Mare . . .'

'Mare Tenebrosum.' She avoided his eyes, but only for a moment. Then she looked back at him defiantly. 'Munk and I don't know much more about it than you do. The Ghost-Trader was talking about an endless ocean in another world . . . and a Maelstrom that's some kind of a gateway to it. Sometimes beings from this Mare Tenebrosum come over to us, creatures like the Acherus. And the Ghost-Trader wants to make sure, somehow, that it doesn't get even worse, that the gateway doesn't open fully and . . .' She stopped short, and angrily shook Walker's hand off her shoulder. All the anger dammed up in her since the death of Munk's parents suddenly broke out, ready to turn on whoever happened to be standing next to her, in this case Walker.

Not that he was exactly an innocent victim, she thought furiously.

'The Maelstrom is after Munk and me because we're the last two polliwiggles,' she went on, her voice still angry. 'I've no idea why it wants to kill us for that. But I've lost my crew, Munk has lost his parents, we've been on the run for days. Kendrick's men chased me all over Port Nassau, and then we were all of us nearly roasted alive. Do you really think if either of us knew a way of getting out of this we'd keep it to ourselves?'

Walker looked at her, baffled. 'I've heard a great many weird and wonderful sailors' yarns in my time, but this beats all!'

Jolly uttered an angry sound, turned away and went back to the rail. 'Oh, this is pointless.'

Walker smiled. 'You didn't let me finish what I was saying.'

'I'm sure I missed something amazingly witty.'

His smile turned to a broad grin. 'I was going to say that until a few minutes ago I'd have called anyone crazy if he told me a boy could conjure up gold doubloons out of a few seashells. But I saw what your friend did just now with my own eyes. And if that's true, then perhaps the rest of the yarn you've been spinning us is true too.'

Jolly looked at him appraisingly. 'Meaning?'

Walker exchanged a glance with the pit bull man. 'Meaning Buenaventure and I will help you. We'll take the two of you to Tortuga. And further too if necessary.'

Munk raised an eyebrow distrustfully. 'Why this sudden change of heart?'

Soledad got in before Walker. 'For your sake, Munk. Our unselfish captain here scents great wealth. He's picked you as his personal doubloon mint.' She shot the pirate a reproachful glance. 'Isn't that so?'

'Ah, well . . .' Walker sighed and turned both hands up in a mock-apologetic gesture. 'I'll admit I haven't always been a great philanthropist. But who could resist the charms of a princess and her two young friends?' His white teeth flashed as he sketched a bow in Soledad's direction.

She shook her head. 'I have nothing to do with this business . . . strange seas and creatures, a gateway to another world. *This* is my sea, and I'll be content if I can stake my claim to it. I don't care about the rest.'

'There won't be much of the Caribbean Sea and the pirate realm left if the Maelstrom opens wide enough.' Jolly suddenly heard herself sounding as if the Ghost-Trader himself were speaking with her voice. But the words were her own, and if they carried conviction it was only because she herself was coming to believe all these things. First the Acherus, then the great armies of the Deep Tribes. The world was in turmoil, and at the centre of all these changes a gigantic Maelstrom was swirling somewhere in the vast expanse of the ocean.

Soledad thought over what Jolly had said. 'The Ghost-Trader knows more about it, does he? And he's going to meet the two of you on Tortuga?'

'That's what he said, anyway.'

'Then I'll stay with you as far as Tortuga. I want to hear what he has to say. And find out if the situation's really so serious.'

Griffin had been listening for some time in silence, but now he spoke up. 'Do you doubt it, after what we've just seen?' He kicked a dead fish across the deck to Soledad. If he had hoped the princess would shrink away from it in disgust, he was mistaken; she neatly caught the corpse under the toe of her boot.

'I've never known anything like it myself, anyway,' Griffin went on, 'and what Jolly says is at least an explanation.' He grinned. 'Not a very credible one, but an explanation. And I'd rather fight against whatever's responsible for it here than wait about in port somewhere for ten thousand kobalins to come on land all of a sudden, wondering whether human flesh may taste as good fresh as salted.'

Jolly gave Griffin a grateful smile, but noticed at the same time that Munk didn't look too happy with the pirate boy's decision. Well, at least he'd saved Griffin from being thrown overboard.

Soledad was still hesitating, but then she slowly nodded.

'You could be right, boy.' She turned and set off back to her place at the wheel. As she went, she nodded briefly to Jolly. 'Will you come with me for a moment? I want to talk to you.'

Walker's face darkened. 'Secrets?'

'*Girl* talk,' said Soledad with a sly smile. 'You wouldn't understand a word of it anyway.'

'Oh, I can be very understanding,' Walker protested. 'Sensitive, too.'

'Of course. Coming, Jolly?'

Jolly followed her up the steps to the bridge, and

watched as the pirate princess undid the rope she had used to lash the wheel in place.

'You've got yourself into quite something, haven't you?' said Soledad, lowering her voice so that the men on the main deck couldn't hear her.

'Because of the Maelstrom? There's nothing I can do about that. I was going to –'

'That's not what I meant.'

Jolly still didn't understand.

'I mean your two admirers down there.' Soledad nodded in the direction of Munk and Griffin. Walker was just handing them brooms to sweep the dead fish off the deck.

'My . . . admirers?' Jolly laughed out loud. 'Oh, come on, what on earth are you talking about?'

'Either you're not nearly as mature as you make out – or you're blind.'

'Nonsense.'

'Have you really not noticed the way those two look at you? And the way they look at *each other*?'

'They don't get on. So what?'

'It's not enmity flashing in their eyes, Jolly. Or dislike. It's jealousy.'

Jolly laughed nervously, but she avoided Soledad's searching gaze. 'Most of the time Griffin is a monster and a cheat. And Munk's still wet behind the ears, a boy playing with shells.'

'I didn't say *you* were in love with either of them, it's the other way around. Although I'm not so sure that . . .'

'Oh, don't worry about that!'

Soledad smiled surreptitiously. 'I was only going to advise you to watch out. You seem to be planning something, if you meant what you said just now. Your two friends won't make it any easier. There's no worse enemy than the one in your own ranks.'

'You think one of them might give us away? Out of jealousy?' She shook her head again. 'Because of *me?*'

'Men do stupid things when they stop thinking with their heads.'

Jolly dismissed the idea. 'Why don't you watch out for Walker instead? I've seen the way he stares at you.'

Soledad grinned. 'One man on his own is totally predictable. So long as Buenaventure doesn't start parading his canine charms I can manage Walker. You get used to that kind of thing.' Her eyes were sparkling. 'You're a pretty girl, Jolly . . . yes, I know you don't want to hear about that. But it's the truth. And some day you're going to be a very beautiful woman. It won't do any harm for you to learn to see the amusing side of such situations. And who knows, the gallant captain may yet come in very useful to us.'

'Just like Griffin and Munk.'

Soledad sighed. 'You don't have to admit that I'm right. Just keep your eyes open. And don't do anything that could set them against each other. Because a powder-keg would be harmless by comparison, believe me.'

Soledad turned to the wheel. As far as she was concerned, the conversation was over.

Jolly leaned both hands on the balustrade of the bridge and looked down at the main deck. Munk and Griffin, cursing, were toiling away to clear the dead fish, sweeping their corpses into heaps ready to be thrown overboard. It was a disgusting job, but they were working together like good friends.

But could Soledad possibly have been right? Was the harmony between them deceptive?

A powder-keg, she'd said.

Don't do anything that could set them against each other.

TORTUGA

Walker had been right about one thing anyway, as the encounter with the kobalins had shown: the pigs had to go.

The unknown creature that commanded the armies of the Deep Tribes and had brought the rain down on them couldn't have noticed Jolly and Munk on the *Carfax* – Jolly didn't like to think what might have happened if it had. But they mustn't run the risk of letting the plump, tender animals in the hold lure kobalins their way a second time.

Jolly was still refusing to have the Jean-Pauls simply driven overboard, of course. Munk and Griffin backed her up, while Soledad kept out of the argument. Walker raised hell until it occurred to him that their route to Tortuga would take them past an island where a handful of missionaries had built a small monastery. With Jolly's consent, he set course for this island. He deliberately didn't mention that he was also planning to make a little profit on the side.

They reached the island on the third day of their voyage without going too far off course. No more kobalins crossed their path. There was a favouring wind, the *Carfax* made brisk progress, and Walker held out hopes of reaching Tortuga next day.

With the help of the delighted and grateful monks, they got the Jean-Pauls off the ship. Every one of the huge, well-fattened pigs had to be driven out of the hold, lowered into a ship's boat on a rope, and rowed ashore. The work was tedious drudgery that made them sweat and, contrary to Walker's predictions, set them back a full day. Jolly was happy and satisfied when they handed over the last pig to the monks. In spite of all the dirt and the pig muck, she was sure she had made the right decision.

It was left to her and the two boys to clean the hold and then scrub the deck. Walker supervised them like a slave-driver. Keeping a careful eye on his workers and intent on every speck of dirt, he leaned back at his ease and lit a meerschaum pipe.

'How about lending a hand?' asked Griffin grimly.

'I'm the captain,' replied Walker, shrugging his

shoulders. 'You're not. A small but significant difference.'

'Oh, what the devil, clean your own stupid ship!' Griffin slung his brush furiously into a full bucket. Dirty water splashed all the way to Walker's boots.

The pirate simply grinned. 'Do I scent the spirit of mutiny? There's a penalty of twenty blows with a stick for that, delivered by my loyal and justice-loving steersman.'

Buenaventure's chops twisted into something that might be a pit bull smile.

Griffin snorted derisively, but went on scrubbing. 'Pure harassment! The ghosts could do it just as well.'

The same idea had already occurred to Jolly, but she had been forced to admit that in spite of Munk's encouragement she hadn't had any luck in giving the ghosts orders. She just didn't know how she was supposed to make those misty creatures obey her.

Walker had watched her failed attempts with malicious glee, and naturally refused to use his authority as captain to order the ghosts to clean up the ship. He put the three of them off with the threadbare excuse that the crew was urgently needed for other tasks. So, he said, he was afraid he had no option but to set his passengers to the work that had to be done on board. It was the law of the sea, he said with relish, and unfortunately he was right: even pirates kept certain rules.

'If he grins once more I'm going to throw him overboard single-handed,' whispered Munk, scrubbing even harder.

Griffin pointed to the bag at Munk's belt. 'Can't you turn him into something? How about a Jean-Paul?'

'Too difficult.'

'Then at least make his hair fall out. Or all his teeth.'

'Also too difficult.'

'Good heavens above, you can make gold! Something like this would be easy for you.'

'The Ghost-Trader told me there are few kinds of magic more difficult than changing living creatures – no matter how large or small the change. Inanimate objects, yes. Even the elements sometimes. But a human being . . .' Morosely, he wrung out his cleaning cloth. 'Well, I can't do it, anyway.'

Jolly glanced at Soledad, who was standing at the bowsprit of the *Carfax* and staring into the distance, lost in thought. Of course Walker hadn't ordered the princess to crawl around the deck on her knees, scraping pig-muck off the planks. Jolly doubted whether Soledad would have taken orders from Walker anyway.

'I think I can see another hoofprint there . . . yes, right in front of you, Munk.' Walker contentedly blew a smoke ring. 'And Jolly, put your back into it a bit more, will you?'

Buenaventure made a sound like a dog happily greeting its master and mistress as they arrive home. This time there was no doubt about it; the pit bull man was laughing.

Jolly was so angry that she could have bitten the rim of her wooden bucket in her rage.

But she didn't.

She went on scrubbing.

The island of Tortuga owed its name to the unusual shape of its outline on the horizon. The first French settlers had called it *La Tortue*, the turtle.

Only a few miles lay between Tortuga and the shore of Haiti, one of the largest landmasses in the Caribbean. By comparison, Tortuga was tiny. If the first Caribbean pirates hadn't decided to settle here in the last century, the oval hump with its tropical forests would probably have appeared only on the most detailed of maps.

Buenaventure steered the *Carfax* around the island's inhospitable northern coast, past cliffs and rocky points, sailed around a barrier reef in the south, and came into the fortified harbour. With its two narrow entrances, it could be easily defended. In contrast to New Providence, there was no sandy beach here, only a paved road around the harbour just above the waterline. Beyond this road rose houses with tiled roofs, and a wild, luxuriant jungle of mahogany, ironwood and bougainvillea grew behind the town.

Dusk was already falling as the *Carfax* found a suitable place to cast anchor. If they had to leave in a hurry they could get out of the harbour quickly from the spot they chose. The ghosts reefing in the sails were barely visible as darkness came on. Walker had warned them of the attention that the phantom sailors on the *Carfax* might attract, but his anxiety proved unfounded: the crews of most of the vessels in the harbour had gone ashore, and the few left on deck as watchmen had better things to do than inspect the new arrivals.

The companions left the ship to the ghosts and went ashore. Jolly looked sadly down at the waves below them lapping against the harbour wall. She fought her urge to run out on the water, leaping from wave to wave; it was like an addiction that came over her after she had spent any length of time on land or on board ship. The waves seemed to be whispering her name, the wind tugged at her. At such moments, even the smell of salt water seemed to her tangy and inviting. But she resisted the temptation. She mustn't attract notice now.

When she asked Munk if he felt the same, he shook his head in surprise. 'No, not at all,' he said.

Once ashore they parted. Soledad and Buenaventure were going to the taverns to see if they could pick up any rumours of the Ghost-Trader's presence. It certainly seemed next to impossible that he had reached the island ahead of them, but it couldn't be ruled out – after all, they had lost a day unloading the pigs.

Meanwhile Jolly, Munk, Griffin and Walker sought out the old flag-maker whom the Ghost-Trader had mentioned. Silverhand was well known on Tortuga. Hardly a free-booter's flag was hoisted in the whole Caribbean that didn't come from his workshop, where he adorned the famous death's head not just with a skull and crossbones but some-times with swords, pistols, even beer mugs. Skeletons were a popular subject too, many armed with swords, others with wine goblets in their hands.

'Welcome,' Silverhand greeted them, shaking hands heartily with Walker. He looked at Jolly and the two boys with slight suspicion, although Munk's astonished appreciation of all the flags on the walls quickly won him over. 'Take a look around, my boy,' said Silverhand in a voice that sounded like the hinges of a rusty treasure chest. 'I make two of every flag, one for my esteemed customer, the other for my collection. Every cut-throat who ever made these waters perilous and had a Jolly Roger sewn for him is immortalised here – including those that the Spaniards and the French strung up. Many a flag has sunk to the bottom of the sea forever, others have burned along with the crew. But in Silverhand's workshop they live on in memory of their captains . . . and the gold those captains left here.'

He uttered a raucous laugh. Jolly noticed that his hands were as bony as those of the skeleton on his flags. But Silverhand's most striking feature was his scars. Jolly had met many men who proudly displayed their mementoes of a number of battles. Silverhand's scars, however, had not been made by sword-blades or pistol balls. On their way along the narrow alleys Walker had told them the old man's story: after many years at sea as sailor and ship's mate, even as ship's cook, he had ended up on the vessel of a particularly unpleasant and vile freebooter. This man had the frail seaman keelhauled for some long-forgotten offence – one of the most cruel sentences that could be passed on board ship. The victim was hauled right under the keel of the ship by ropes. Those who did not die were marked for life: depending on the ship's condition, the rough wood could inflict terrible wounds on the poor man. The ship on which Silverhand was sailing had been in a terrible state, its hull thickly encrusted with seashells. Their sharp edges and points had cut his skin to shreds, until it hung off his bones like a patchwork costume.

Today his body looked as if all the pirates of the Caribbean had whetted their blades on it. The scars of old weals stood out, running criss-cross, his mouth was set askew in his face, one eye was missing. Only his fingers had remained intact back then, so after he recovered he was able to earn a meagre wage in a flag-maker's workshop. Soon he had taken the business over, and now he had been supplying the corsair vessels of the Caribbean for over twenty years with the emblems that taught all honest folk the meaning of fear.

'What can I do for you?' asked Silverhand, leaning his frail frame against a stack of black bales of cloth. Jolly put his age at eighty at least, ancient for this part of the world, where most men died young on the gallows or under fire.

'Show him the spider,' Walker told Munk. Munk took the little box out of the bag at his belt, opened the lid and handed it to the flag-maker.

'A vicious creature, I'll be bound,' said the old man when he had taken a good look at the spider's corpse. 'So you're not here because you're interested in my flags.'

'I think they're terrific,' said Munk, and he meant it.

Silverhand gave his wry grin. 'Good lad. So tell me why you're showing me your spider.'

'Well, it's really –'

'*My* spider,' Jolly interrupted him. 'I belong to Captain Bannon's crew. My name is Jolly.'

'Bannon?' Silverhand scratched the back of his bald head, which was as scarred as every other part of his body. 'A bad business, that. I heard the *Maddy* had gone to the bottom. A bad, bad business.'

Jolly told him what had happened.

'Spiders, ah, well.' Silverhand brushed the top bale of fabric with his hand as if he had just that moment found one there. 'Handsome creatures, in my opinion. But dangerous. Very dangerous. Deadly as the plague.'

'I was wondering whether perhaps, on all your travels, you'd ever seen one like this.'

'Is that why you came? Because I've been around the world more than any other seaman?'

Jolly nodded. 'So we've been told, anyway.' She looked round, and noticed that Walker was listening attentively to every word she said, with astonishment in his face as he looked at her.

Curiously enough, it was Silverhand who provided the explanation for that. 'You have a lot of Bannon in you, child.

The way you talk, the determination in your eyes. How long were you with him?'

'As long as I can remember.'

'Then you must be the little polliwiggle he landed.'

She nodded again, although she was feeling bad.

'There's plenty of fellows were damned envious of him. He had luck, he certainly did. Back then polliwiggles were the most valuable treasures you could imagine. I wasn't going to sea much at the time, but everyone was talking about 'em. Here and in the taverns and on board ships. There was some would shrink from nothing to get hold of one. Murder, they'd commit downright murder to get their hands on one of you.'

Jolly's discomfort was growing. She hadn't forgotten what Munk's father had suggested: Bannon might not have bought her in the slave market after all, he could have killed her parents and taken her away with him.

'The spider,' she said in a voice that shook, pointing to the little open box in Silverhand's bony fingers. 'Would you take another look at it?'

But the old man's one sound eye was still turned on her, as if all the others had suddenly left his workshop. He was assessing her, measuring her up, rummaging around in her thoughts as if in a chest of drawers.

'Silverhand!' It was Walker's voice that finally broke the spell. 'We don't want to waste more of your time than we have to. Have you ever seen spiders like this or not?'

The old man looked away from Jolly, although with reluctance, and stared down into the box again. 'Hm,' he said slowly. 'A rare specimen, for sure. I'd wager it comes from the mainland. At least, I've never seen one with a pattern like that in the islands.'

'Are you sure?' asked Jolly.

'Not sure, no. But I'd have to be very much mistaken.' He handed the little box back to Munk, who immediately put it away again.

Jolly was disappointed by Silverhand's vagueness. Why had the Ghost-Trader bothered to send her here?

'Do you know where on the mainland it might come from?' asked Munk, seeing Jolly's disappointment.

'No, no idea.'

Walker joined in again. 'Are you absolutely sure you don't?' He took out one of Munk's doubloons and flicked it over to the old man with his thumb and forefinger. Silverhand caught it, swiftly pocketed it, but then just shook his head for a second time. 'I'm sorry. If I knew I'd tell you.'

Walker took a deep breath, clapped Jolly on the shoulder and nodded to the old man. 'Thanks for your help,

Silverhand. See you some time.' So saying, he led Jolly and the two boys to the door.

They were just about to leave the workshop when Silverhand's croak of a voice stopped them.

'There could be a possibility,' he said.

Jolly spun round. 'What kind of possibility?'

'The Oracle.'

Walker's eyes narrowed. 'God in heaven, man, we don't need a soothsayer, what we need is –'

Impatiently, Jolly interrupted him. 'Where do we find this Oracle?'

Silverhand gave her a tight-lipped smile. 'Down by the harbour, the ship with the finest figurehead there. A mermaid it is, but bigger and better than all the rest. Just follow the crowd, there's always a crowd there at this time of day.'

'Who's on board this ship?' asked Walker suspiciously.

'On board?' Silverhand chuckled. 'Not a human soul. The old tub's a wreck, won't go to sea any more. But it speaks. That darn figurehead speaks.'

Walker shook his head. 'What are you talking about, Silverhand?'

'It's the truth, believe you me! Old Silverhand's got no need to lie to you.' His glance probed Jolly's mind like the blade of a knife. 'The figurehead's the Oracle. And if it likes . . . but only if it likes . . . it'll tell you the answer to your question.'

THE VOICE IN THE FIGUREHEAD

'I'll torch that whole darn wreck!' bellowed a pirate coming along the harbour towards them. Two other men were holding his arms as if to lead him away. He kept trying to break free and turn back. 'There won't be anything left of it – not a goddarn plank. That . . . that thing's ruined me. Ruined me, d'you hear? Says my ship will sink on its next voyage . . . who's going to sign on with me now? That monster! It's the devil's work, I tell you! The devil's work and witchcraft!'

His two comrades were trying to calm him down, but the pirate wasn't listening to them.

'I'll finish it! What do I care if it's made of wood or flesh and blood? I'll burn it, that's what you do with a witch! No one treats me that way! No one!'

The two men led their indignant companion into a side

street. 'Come along, Bill, you'll feel better once you get a drop of drink inside you.'

Jolly and the others had stopped, and watched the three disappear into a tavern. 'Ruined me, that's what it did!' they heard the man complain again through an open window, and then his voice was drowned out by the noise of the tavern.

'Did he say witch?' asked Griffin, frowning.

Munk hooked one thumb into his belt. 'Do you think he meant the Oracle?'

'Oracle! Stuff and nonsense!' said Walker, snorting. 'Silverhand's not right in the head, everyone knows that.'

A large number of pirates had assembled down at the harbour by the light of freshly kindled torches, among them a few maidservants and pirate trollops, small children with dirty faces, and a handful of cabin boys of Jolly's age who had ensconced themselves on a stack of chests and barrels. The flames shone on their faces, lighting them up with gold against the deep blue of the evening sky.

Walker stopped one man. 'What are you all doing here?'

'The Oracle's speaking.'

'Where do we find this . . . er, Oracle?'

'See the old tub over there? The wreck with only its bows

still rising above the water? The figurehead – well, it answers any questions you ask it.'

'Does it have a name?'

'The Oracle.'

'Ah . . . yes, I might have known it. Thanks, friend. I'll drink to your health later.'

The pirate, who was wearing a battered three-cornered hat on his head, examined him with new interest. 'Hey, I know you! You're Walker, right?'

Jolly surreptitiously pinched the captain's arm.

'Walker? Is he here on Tortuga, then?' Walker shook his head. 'Sorry, friend, you've got the wrong man.'

The pirate looked suspicious and leaned forward, almost as if he were planning to sniff at Walker to find out the truth. 'I saw the *Carfax* lying in harbour.'

'You did? Fancy that.' Walker gave him a brief nod and then turned away. 'Goodbye, friend, and thanks for the information.'

Uneasily, Jolly saw out of the corner of her eye that the man was watching them as they approached the crowd. They quickly pushed in among the throng of men and women to escape his distrustful gaze.

'Do you think they'll look for us here?' Jolly whispered into Walker's ear.

'Who, this Maelstrom of yours?'

'Kendrick.'

Walker thoughtfully massaged his temples. 'If he really got away from New Providence then Tortuga's an obvious place to go. Most of 'em here accept him as the pirate emperor. Of course the *Carfax* is faster than his ship. On the other hand, we've –'

'Lost a day,' she said gloomily. 'Yes, I know.'

'Not including the extra time the weight of your friends the pigs cost us over the first three days.' But he was too anxious now to take Jolly seriously to task. 'Yes,' he added after a brief pause. 'Kendrick could be here.'

'And there could be a price on my head, and Soledad's?'

'It's possible.'

Jolly bit her lower lip, and wished she could disappear from view among the pirate horde. The disreputable crowd smelled bad, of spirits and beer, smoke and sweat. All the same, she was suddenly glad of it, since it hid them from the eyes of the man whom Walker had spoken to. When she looked around in search of him, she couldn't see him anywhere.

'Problems of some kind?' asked Griffin. In the crush, she had lost sight of him for a moment. Munk was right behind him.

'No, it's all right,' she said faintly.

'What about this Oracle?' asked Munk. 'Do you want to go and ask it yourself, or shall I?' The little box containing the spider was in his hand. Its lid was closed.

'I'll do it.' Jolly took the box.

'That's not a good idea,' Walker said. 'If they really are looking for us . . .' He stopped, shaking his head, as Jolly ignored his warning and pushed her way through the crowd.

Ahead of her the noise was even louder, but all the heads hid her view of what was going on there. Jolly made herself as thin as possible, and once even slipped through the legs of a gigantic freebooter. Munk tried to follow her, but she was much nimbler and reached the front of the crowd long before him. Someone swore as she pushed by, but did not thrust her aside when he saw that she was smaller than he was, and he could see over her.

The figurehead rose above the quay in the light of several torches that had been planted around it.

The mermaid's face, like her perfect body, was made of dark wood. Blank eyes looked over the heads of the crowd majestically, in spite of the pitiful condition of the rest of the ship. Her features were cut like stone. Only the flickering torch flames gave an illusion of life where there couldn't possibly be any.

The figurehead was twice as tall as a man, and stood almost upright because the stern of the galleon had sunk into the harbour basin. Only part of the foc's'le, the bowsprit, and the figurehead itself rose from the water, which was black as night. The rigging had rotted and fallen apart long ago. The wooden figure was about five paces away from land, too far for anyone's bare hands to reach it.

A dozen men and women were shouting at the same time, all of them trying to get their own questions out. Two girls were literally fighting, scratching and hitting each other because each claimed it was her turn next.

'Is it like this all day?' Jolly asked an old seadog who was watching the show with cheerful calm.

'All day? Oh no.' He puffed at a little pipe that had seen better days. 'The Oracle speaks only at dusk, from sunset until it's fully dark. After that it says nothing until next evening.'

'Oh,' said Jolly, disappointed, for the sun had sunk into the sea long ago, and the first stars were already twinkling in the sky.

'Too late!' called someone from the crowd. 'It's too late for today!'

'We haven't heard the poem yet,' shouted someone else. 'We want to hear the poem!'

Jolly turned back to the old pirate. 'What sort of poem?'

'Ah, well, the Oracle recites a poem at the end, see? Every time. It's kind of traditional.'

Jolly was surprised, but supposed this might be usual among oracles. After all, she'd never met one before.

'Is its poetry good?' She asked only to hide her disappointment. Now she'd have to wait until tomorrow evening to ask about the spider.

'Good? By Neptune's seaweed punch!' The old man turned his eyes to heaven. 'Never heard a worse poet in my life. Terrible stuff it is, by Davy Jones! But there's a few here as take note of it all and turn it into songs for the taverns.'

She laughed too, out of politeness, but stopped short when a rasping voice spoke from the mouth of the inanimate figurehead.

'Silence! Hush! A little consideration for those who appreciate good poetry, if you please!'

Jolly stopped short. So that was the voice of the Oracle. It was neither masculine nor feminine.

'Silence!'

The audience duly fell silent.

Munk slipped through the spectators to join Jolly. 'This is crazy, right?'

She just nodded and listened.

The Oracle audibly coughed and then raised its rasping voice again:

> *Oh, once there lived a bold corsair,*
> *Sharp was his sword and black his hair,*
> *Frutti di mare was his fare –*
> *But oh, he had no ship.*
>
> *Women and children he cut down,*
> *He chopped off heads, left men to drown,*
> *He'd plundered all of Kingston Town –*
> *Alas, he had no ship.*
>
> *Rum's good for breakfast, so he said,*
> *Rum's nice for dinner, or instead*
> *Of lunch, let's drink rum till we're dead –*
> *Yet still he had no ship.*
>
> *He took all his ill-gotten gold.*
> *Heard of a ship soon to be sold,*
> *Out drinking went that corsair bold –*
> *Next day the ship was gone.*
>
> *He learned a lesson that sad day:*

Ships sometimes their own anchors weigh.
They hoist sail and they go away,
No captain do they need.

Our bold corsair just stayed around
On land, was glad when safe and sound
The wrecks of several ships he found –
And built himself a house.

Jolly, bemused, looked into the torchlight. No one said a word.

'Er,' said Munk at last, looking as if he had toothache. 'That was . . .'

'Not very good?' Jolly suggested.

At the same moment loud shouts of applause rang out. The pirates rivalled each other in their cries of 'Bravo!' Hoarse-voiced men who couldn't tell a poem from a curse praised the Oracle's sublime poetic talent. Others prophesied a great future for it as pirate poet laureate.

Jolly looked at Munk. 'They don't mean it seriously, do they?'

Baffled, Munk shook his head. 'I suppose pirates don't necessarily *have* to know anything about art.'

Griffin's face emerged from the crowd, glowing with

enthusiasm. 'Hey, that was crazy, right?'

Jolly and Munk exchanged another glance. 'Totally, *really* crazy!' they said in chorus. Munk made a gesture of sticking his forefinger down his throat, and suddenly Jolly had to laugh so hard that she could hardly catch her breath.

'What's up?' asked Griffin, taken aback.

Jolly just laughed even louder, Munk joined in, and suddenly even the old sea-dog grinned before he put the pipe between his lips again and walked away. After a few paces he disappeared into the darkness.

Jolly was gasping for air, and finally managed to breathe again, but she still couldn't calm down. Munk was rubbing his stomach.

'Look, could one of you kindly tell me . . .' Griffin began, but he was interrupted by a hand that came down on his shoulder and pushed him aside.

Buenaventure was standing behind him, looking as if he had just sprung out of the paving stones.

'We must get away!' said the pit bull man. 'Kendrick's bounty-hunters are after us!'

The last of Jolly and Munk's laughter died away as they realised that he meant it.

'They're looking for us,' said Buenaventure. 'Everywhere.'

Walker appeared beside him. 'What are you all waiting for?'

Next moment Soledad turned up too, her hair damp with perspiration, strands of it sticking to her face and a hunted look in her eyes.

'Run!' she cried.

Jolly seized Munk's hand, and together they took to their heels.

The door of a tavern lay at the end of a narrow blind alley.

A badly spelled handwritten notice on it informed passers-by that the tavern was closed today for clearing up after 'serten insidentz' the previous day.

As there was no other way out of the alley, and Walker thought it would be a bad idea to go back and look for another hiding-place, Buenaventure raised his hand and hammered on the wood of the door.

'Can't you folks read?' bellowed a voice inside. 'Ah, the devil, of course you can't, you uneducated riff-raff! I might have known it. Brainless fools!'

'Delightful manners they have around here,' murmured Soledad.

The door was opened just a crack. A bald-headed man with a swollen eye stared at them. Buenaventure had

277

stepped back, but obviously the sight of Walker alone was enough for the landlord.

'We're closed,' he said in unfriendly tones, and was about to shut the door again.

'Hey there!' said Walker, hastily shoving his foot in the doorway. 'A good landlord never turns guests away.'

'Guests can go to hell for all I care. This entire island can drown itself in the sea. I don't want no more to do with you and your kind.'

'Think again, why don't you?' said Walker in an amiable tone, beckoning the pit-bull man forward. 'Because otherwise my friend here will piddle against your leg – figuratively speaking, of course.'

The landlord looked at Buenaventure, unimpressed. 'No dogs allowed in here. They smell, they do their business all over the place and they beg for scraps under the table.'

'I hear voices the other end of the alley,' said Griffin. 'We ought to hurry.'

Buenaventure shrugged, laid both his huge hands against the door and pushed it in, taking the landlord with it.

'Uncouth folk,' said the man angrily, waving his hands in the air. 'Females with 'em and all, common trollops most like, and –'

Soledad planted herself angrily in front of him, hands on

her hips, and put her face extremely close to his. 'If you value your life, landlord, and more particularly if you value your teeth, shut your gob this moment!'

Surprisingly, this impressed the landlord far more than the menacing appearance of the gigantic dog-man. He looked at the princess incredulously for a moment, then muttered something that they couldn't make out and set off for the bar.

'Sit down, then,' he cried. 'Take the candle there with you, light as many more as you fancy. What'd you like to drink?'

Walker shot the bolt on the inside of the door. 'I see you're a man with a generous heart and a noble mind. We appreciate the honour of being welcomed into a gentleman's house.'

'All right, all right, that'll do.' The landlord angrily dismissed the subject and went round behind his bar.

They ordered beer, and rum and water, as well as all the dishes the kitchen had to offer – there were exactly two: potato bake and chicken soup.

'No fish?' asked Walker, disappointed.

'No fish.' Their host disappeared into the kitchen.

The tavern was in poor shape. Half of the furnishings had been demolished during yesterday evening's 'incidents'. Jolly saw dried bloodstains here and there on the untidy straw that covered the floor.

Half an hour later, long after the food and drink had been

served, there was a vigorous hammering on the door.

Walker, Buenaventure and Soledad immediately reached for their weapons. Jolly and the boys jumped up. Griffin drew the sword he had brought from the *Carfax*. Jolly took out her dagger.

'I can't see you,' said a voice on the other side of the door. 'But I know you're in there.'

Walker's lips were as thin as lines drawn in chalk. 'Isn't that —?'

A smile flitted over Jolly's face. 'Yes,' she said. 'The Ghost-Trader.'

'How did you find us?'

The Trader gave Jolly an indulgent smile. 'There are ways and means,' he unctuously began, 'that are beyond your powers of imagination, and —'

'Yes, of course. But *really*, how did you find us?'

His smile grew even broader. 'I eavesdropped on the men looking for you. They're combing every part of this town, and you were last seen around here. And if I know Walker, he was bound to take you to a tavern . . .'

The pirate wiped the froth of his beer off his upper lip and raised one critical eyebrow.

'. . . and as he's shrewd enough not to choose one where

Buenaventure would immediately attract attention to you, it had to be one that was closed. So I found this one, and then I had only to listen at the door to be sure.' He looked around at them sternly. 'Bounty-hunters on your heels could just as easily have done the same. There seem to be a great many of them about.'

Soledad nodded. 'Buenaventure and I heard about it in a pothouse down by the harbour. Kendrick has set a pretty large sum on my head – and yours too, Jolly.'

Walker scratched his head. 'Then perhaps this might be a good time for our ways to part.'

The princess grinned at him. 'Kendrick knows you and Buenaventure got us out of Port Nassau. You'll be on his list too now.'

'Wonderful,' said the captain gloomily.

Buenaventure uttered a kind of growl. Probably only Walker could say for certain what he meant by it.

'How did you get here yourself?' Jolly asked the Ghost-Trader.

He stroked the dark feathers of the two parrots sitting on his shoulders. 'Fast as the wind.'

'Yes, I know, I know,' she said with an exaggerated yawn, imitating his deep voice. 'For there are ways and means beyond our powers of –'

The Ghost-Trader interrupted her. 'In this case there really are.'

She tightened her lips and looked intently at the Trader. His face was grave again in the shadow of his hood. She wondered whether it didn't look a little more lined than a few days ago.

'The sea eagle brought bad news back to New Providence.' He emptied his glass of rum in a single draught, but did not order another. 'Greater danger threatens than I had feared.' He paused. His one eye rested on Jolly for a while, then his gaze moved to Munk. Jolly thought she saw grief in it, but determination too.

'It's time for us to arm ourselves,' said the Ghost-Trader. 'The hunt is up, the polliwiggles are expected.'

'By the Maelstrom?' asked Griffin.

The Ghost-Trader seemed to notice the pirate boy for the first time. Then he looked at Jolly. 'You've told them all about it?'

Jolly shivered under his searching look, but nodded. Then she told him about the armies of the Deep Tribes, and the invisible being that had led them.

The Ghost-Trader clenched his right hand. 'That only confirms what our allies in the east have told me.'

'*Our* allies?' asked Walker sceptically.

'The allies of all free men,' said the Trader sharply. 'And all who wish to remain free.'

Walker snorted derisively, but said no more. Jolly sensed that he felt far more respect for the Ghost-Trader than he would admit. Even Buenaventure made no sound. The landlord, in all seriousness, had offered him a bone just now. For a moment Buenaventure had looked as if he would like to eat the man rather than the bone. But then he merely ordered another beer.

'Who are these allies?' Munk asked him. 'And where are we expected?'

'I can't tell you yet. Not here, where the walls have ears.' He cast a meaning glance at the landlord, who was behind the bar polishing the same set of glasses for the third time. 'But you'll meet them if we get off this island safe and sound.'

'If? Do you think we might not, then?' asked Jolly.

Walker opened his eyes wide in alarm. 'The *Carfax*! Kendrick will try to sink her.' He jumped up so quickly that his chair fell over. 'Dammit, we must get to the harbour!'

'Keep calm,' said the Trader, 'and sit down again. The ghosts are taking good care of your ship. If Kendrick tries to board her he'll get an unpleasant surprise.'

'You've been on board, haven't you?' asked Jolly.

'Just now, yes. And I told the ghosts to kill anyone who sets foot on deck without permission.'

Jolly shuddered.

'Was Silverhand able to help you over the spider?' asked the Trader.

'No. He just said it probably comes from the mainland.'

Sighing, the Ghost-Trader shook his head.

'He sent us to that Oracle in the harbour,' said Jolly.

The Ghost-Trader dismissed this news. 'I saw the last living oracle before . . . oh, long before the days of the Wild Hunt. In Delphi. Whatever it is down there in the harbour, it's certainly no oracle.'

'In the *Dolphin*, did you say?' Walker pricked up his ears. 'I know a tavern in Jamaica called the *Dolphin*.'

'That's not what I meant,' replied the Ghost-Trader with a glance of reproof.

The pirate, his feelings injured, grinned wryly and looked back into his tankard.

'In any case, Bannon must wait.'

'No!' Jolly's eyes flashed with anger as she looked at the Trader. 'I only let myself in for this whole crazy business because of him.'

'Many heroes have gone on their travels for far less, and come back with the crown of the world instead.'

'I don't want any crown,' she said crossly. 'I want to find Bannon.'

'Wait a minute.' Griffin joined in. 'It was you who told us all about the Maelstrom. And how important it is to stand up to it. Doesn't that matter any more?'

Munk had turned to her as well. 'Griffin is right, Jolly. If polliwiggles are necessary to put an end to this thing, then we must both try to do it.'

Jolly looked at the Ghost-Trader again. 'Munk can help you. He's a much better polliwiggle than I am. He can give the ghosts orders, and then there was that business with the shells . . .'

'You could do it too if you'd only give yourself a chance. And even more, perhaps.'

'Me? Nonsense. I don't know anything at all about magic. And ghosts give me gooseflesh. I can run over the water, and that's all.'

'Where I'm taking you, you'll learn about magic.' The shadows round the Ghost-Trader's eye were suddenly deep as a well. Jolly felt dizzy. 'You will understand it all in Aelenium.'

'In –'

He cut her short with a gesture, and cast another warning glance the landlord's way. 'Quiet! Too much has been said already.'

'Anyway, I'm not going anywhere I can't find Bannon.'

'Bannon is dead,' said Walker abruptly. 'Everyone knows that.'

'He isn't!'

'The ship must have sunk, Jolly. If it hadn't, someone would have found it. Believe me, there can't have been any survivors.'

'So what about me?'

'You're a polliwiggle.'

She felt tears shoot to her eyes, which annoyed her so much that she remained grimly silent.

Griffin put his hand over hers and gently stroked it with his forefinger. She was about to pull her fingers angrily away, feeling she would like to slap him – anyone! – but then she thought it didn't feel so bad after all, and even comforted her a little.

Out of the corner of her eyes, she saw Munk turning away.

Good heavens, she thought, what am I doing here? Although it was all really quite obvious – she had to find Bannon, someone had to overcome the Maelstrom – she felt more bewildered than she had ever been in her life before.

The Ghost-Trader spoke up again. 'What matters now is to take the two polliwiggles to the place where they are expected. Walker, will you help us with the *Carfax*?'

The pirate looked anything but pleased at the prospect. 'There was talk of certain treasures . . .'

The Ghost-Trader's face paled with anger, but he said nothing.

'Oh, very well,' said Walker hastily, 'perhaps it'll do if the boy works his doubloon magic a few more times.'

'Doubloon magic?' The Trader's surprised glance moved to Munk.

Munk hunched down in his chair and shrugged his shoulders.

'Ah, yes,' said the Ghost-Trader suddenly. 'Of course – the doubloon magic!'

Walker nodded enthusiastically. 'And you say Jolly will learn that kind of thing?'

Jolly wasn't listening any more, but the Trader nodded. 'Oh yes, indeed.'

Walker thought about it. 'Hm. Couldn't I . . . I mean, I'm sure I'd be quick to learn, I could –'

'Can you walk on water?' the Trader asked him.

'Er . . . no.'

'Then forget it.'

Walker sulked for a moment or so, then straightened his back and let his breath out sharply. 'Anyway, the *Carfax* is at your disposal. Isn't that right, Buenaventure?'

The pit bull man waved a hand and emptied an entire tankard of beer at a single draught.

The Ghost-Trader rose to his feet. He threw a handful of coins on the table. 'That's decided, then. We must get off this island as quickly as possible.'

They set off, leaving the relieved landlord of the tavern behind on his own.

Out in the streets, the smell of a fire drifted towards them. They heard excited voices in the distance.

Walker turned pale. 'It comes from the harbour! The *Carfax*!'

THE WISDOM OF WORMS

The mermaid was burning.

It looked as if someone had thrown a cloak of flames over her. The fire was leaping high around her wooden body. Her head had disappeared in a greenish-yellow blaze, and her coal-black face showed through the fire only occasionally. Her empty eyes looked accusing, almost reproachful.

The voice of the Oracle had fallen silent.

Men and women were running frantically about on the quay. Several chains passing buckets from hand to hand had been formed, to prevent the flames from spreading to other ships moored nearby. The wreck itself was past saving.

Jolly and the others had run the last part of the way, afraid that Kendrick's bounty-hunters really had succeeded in setting the *Carfax* on fire. But when they emerged from an alley and came out on the quayside, they saw Walker's ship lying intact in the darkness. If anyone had tried attacking her, the ghosts had beaten the assailants off. At the moment all on board the ship looked peaceful.

As Jolly came to a halt in the turmoil around the burning figurehead, and peered through the smoke and fire with streaming eyes, she saw Bill, the angry sailor they had met just now, being knocked to the ground and tied up by several men.

'Did he do it?' she asked one of the pirates.

The man nodded grimly. 'Threw an oil lamp at her head, so he did!'

'It was her fault!' screeched Bill, defending himself desperately against the men holding him. 'It was her –' But a blow from a fist silenced him.

'String him up!' shouted a woman.

'Burn him!' cried another.

Several pirates banded together and looked as if they were about to carry out these demands. But then a troop of uniformed Frenchmen from the fort above the town appeared and took Bill the fire-raiser away. For a moment it seemed that some of the pirates were thinking of forcing the soldiers to hand over the culprit, but then reason prevailed: the French garrison on Tortuga tolerated the pirates' activities so long as they paid their dues, and it would have been stupid to risk such a lucrative arrangement just for a burning wreck.

'To the *Carfax*!' cried the Ghost-Trader, turning to his companions. 'This is our chance to get away unnoticed!'

All of them joined him but Jolly. She stood there sadly, staring past the chains of buckets and into the fire. Another opportunity to learn something about Bannon's fate gone!

The burning bows of the wreck rose above the water like a pyramid of fire. Its heat blew painfully into Jolly's face. Around her, the air flickered.

She went to the edge of the water. Someone almost ran into her, spilled half a bucket of water, and shouted at her either to get out of the way or to help. Jolly took no notice. Instead, she looked down into the harbour basin, to the place where the waves, now shining like fire, disappeared under a ring of dark smoke.

There was something down there in the water.

Something moving.

It was not quite as long as her arm, pale and hairless as a newborn baby, and it was writhing and coiling in the water as if desperately trying to stay afloat. But smoke and the brightness of the fire kept Jolly from seeing properly, and she wasn't sure. Perhaps it was just a piece of drifting wreckage.

But no, it *was* something alive. Something that would probably drown if she didn't do anything to help it.

Glancing briefly over her shoulder, Jolly saw that her

companions had stopped, heard Munk and Griffin call her name at the same time – and then she jumped off the quay and came down on the water.

Her landing on the waves was hard and hurt her knees, but it didn't unbalance her. She ran straight on, fervently hoping that the people on shore were too busy to notice her.

Running fast, she approached the thing in the water. The heat was even worse down here, building up between the burning wreck and the harbour wall. Sparks floated through the night in golden swarms, came up against the ship next to the wreck, but went out there without lighting another fire. Members of the ship's crew were standing behind its rail, pouring buckets of water down the hull. One man spotted Jolly and shouted something to his comrades.

She took no notice, but ran on.

One thing she now knew for certain: whatever was writhing there in the water wasn't a child.

It wasn't even a human being. In fact it looked rather like . . . yes, like a worm.

Except that this worm was almost two feet long and as stout as a man's thigh.

'Help!' shouted the worm, although she couldn't see any mouth on it. 'Help me, you stupid thing! I'm drowning!'

She knew that voice.

Jolly picked the worm up with both hands and lifted it out of the water. Then she ran on, back into the darkness of the harbour basin, away from the fire and the shouting crowd, away from the heat, the smoke, and the hundreds of eyes watching her.

'What are you?' she asked the slippery thing in her hands. '*Who* are you?'

'Stupid question!' replied the worm, and all the fear had left his voice. 'Who do you think I am, you silly girl? I'm the Oracle . . . I am the Hexhermetic Shipworm!'

No one really welcomed the creature that Jolly brought aboard the *Carfax*. Least of all Walker, who reminded them that shipworms ate wood. And what else was the ship on which their lives depended out at sea made of?

'I can feed him,' said Jolly. She thought she'd seen some planks in the hold, wooden beams and boards kept there for repair work. Surely Walker could spare a few.

'If he starts eating my ship he goes overboard.'

'Oaf!' retorted the Worm.

'What did he say?'

'He said thank you,' Jolly was quick to assure Walker.

'Thank you, huh!' muttered the Worm. 'That boor isn't worth the wood they'll use for his coffin.'

Walker was already on the way up to the bridge. 'And no poetry!' he called back over his shoulder before joining the Ghost-Trader and Buenaventure, who were standing there at the wheel, deciding what course to set. 'One bad rhyme on my ship and –' He drew one finger across his throat.

Jolly held the Worm in front of her with both hands and stared at his face – or at least, at the end where she assumed his face was.

There were no eyes to be seen, just a broad horny plate with a mouth opening below it. He had six stout, stumpy legs, and his body twitched frantically when he was in a bad temper.

'How about saying "Thank you for rescuing me, Jolly?"' Her eyes flashed angrily. 'And kindly stop insulting my friends.' Secretly, she was surprised at herself: was Walker her friend, then?

Consideration of this question must wait, for the Worm now launched into a torrent of abuse and bad language.

'Walker's right,' said Griffin, inspecting the strange creature. 'We ought to throw him overboard.'

'Oh yes?' retorted Jolly. 'I seem to remember, that was just what was supposed to happen to someone else. Weren't you glad when Munk stopped it?'

The corners of Griffin's mouth twitched, but he said no more.

Munk came to his aid. 'That was different, Jolly. This . . . this thing isn't a human being. He's ungrateful and outrageous and he knows more swearwords than Walker and Buenaventure put together. What's more, he looks as if he stinks.'

'I do *not* stink!' said the Worm indignantly. 'You little . . .'

'Quiet!' Jolly had to think, and she couldn't do that if everyone else was talking. The only one who kept out of the argument was Soledad. The princess stood a few steps away, looking through the forest of ships' masts at the quay. The wreck was still burning, and the smoke now drifting over the harbour basin could help them to make their getaway. The ghosts had been busy for some time, making the ship ready to set sail. Her mighty winch creaked as some of the misty beings raised the anchor.

The Worm cleared his throat. 'I would like to make it perfectly clear that I do not –'

'Get him below decks,' Munk interrupted. 'Walker keeps looking this way, and the Ghost-Trader doesn't seem too happy either.'

'That fellow was giving me a very nasty look when Jolly

brought me on board,' spluttered the Hexhermetic Shipworm. 'What's he got against me?'

'*What's he got against me?*' Griffin imitated the Worm in a squeaky voice. 'I've heard that lime is a good way of dealing with shipworms. And salt.' A wicked smile flitted over his face. 'We could always try salting him. Perhaps he'd shut up then.'

'Yuk!' said the Worm, horrified, and curled up in Jolly's hands into something more like a ball than a worm.

Jolly reassuringly patted his horny plate. 'Don't worry, the Trader was just afraid you might be a creature of the Mael . . . might be one of our enemies,' she quickly corrected herself.

'Maelstrom, eh?' asked the Worm, uncoiling again and stretching out to his full length. 'Were you just about to say Maelstrom?'

Jolly exchanged a doubtful glance with Munk and Griffin. The two boys looked as unsure as she herself felt.

'Yes,' she said at last. The Trader had considered the Shipworm harmless, so she assumed she could trust him.

'M . . . M . . . Maelstrom,' stammered the Worm, and uttered another unnerving sound, this one like a tuneless bosun's whistle.

'What's the matter with him now?' Griffin rolled his eyes.

Munk went to the cargo hatch over the hold and opened

it. 'Get him down there first. Then we can go on talking.'

Jolly nodded and began down the steps. She turned back to the pirate princess once more. 'Anything suspicious?'

'Two ships are setting sail over there. It could be just chance – or maybe not.'

'Hell!' Griffin followed the direction of Soledad's eyes, but Munk drew him over to the hatch.

'Walker and Buenaventure know what they're doing.'

Jolly went ahead, followed by the two boys. The stink of the pigs still lingered in every nook and cranny of the empty hold. She doubted whether she'd ever be able to look at a pig again without feeling her stomach turn.

'Over there,' she said, pointing to the stack of wooden planks. 'I should think Walker can spare a bit of that.'

'What do you mean, a bit of it?' The Worm slipped out of her hands and scurried over the floor on his short legs much faster than she would have thought possible.

'Hey,' cried Griffin, 'watch out!'

'He'll eat a hole in the hull before we know it,' prophesied Munk gloomily.

It had struck Jolly already that whenever things got serious the two boys were of the same opinion – which didn't often agree with hers. At least they didn't share Soledad's presentiments.

She took a step after the Worm and managed to grab one of his scurrying little legs. He squeaked and swore like a drunken ship's cook.

'I wish to protest in the strongest possible terms! This is no way to treat a Hexhermetic Shipworm!'

Jolly picked him up. This time her hands clutched him firmly, and soon he stopped wriggling. 'You're hungry, right?'

'My stomach's rumbling.'

'Then kindly listen to me. You eat only what I give you, understand? No holes in the ship's side. No nibbled masts. Is that clear?'

The mouth opening twisted into something that might have been an angry pout. The Worm was sulking. 'Oh, all right,' he said sullenly.

'Er . . . Jolly?' Munk raised a hand as if for permission to speak. 'Ask him how much of this stuff he eats a day.'

'Ask him yourself.'

'I'm not *deaf*!' protested the Worm again. 'And I speak your language, boy.'

Munk repressed a sharp retort. 'Then answer me.'

'A plank a day ought to be enough to keep me from dying of malnutrition.'

'A *whole* plank?' Griffin groaned.

Jolly could already see Walker's expression when he

heard this news. 'You don't really need that much, do you?'

'Are you lot prepared to take the responsibility if I starve to death?'

'Could be,' said Griffin, earning a nasty look from Jolly.

Naturally, the Worm's sheer cheek annoyed her as much as it did the boys, but something told her there was more to him than astonishing reserves of impudence. She was about to say something sharp to him when he slid out of her hands again, and scrambled up the pile of wood at a pace that took even Griffin and Munk's breath away.

With an indescribable noise, the Worm ate his way along one of the planks at the speed of light. He fitted his mouth opening over one end and then simply walked forward, while his munching equipment reduced the wood to a cloud of sawdust and splinters.

He had already demolished half the plank when Jolly grabbed his back legs and held him tight. His jaws went on grinding and chewing, but now they were taking in nothing but air. After a few moments he gave up. Instead, a now familiar torrent of curses and insults swept over the three young people.

'Right,' said Jolly. 'Now you're going to answer a few questions.' Turning to Griffin, she called, 'Better close the hatch. We don't want Walker hearing this.'

'Are you going to torture me?' said the Hexhermetic Shipworm.

'Torture you?' Jolly stared at him blankly.

Munk was quicker to react. 'Yes, you bet we are,' he said in a menacing tone. 'You should know that I'm a Grand Master of shell magic, and if I want to I can turn you from a Hexhermetic Shipworm into a Grasseating Grub in the twinkling of an eye.'

'You . . . you'd do a thing like that?'

Munk took a handful of shells from the bag at his belt. 'I can see,' he announced in a tone that boded no good, 'that what you need is proof of my magic arts.'

'Oh no, no.'

'Quite sure?'

'Jolly!' cried the Worm accusingly, 'why didn't you leave me to drown? A quick death would have been better than the company of uncivilised folk like this.' As he spoke his voice rose higher and sounded shriller.

Jolly bit back a grin. 'Well, they're boys, you see. They're stronger than me. They can do anything they like to you if they want.'

'And oh, don't they just want!' said Griffin.

After a moment's hesitation, the Shipworm shook his back legs free, cast a melancholy glance at the rest of the plank, and then sighed. 'All right, all right, I bow to brute force.'

'What do you know about the Maelstrom?' asked Jolly.

The Worm settled on the stack of planks and swallowed. 'Well . . . it's big.'

'You've seen it, then?'

'Not personally, no. But I've heard about it.'

'Who from?'

'Never heard of the wisdom of worms? We have knowledge far greater than anything you can imagine, you pale, ugly, two-legged creatures.'

Griffin rolled his eyes. 'Another show-off!'

'Well?' said Munk. 'Who told you about the Maelstrom?'

'Other worms. Brothers and sisters who once lived in the wood of ships that were sucked into the Maelstrom. Mostly they were swallowed with all hands, but a few broke apart first, and occasional pieces of driftwood returned to civilisation. The inhabitants of the driftwood spread news of the Maelstrom everywhere. There are shipworms on every vessel and every island – although most of them are smaller than me, of course, and they don't have my brilliant mind.'

'Where exactly is the Maelstrom?' The Ghost-Trader could have answered this question for them, but as long as he kept it a secret the Worm might be able to help them.

'In the Atlantic, some way from the outermost islands.'

'Can you be a little more precise?' asked Griffin impatiently.

'North-east of the Virgin Islands. It's said to spring from the ocean bed in a place that bears a name from the time when there was still life deep down there, not just a few sightless fish. It was called the Rift in those days.'

Jolly remembered one of the many maps that Captain Bannon had kept in his cabin. He had often studied them with her, had taught Jolly the meaning of the strange signs, lines and nautical terms, and explained how he sailed the ship safely through the Caribbean with the help of all the information they gave.

The Virgin Islands lay on the edge of the Caribbean island groups, forming the most northerly point of the Lesser Antilles. Beyond them there was nothing but thousands of miles of open sea, an endless horizon, an empty waste of waters above fathomless depths. There were regions in those parts where no ship ever cruised – they might have been tailor-made for the powers of the Mare Tenebrosum.

'What else do you know about the Maelstrom?'

The Shipworm writhed uneasily back and forth. 'Well,' he began, 'what do *you* three know about it? Particularly that powerful master magician of yours!'

It took Munk a moment to realise that the Worm meant him and not the Ghost-Trader. He looked as if he didn't feel very comfortable about it.

'That's none of your business,' he said quickly, and as if to confirm it put one hand in his bag of shells.

The Worm drummed his legs on the wood the way people sometimes drum their fingertips on a table when they're impatient. 'Things are going on everywhere among the islands,' he said, and for the first time he sounded thoughtful. 'Strange creatures are out and about, and the kobalins are on the move in shoals, quite contrary to their usual habits. Once upon a time the Deep Tribes fought each other, but now they're uniting into mighty armies, all going in a certain direction.'

'North-east?' asked Griffin.

'That's right.'

'We've seen them,' said Munk.

'Then I wonder why that one-eyed fool gave the order to set the ship's course north-east.' The Shipworm ground his jaws as if he had found a couple of delicious wood shavings between them. 'We'll all be swallowed up if we come too close to the Maelstrom.'

'He's right,' Griffin told Jolly and Munk. 'I heard it

myself – the Ghost-Trader has set a north-easterly course.'

'Aelenium,' said Jolly, deep in thought. 'That was the word he mentioned. Our destination, I think.'

'Well, it's no island that I ever heard of,' said Griffin.

'Perhaps it has some other name too,' said Munk.

The Shipworm had paid attention when Jolly spoke the name, but now he was looking as if butter wouldn't melt in his mouth. She had noticed, all the same. 'You know what this place Aelenium is, don't you?'

'Do I?' The horny plate of the Shipworm's head turned longingly in the direction of the half-eaten plank. 'If I wasn't so ravenously hungry then . . . perhaps . . .'

Jolly leaned threateningly over him. 'You *do* know.'

'Maybe.'

'We could pull his legs off one by one until he –'

'Griffin!'

'My stomach's rumbling again,' said the Worm, unimpressed. Obviously he had realised that Jolly wouldn't let the others use violence. 'And when my stomach's rumbling I can't think. Or remember anything. Definitely not things so many miles away . . . things in which some people here may have a certain interest.'

'You're a monster,' said Jolly.

'Can I have something to eat now?'

'Only if you promise to tell us all you know about Aelenium afterwards.'

'Very well.'

Jolly pointed to the half-plank. 'And only the rest of that one, understand?'

The Hexhermetic Shipworm fell on his meal. In no time the plank was a small heap of fine sawdust with two or three leftover shavings which he greedily collected in his jaws. 'One should never let anything go to waste,' he said, chewing. 'Never let anything go to waste.'

'We're gathering speed,' said Munk, allowing his eyes to wander to the creaking side of the *Carfax*.

Griffin nodded. 'About time too.'

Jolly put her hands on her hips and looked expectantly at the noisily munching Worm.

'Aelenium,' she reminded him.

The Worm heaved a heart-rending sigh, then took up his position in front of them on his six stumpy legs and launched into a poem.

Aelenium the fair,
Oh, would that we were there
Where all the . . .

'That'll do!' Jolly tapped her forefinger smartly on his horny plate. 'No poetry, Walker says, and that means down here too.'

'No rhymes,' Griffin confirmed.

'No verse,' agreed Munk.

'No sense of the poetic imagination!' cried the Worm indignantly, but thought better of letting himself in for another quarrel. 'Aelenium isn't an island,' he said after a short pause. 'Aelenium is a city.'

'A city in the middle of the sea?'

'That's right.'

'Nonsense.' Griffin dismissed the notion. 'He just wants to eat the ship from under us, that's all.'

'No, I don't . . . or do I? I'm telling the truth, anyway!'

Munk frowned. 'You mean Aelenium is a *floating* city?'

'Got it at last.'

Jolly narrowed her eyes. 'Something like a ship, then?'

'No, different. More peculiar. Aelenium lies at anchor on a chain many miles long that goes down to the very bottom of the sea-bed. And it's not, I am sorry to say, made of wood.'

'What is it made of, then?'

The Worm suddenly quivered. A movement ran through his body like a wave – and vented itself in a loud belch.

At the same moment the ship shook. Jolly and the boys

lost their footing. She managed to grab a supporting beam in the ship's side, but her hands slipped, and wooden splinters bored into her palms. She let out a cry of pain, saw blood between her fingers, and instinctively let go.

Griffin caught her. Not particularly gallantly, not even on purpose, she suspected – but his hands shot out and seized her before the back of her head could hit the planks. He had got to his feet faster than either of the others after his own fall. He really is *devilishly* fast, thought Jolly.

'Thanks,' she managed to say, wiping the drops of blood off her hands on her trousers and looking for Munk. He had fallen against the side of the ship some way off, and was holding his head and swearing quietly.

'Are you all right?' she asked anxiously.

He nodded, and made a face as if he were in pain. 'My head hurts. But it'll soon pass off.'

'Sure?'

'Yes.' He was more cautious this time and didn't nod again.

They all three looked at the Hexhermetic Shipworm.

He had rolled off the pile of wood, but he got up on his short legs again – and belched once more.

This time the *Carfax* didn't shake.

'It was a cannon shot, that's what it was!' said Griffin.

'A ball must have hit the water close to the hull!'

Behind them, the cargo hatch was flung open. Soledad leaped down the top steps into the hold, looked for them in the dim light, and finally found them around the stack of planks.

'Come up on deck!' she called. 'We're under attack! Kendrick's bounty-hunters have found us!'

A SEA BATTLE

Two ships had taken up the pursuit of the *Carfax* by moonlight.

One was a two-master, a schooner with a narrow hull and a large spread of sail, enabling her to make good speed. The vessel's shallow draught made her agile and specially suitable for sailing close to shore.

'Not many cannon,' said Walker as Jolly and the boys joined him on the bridge. 'She's fast but not particularly dangerous.'

'Oh, but she is,' said the Ghost-Trader in ominous tones. 'She'll try to bar our way so that the other ship can take us. These two aren't rival bounty-hunters, they're working together.'

Walker fell silent as he considered this possibility.

Jolly looked at their second pursuer, a sloop like the *Carfax* lying almost as low in the water as a fully laden merchant ship – with the difference that the cargo she carried was guns, certainly more of them than they had at their own disposal. If the schooner managed to pass them and cross their path, they'd be easy prey for the sloop with its superior fire-power.

The bounty-hunters must have been waiting for the *Carfax* to leave the harbour. In a confrontation on land too many other pirates would have joined in, greedy for the price that Kendrick had set on Jolly and Soledad's heads. Out here, however, no one was going to interfere with their handiwork.

Walker barked orders from the bridge, Buenaventure's great hands clutched the wheel, and Soledad stood perfectly still at the rail with a throwing-knife in her hand, as if she expected the bounty-hunters' crews to board them at any minute.

Usually sand was sprinkled on the decks of a ship at the beginning of a battle, to keep the crew from slipping and wasting precious time. In view of the ghostly sailors who manned the *Carfax* that wasn't necessary; the weightless, misty crew hardly touched the deck anyway. Many of them were now crowding round the cannon, making them ready for the fight.

The further they left Tortuga behind, the fresher the

wind was. Their bows ploughed through the foaming spray, and dull booming and thudding sounds came from inside the ship. The schooner was still level with them and sailing close to the wind. The bounty-hunter's crew fired their guns several times more, but all the cannon-balls fell into the churning waves not far from the *Carfax*. The ship shook every time, but there was no direct hit that could cause damage. Walker refrained from wasting powder and shot in the same way, and held back his order to fire until both ships were in a better position for him to fight. After some time the schooner too gave up firing at the *Carfax*, particularly as her aim was only to bar the course of Walker's ship and not try to sink her single-handed. That job was left to the sloop coming up behind the schooner.

'They're fools to squander their first broadside that way,' said Jolly to Munk, without taking her eyes off the enemy ship. 'The first charge is usually the most carefully loaded and aimed – the crew still has time for it at the beginning of the fight. But they have to move faster in the heat of battle and the shots aren't so well aimed.'

'Do you know these ships?' asked the Ghost-Trader, turning to Walker.

'That schooner's the *Natividad* under Captain McBain.

He's not a bad fellow unless you happen to have passengers with a price on their heads aboard.' Walker gave Jolly and Soledad a dark look.

'Think of the treasure,' said Jolly.

'Believe me, I'm thinking of nothing else.'

'But you should,' the Ghost-Trader told him. 'For instance, how you and your hairy friend are going to get us out of here alive.'

'I could always hand the pair of 'em over.'

There was a whirring sound, and something buried itself in the rail beside Walker's hand with a dull impact. Soledad's throwing-knife. The blade had gone in barely an inch from his little finger.

'You just try it,' she called, 'and the next knife goes between your eyes.'

The captain beamed. 'Your charms are as beguiling as ever, fair princess.'

'A lot of men have said that – and it was the last thing they ever said too.'

He laughed quietly and turned to Buenaventure. 'No closer to the wind,' he ordered. And he called to the gunners on deck, who were almost invisible in the moonlight, 'Get ready to fire!'

Torches flared in the darkness.

Munk leaned over to Jolly. 'You said it wouldn't be a good idea to fire now.'

'Not now – but maybe in one or two minutes. If the schooner holds on course it will bring her closer to us. Walker wants to play safe and be sure we're ready at the best possible moment.'

'Bannon has taught you a lot about fighting at sea,' said the captain appreciatively. 'Not bad for a little toad polliwiggle.'

Griffin bit his lip. 'Here we go, any moment now.'

'What about the sloop?' asked Munk.

'Still too far behind us,' said Jolly. 'The *Natividad* has made the mistake of challenging us too early. Instead of firing on us, she should have put all her efforts into getting ahead to cut off our course.'

Walker agreed. 'McBain was always an impatient fellow. He's trying to act on his own initiative, and that can only be good for us.'

'Do you know the captain of the other ship?' asked the Ghost-Trader.

'I know the ship, she's the *Palomino*. Until recently she belonged to a corsair from the Lesser Antilles, but they say he lost her to another captain at dice. Constantine, that was the name of the man who won her.'

'Yes, Constantine,' Soledad confirmed. She had taken three swift strides to join them on the bridge, where she pulled her throwing-knife out of the rail. 'He was a friend of my father's once. Then he was among those who betrayed him. It was through Constantine that Kendrick got his chance to kill my father.'

'Aha!' said Walker. 'Well, that gives the whole business a certain piquancy, wouldn't you say? It's getting personal now.'

Did Soledad hope to cross swords with her father's betrayer? The light of battle was blazing in her eyes. The Ghost-Trader looked at her in some concern. What would he do? He wasn't going to allow anything – or anyone – to thwart his mission.

Jolly's eyes wandered over her companions, all of them waiting in suspense, and suddenly she felt grief. Deep, inexplicable grief. Perhaps not all of them would see the end of their journey.

The *Natividad* fired again.

Something hissed away overhead. But before they all fully realised that they had just been within an inch of death, Walker roared, 'Devil take it, they must have heavier guns on board than I suspected!'

'Fire now,' said the Ghost-Trader calmly. 'At once.'

'You're right.' Walker swung round and barked out his

orders across the deck. Seconds later the cannon of the *Carfax* were spitting death and destruction at the *Natividad*.

Whatever the ghosts at the guns had been in their first lives, they knew how to handle cannon. And how to score a direct hit with the first shot.

The thunder of the guns shook the *Carfax* to her keel. For a moment her masts and rigging quivered as if the ship had run aground. Yellowish gun-smoke wafted back over the deck and was swept away by the wind. Munk, who had never been in a sea battle before, narrowed his eyes as the acrid smoke passed over him. But Walker took a deep breath as if he relished it, and Jolly set her hands more firmly on the rail as if to brace herself against the wind and the smoke of the cannon.

The storm of iron swept over the decks of the *Natividad*, tore away parts of her rigging, and sent shredded canvas from the sails falling on the bounty-hunter's crew. Two balls knocked holes in the schooner's hull above the waterline, and the cries of injured and dying men came from inside the ship. Splinters flew like daggers in all directions. The cannon had hit the gun-deck of the *Natividad* and destroyed several of its guns at a stroke.

One figure stood grimly up on the bridge, untouched by the destruction on board the ship, shouting orders: Captain

McBain. He had no intention of giving up because of a single direct hit. His furious voice echoed over the gap between the ships, and sent a shudder down Jolly's spine.

The ghosts immediately set about reloading the cannon, but those guns still intact on the *Natividad* were ready to fire.

'Their turn now,' whispered Griffin. For the first time Jolly saw real anxiety in his face. Somehow it didn't seem to suit the cheerful, high-spirited boy she knew.

There was no point getting behind cover. Cannonballs could crash through the rail or the side of the ship. The companions might just as well stand here waiting for the enemy to attack; none of the adults even thought of sending Jolly and the boys below. They were treated as equals, full members of the crew. It was almost like being back on the *Maid Maddy*, when Bannon and his crew plunged into yet another apparently hopeless venture, but emerged victorious at the end of the battle.

The thunder of cannon banished Jolly's memories. Smoke poured from the gun-ports of the *Natividad*, shrouding the whole ship in mist.

'Watch out!' shouted Walker, and now they did all duck their heads.

Iron fanned out over the deck of the *Carfax*, wood

316

cracked, parts of the masts and rigging broke away. Jolly saw one ghost hit by a cannonball. It scattered into scraps of mist which immediately came together again. She realised how superior their own crew was to the bounty-hunter's and plucked up courage, particularly when Walker cried, 'None of the masts damaged! No leak in the hull!' Exuberant in this moment of triumph, he clapped Buenaventure on the shoulder. 'We've got 'em now!'

The *Carfax*'s next broadside exploded across the waves, and the smoke billowing around the *Natividad* didn't come from her own guns this time. One ball must have hit the magazine, for fire broke out on the deck of the schooner. When the smoke around the bridge cleared, Jolly saw with a shudder that Captain McBain had disappeared – and a large part of the superstructure with him.

Walker was more jubilant than ever, Buenaventure uttered an enthusiastic yelp, and even Soledad was in such high spirits that she flung her arms around the captain's neck in her relief – if only for a moment. She moved back almost at once, surprised by herself, and brushed her clothing down. Walker grinned and whispered something to the pit bull man which made him burst into yelping laughter.

The Ghost-Trader's gloomy expression did not lighten. 'They're turning away,' he said quietly. Jolly wondered why

317

the wind had not blown his hood off his head. It was as if the power of the elements couldn't touch him, as if the winds avoided him.

And where were the two parrots? She hadn't seen Hugh and Moe since the beginning of the battle.

Walker waved to the *Natividad*, and watched with satisfaction as they left the crippled schooner behind.

'What about the *Palomino*?' asked Griffin, and glancing back over the stern of the ship he answered his own question. 'She's still following us.'

'She's slower than we are,' said Walker.

'That's possible,' said the Ghost-Trader, 'but not very probable.'

The captain looked at him in surprise. 'What do you mean?'

With his long arm, the Trader pointed to the mainmast. The top of it was just bending over, along with the crow's-nest and the topsail. There was a painful creaking, cracking sound, and then the entire upper part of the mast fell to the deck. It crashed on the planks amidst a tangle of torn rigging, burying several barrels of drinking water under it. Ghosts scattered like smoke, formed their ghostly bodies again somewhere else, and came hovering back to set about the repair work.

'Damn it!' exclaimed Walker.

Soledad ran to the balustrade and looked down at the main deck. 'One of their balls must have grazed the mast.'

Walker reacted at once. Wasting no more time, he discussed their next move with Buenaventure. Then he turned to his passengers. 'I think it will work. Even if we don't happen to have a carpenter among our ghosts, we won't be losing much speed. At least we can maintain our distance.'

'What about the *Palomino?*' asked Jolly.

'She'll follow us, that's certain. And even attack if we do slow down.'

'We can't run before them for days on end,' said Munk. He looked as if he were thinking hard about something, and Jolly noticed that his right hand lay on the bag with the shells in it.

Walker raised one eyebrow disapprovingly. 'It's only been an hour so far, boy. We'll have to wait and see what time brings. Perhaps some advantage we aren't expecting yet.'

'Or perhaps the end,' said the Ghost-Trader.

Jolly ran to the rail at the stern and looked at the bounty-hunter's ship. The *Palomino* was following at a distance of a mile, maybe less. A tough race lay ahead of them.

Now it all depended whose side the wind and the sea were on. Both, she knew from Bannon, were unreliable allies.

Next afternoon the *Palomino* was still the same distance behind, following them like a shadow, and the sight of her outline on the horizon made them all feel downcast. As long as the enemy ship was behind them, her guns were no threat. But if she succeeded in catching up and showing them her broadside, they were done for. Everyone realised that, even Munk, who had learned more about seafaring and fighting on the high seas in the last few hours than he could ever have imagined in his wildest dreams.

Jolly climbed to the bridge, where Buenaventure stood alone at the wheel. 'What course are we following?' she asked.

The pit bull man glanced at the distant horizon in the west once again, then at Jolly. Every time she looked into his round, brown dog's eyes she felt a strange melancholy, in spite of the menace and strength that the gigantic steersman radiated. The tip of his tongue showed red between his teeth.

'We're going east,' he said in his morose voice. 'And north.'

'I know that. I thought perhaps you could tell me a few more details.'

Buenaventure's chops moved in a pit bull smile. 'He's not telling you anything, eh?'

'No, nothing at all.' Jolly followed his gaze to the Ghost-Trader, who was standing in the bows with one hand on the rail, the other on the silver circlet beneath his robe. The two black parrots were sitting on his shoulders again like stuffed birds, their feathers ruffled only by the wind.

'He's not talking to anyone any more. Not even Munk. I think he's seriously worried.' And not about me or Munk or any of the others, she thought. Only about Aelenium. That's where it's all leading.

The Hexhermetic Shipworm had refused to tell them any more about the floating city. He was sulking. Walker had put him in an old metal bird-cage which he had brought up from the captain's cabin in a fury and placed on deck. Jolly had to admit that the captain had good reason to be angry: when he had gone down to the hold last night to see what reserves of wood, masts and planks had been loaded there, he had discovered that the Shipworm had not been inactive during the sea battle – and had consumed a good half of all their stocks of spare wood.

Jolly had thought Walker would never stop shouting. Particularly when the Worm offered to compensate him for the loss of the wood by reciting a poem.

She had no sympathy with the Worm. He was greedy, dishonest, and generally insufferable. It was little short of a miracle that Walker hadn't thrown him straight overboard.

Now the Hexhermetic Shipworm was sitting in his prison at the foot of the mainmast, nursing a grudge in silence. The bird-cage was shaped like an onion dome. Walker had reinforced its door by adding a padlock. The Worm had spent his first few hours in the cage cursing non-stop, until Griffin threatened to slice him up with a boarding knife. After that he just muttered now and then about being robbed of his freedom, improper behaviour, and the way his stomach was rumbling, but most of the time he kept silent.

Buenaventure brought Jolly back from her thoughts. 'If all goes well, our voyage will last eight or nine days. Once past Haiti, we leave the Mona Passage on our starboard side, and then we must go further out into the Atlantic. Or so your one-eyed friend says, anyway. But I don't know if it'll work.' He saw the look in her eyes, and the dark skin on his forehead crinkled. 'Why are you staring at me like that?'

'I . . . I didn't know that . . .' She was bewildered by his unexpected torrent of words, but interrupted herself, shaking her head. 'I'm sorry.'

322

'I can talk like anyone else,' he said, 'if that's what you mean.'

'But you don't. Or not very often.'

'Only when I have something to say.' He looked back at the sails and the sea again. To the south, many miles away, the coast of Haiti was passing by, little more than a dark line on the horizon. The sun burned down from a deep blue sky, the wind was blowing strongly, driving them forward fast. The air smelled fresh and tangy.

The distance between the *Carfax* and the *Palomino* was still much the same. Sometimes the enemy ship came a little closer, then it fell back again. If the weather didn't change this nerve-racking chase could go on in exactly the same way for days on end.

'What did the Trader tell you?' asked Jolly. 'About the place where we're going, I mean.'

'Only that it's in the Atlantic, beyond the Caribbean Sea, and its name is Aelenium. I've never heard of such an island, but to be honest that doesn't interest me. I'm just glad to be left in peace to steer the ship. Walker looks after our business and decides where we go. Usually, anyway.'

Jolly sighed. 'Then I won't bother you any more.'

He let her reach the top of the steps before he spoke again. 'You can stay here if you like.'

Jolly turned to him.

Buenaventure's chops lifted. 'Can I ask you something too?'

'Of course,' she said.

'What does it feel like, being able to walk on the water?'

She went up to the wheel and leaned back against the balustrade. 'I don't know what it feels like *not* being able to.' She thought for a moment. 'I can't stand it for very long on land. Or at least, not far from the sea. Bannon once went into the Yucatan jungle because someone told him old Henry Morgan had hidden a treasure in a temple there. I couldn't go with the expedition. Or rather, I tried, but on the third day Bannon sent me back to the ship with two of the men. I could hardly breathe, my feet felt as heavy as cannonballs, and in the end I could scarcely move my legs. Just as you don't know the feeling of running over the water, I don't know how anyone can walk on land for long.'

Buenaventure thought for a while. 'We never stop to think about it. We walk on land just because we can. It's taken for granted.' After a brief pause, he added, 'I think I know what you mean.'

She smiled at him. 'It's exactly the same for us polliwiggles. We walk on water because we can. Other people think nothing of walking down a road – and in the same way leaping from wave to wave is nothing special for us. Well, perhaps with the difference that you don't have to watch out for kobalins and sharks walking down a road.'

The pit bull man flicked the tips of his ears. 'That was probably a stupid question of mine.'

'Oh no!' Impulsively, she went up to the steersman and gave him a hug. She only came up to his waist. 'Just wanted to say thanks!'

He almost let go of the wheel in his surprise. 'What for?'

'For helping us.'

'You're paying us for it.'

She let go of him and smiled. 'Not for everything,' she said. 'Certainly not for everything.'

Buenaventure the pit bull man, veteran of the mines of Antigua, returned her smile, and from then on they were friends.

FIRE AND SMOKE

On the fifth day of their flight Walker summoned them all to his cabin, leaving only Buenaventure behind on the bridge. The pit bull man probably knew what Walker had to tell them anyway. Sometimes there seemed to be an invisible bond between them; each knew what the other was thinking, and they acted like two halves of a single man.

'I've had enough of this,' said Walker energetically, leaning both hands on the table in his cabin and the sea-charts spread out on it. 'We must shake the *Palomino* off. I'm sick of the sight of her.'

Through the small portholes behind his back they could see their enemy's ship on the horizon. She was still following in their wake. Walker had hoped that the captain of the bounty-hunter would be forced to give up because his crew had so many more mouths to feed than theirs, but that hope had proved unfounded. Captain

Constantine had prepared for a long chase.

Only now did Jolly get some idea of the height of the price that the pirate emperor must have set on her head and Soledad's. It made her feel quite ill.

'We have to reach the islands to the south,' said Walker, tapping one of the charts with his forefinger. 'This silly game of cat and mouse is getting me down.'

'You want to face them?' asked the Ghost-Trader.

'If I can choose the battleground – yes.'

'So you have an idea, then?'

'There's a group of small rocky islands, little more than a few peaks and ridges sticking up out of the sea. It's not far away; we could be there by evening. And perhaps we may manage to shake them off there.'

Soledad spoke up. 'You're going to try to run Constantine aground on a reef?'

Walker shrugged. 'I'm not sure if he knows his way around here – but I've been in these parts many times, and there were some Spaniards who bitterly regretted following me.'

The Ghost-Trader still wasn't convinced. 'How much time will we lose?'

'Half a day, perhaps a whole day. No more.'

The shadows under the Ghost-Trader's hood seemed to

turn even darker, as if his face were sinking into uncertain depths. 'I'm not sure that this is a good idea. Once we reach Aelenium they can't touch us.'

'*If* we reach Aelenium. And then what about Constantine? Will your friends sink him? If not he'll sail back to Tortuga or Haiti and tell your little secret to all and sundry.'

Soledad agreed with the captain. 'We must shake him off.'

'He's one of those you want to see dead, Princess.' The Trader looked at her. 'But there are more important considerations.'

'I don't want to *see* him dead,' she replied coldly. 'It will satisfy me to *know* he's dead.'

'Your severity won't help you if the Maelstrom prevails.'

Soledad held his gaze for a long time, but then she turned away.

'I am the captain of this ship,' said Walker emphatically. 'And I make the decisions.' Perhaps that was why he had assembled them in the cabin, as if their surroundings underlined his right to command the *Carfax*.

The Ghost-Trader slowly nodded, and his parrots imitated his movement. 'Do as you think right, Captain. But never forget what's at stake.'

And that's the question, thought Jolly. What, for heaven's sake, really is at stake?

Griffin pointed to a slim container standing on a wooden shelf between leather-bound books. 'What's that?' he asked, although surely he could see it was an urn.

'My mother,' said Walker. 'God keep her soul, devil of a woman that she was.'

Jolly raised an eyebrow. He noticed, and smiled.

'The bravest, most depraved and pitiless, most bloodthirsty woman pirate in these and all other latitudes!'

'Was this her ship?' asked Jolly.

'Indeed it was. She designed it, she had it built. She was the first woman captain in the Caribbean, and by God, she was the best.'

'A woman pirate captain?' It took Jolly's breath away. She had often dreamed of being such a captain herself, but she hadn't known that it had ever been done before.

'A freebooter body and soul,' agreed Walker with great pride and a little melancholy. 'More men went to their deaths for her than I can count . . . and I'd have you know I can count up to a thousand.' He gave her a broad grin. 'On a good day.'

A woman pirate. Captain of a ship. Commanding a whole pirate crew.

Just for that, thought Jolly, it's worth seeing this through.

She cast a last glance at the urn, and it was as if a voice were speaking to her. *You can be like me, Jolly*, said the dead woman pirate in her head. *You can be like me, if only you want to.*

And at last she understood what the Ghost-Trader meant when he said it was the future at stake. No empty phrases, no vague, indefinite aims without shape or value.

The future. The idea echoed in her mind.

Perhaps that really was worth fighting for.

Hours later, Munk was sitting cross-legged in the bows of the *Carfax* when the first jagged rocks appeared on the horizon. He had spread his shells out on the planks in front of him. He kept arranging them in new patterns, then impatiently jumbled them up again, sorted them out once more, exchanged one shell for another, or stared down at them, brooding and rubbing his temples.

After her moment of exhilaration in Walker's cabin, Jolly was overtaken by another and completely opposite feeling, one that she had suppressed for far too long. Dull, gnawing despair took possession of her.

She couldn't stand the inactivity and the brooding

atmosphere on board any longer. It wasn't just the loss of Bannon eating into her heart, or her grief for him and her friends on the *Maid Maddy*. What troubled her was the loss of her former life among the pirates, playful and free as air. Just now she'd rather be anywhere else, not here, not under the watchful eye of the Ghost-Trader. Even his silence conjured up ominous presentiments and fears.

In her old life on board the *Maddy* she had often climbed up to the crow's-nest, had even gone on watch when it wasn't her turn of duty, just to be alone, think, be free of everything for a while: free of the deck, the crew, even the sea. She remembered that now, when their cramped conditions aboard the *Carfax* were so uncomfortable that she felt she could hardly breathe.

She swung herself up into the shrouds, and climbed the rigging to the top of the mizzen-mast, the third of the *Carfax*'s three masts. The taut ropes hardly gave at all under her light weight. The hemp cut into the palms of her hands, but she relished its pulling and scratching because it reminded her of the old days. If she closed her eyes now, halfway up the mast, she could imagine everything was the way it used to be, with Bannon and the others. For a moment she felt light at heart and carefree, the wind blew around her face and acted like a tonic, getting her up and about and feeling like herself again.

The mizzen-mast had no lookout platform, but she didn't mind that. She sat on one of the two topmost yards, held on to the mast with one hand, and swung her legs.

A long way below her lay the deck of the *Carfax*, now looking to her very small and insignificant among the great blue expanse of the ocean. The Trader was as tiny as an insect, and suddenly lost all his menace. Even the ghosts were only pale phantoms from this height, vague and indistinct above the red cedarwood of the planks on deck.

If she leaned a little way to one side she could see past what remained of the sails and rigging on the mainmast, past the foremast, and look down at Munk bending over the shells that he was moving with practised ease over the wood. He was very far away now too – but he was far away even when she was standing right beside him. Over the last few days he had retreated further and further into himself, speaking and eating even less than before. The change in him that had begun after his parents' death was proceeding faster and faster now, and she felt quite nervous as she wondered where it might lead. The Munk who had cheerfully scrubbed the deck with her and Griffin was gone;

so was the interested boy of a few days ago, marvelling at the sight of his first sea battle. Munk had started down a path that led through deep shadows, and she wasn't sure whether there was any daylight at the end of it.

But she didn't want to think of that now. Her eyes followed the flight of the gulls that accompanied the sloop on her course. For a moment Jolly was overcome by the strange feeling that she could imitate them, simply take off from the yard and swoop above the sea. Who knows, she thought with wry amusement, perhaps polliwiggles can do even more than just walk on water? How was she going to find out whether she could fly if she didn't try it?

She had to force herself to abandon that idea, and did not entirely succeed. To distract her thoughts, she looked at the *Palomino*.

The bounty-hunter was sailing in their wake, small as a toy or one of the tiny model ships that Bannon sometimes put on his sea-charts when he was planning battles or ambushes.

Yes, she thought, it really did help to come up here. A new perspective, a new point of view. And a sense of boundless, absolute freedom. Even if she was pretending to herself, for a moment she wanted to believe in it, wanted to be like the gulls, like the foam on the waves, like the wind over the endless waters of the sea.

And then Griffin was suddenly beside her.

She hadn't noticed him following her. He nimbly pulled himself up from the top of the shrouds to the other yard of the mizzen-mast. Now they were sitting side by side, faces turned to the bows, separated only by the sturdy wooden post of the mast.

'Am I in the way?' he asked.

She was tempted to say yes, but then it struck her that no, he wasn't in the way at all, she was even glad to have him near her. This sensation was almost more curious than her impulse to dive into the air just now.

'No, I was only looking for . . .' She stopped, but he finished the sentence for her.

'Somewhere to be alone?'

She smiled. 'Maybe. Yes.'

Griffin nodded, as if he understood exactly what was going on inside her. And yes, she thought, he does understand.

He noticed her looking at him, inspecting his profile, and quickly pointed down at Munk.

'He's been doing that with the shells for days now,' he said, lowering his voice. 'Does he really think it'll help us somehow?'

Jolly sighed softly. 'At least he's doing something.

The two of us can only sit about up here waiting.'

'That's a fact.'

'Perhaps he really will think of something. I've seen him conjure up a gust of wind myself. If he tries hard . . . I mean, I don't know how this kind of thing works, or even if it's possible . . . but if he tries hard maybe he can make us go faster.' She shook her head. 'Or do something else. I've no idea what.'

'Turn us all into frogs?'

She grinned. 'Would you like that? Being a frog.'

'Only if a princess finds me and kisses me.'

Jolly looked down at Soledad, who was practising throwing her knives at a target on the mast and ignoring the angry Shipworm. He was sitting in his onion-dome cage only a few feet below the target, and he flinched every time Soledad threw a knife.

'She's very beautiful, isn't she?' said Jolly.

'Yes.' Griffin smiled. 'But *she* isn't the princess I meant.'

Jolly's eyes met his. There was a sharp remark on the tip of her tongue, but then she realised that he was serious, and her sarcasm died away, unspoken. 'You're laughing at me,' she said, although she knew better.

'Has he kissed you?'

'Munk?' She laughed nervously. 'Of course not.'

'But he'd like to.'

'What makes you think that?'

'Because I've been talking to him.'

'About me?'

Griffin nodded. 'And what it would be like to kiss you.'

His frankness took her by surprise. She suddenly had a lump in her throat. 'You're totally crazy, the pair of you. Don't you . . . well, don't you have anything better to do?'

'Count flying fish? Or sharks' fins?' He laughed, and all the little blond braids on his head whirled about like tendrils of waterweed. But then he turned serious again. 'Although that was before Munk decided he'd rather talk to his shells than us.'

She wanted to change the subject, but his honesty, and even more the strange look on his face, which she couldn't avoid, left her no peace. He was unsettling her, and that made her shy.

Jolly had *never* felt shy. Until today.

'May I?' he asked straight out.

She felt panic-stricken. 'May you what?'

'You know what – may I kiss you?'

'Good heavens . . . no!'

'That's a pity.'

She glanced quickly down at the deck to make sure none of the others was listening. Wasn't Soledad glancing surreptitiously up at them now and then?

'You're impossible,' Jolly told Griffin.

'I'm a man.'

Now it was her turn to laugh. 'You're a bold rascal, Griffin, a cheat and a big-mouth – but one thing you are *not* is a man.' She pointed back to their pursuers on the horizon. 'And the way things look, your chances of ever getting to be one don't seem too good.'

'One more reason to clear it all up now.'

'You talk as if there was some kind of duel to be fought.' His grin was infuriating her, but at the same time she had a strange, warm sensation inside. It all confused her so much that even her knees were trembling. Or was it the other way around?

'Perhaps, just perhaps I'd let you kiss me if we were stranded on a lonely island – and all the wild boars and tree spiders were otherwise engaged.' She looked at him again as angrily as possible, then let herself fall backwards, and in that brief, alarming moment when there was a complete void around her she seized the yard in both hands, twirled round it like an acrobat, turned in the air and got her hands and feet into the shrouds. As Griffin watched her, open-mouthed, she climbed hastily down to the deck and joined Soledad.

'Will you show me how to do that?' she asked in an unsteady voice, pointing to the knives.

Soledad looked at her in surprise. 'Didn't Bannon teach you?'

'I . . . I'd like you to remind me.'

'You're in quite a state. What's happened?'

Jolly looked Soledad in the eye and realised that the princess had a very good idea of what had just happened.

'Nothing, I –'

'*Aaaarggghhh!*' screeched the Hexhermetic Shipworm. '*Fire! The ship's on fire! Save me . . . save meeee!*'

Everyone spun round.

Flames were flaring up in the bows, making the sky flicker above the foresail. But it wasn't the ship burning.

It was Munk.

Jolly raced forward. Soledad came right behind her. Griffin swung himself down the shrouds and ran to one of the ropes from which buckets hung down over the ship's side.

Munk was sitting cross-legged in the middle of the flames, his hands held out, as if in invocation, over a magic pearl that was hovering in the middle of the circle of shells. He didn't seem to feel the heat at all. The fire came from his skin, his hair, even his eyes – but it was not consuming him.

Munk was burning, and didn't even notice.

He raised his head in surprise as the others ran towards him.

'What the –' he began, and then the entire contents of Griffin's bucket of water hit him in the face. He flinched back, lost control of the hovering pearl, and shouted a warning.

The pearl swept out of the magic circle that had enclosed it until now, rose in the air, turning in narrow spirals, zigzagged from starboard to port like lightning gone mad, flew around Buenaventure in a circle, and then, hissing, shot out over the ship's rail into the emptiness over the ocean.

It was less than a hundred feet away, and could hardly be made out when it exploded. A ball of fire blossomed high above the sea, stood like a second sun in the violet evening sky for a few moments, and then collapsed on itself until it was the size of the pearl again, and at last went out.

The flames round Munk's body had gone out too. He sat there soaking wet, swearing quietly – and immediately began trying to set out his shells in a new pattern.

'Munk!' Jolly crouched down beside him. 'Munk – what was that?'

He raised his face. She was frightened when he bent his feverish gaze on her. His eyes were twitching, his lids fluttering frantically like butterfly wings.

'I can't do it,' he kept murmuring. 'I just can't do it.'

Jolly shook her head and was going to pick up the shells when he struck her arm.

'Dammit, Munk, that hurt!'

'Don't touch!' he said heatedly.

She withdrew her hand, but kept her eyes on his glowing features. Suddenly there was a rustle of black fabric. When she looked up, the figure of the Ghost-Trader was standing over her.

'Leave him alone,' he said firmly. 'Munk mustn't be disturbed just now.'

Jolly leaped to her feet and planted herself angrily in front of the Trader. 'He's ill!'

'No. Just exhausted.'

'Then he must stop for a rest.'

'There are too many hopes resting on him. He can't give up now.'

'But he's shaking. His eyes . . . have you seen his eyes?'

'I tell you, he doesn't need to rest. Not now. What

he needs more urgently than anything is to succeed.'

Munk's voice interrupted them. 'I was so close to it. So close . . .'

Griffin put the wooden bucket down on the planks with an audible bang. 'I'm beginning to think you're all out of your minds.'

'Oh, by every sea-devil in the deeps!' Walker's voice silenced them. Even Munk looked up at the bridge.

Walker was standing there with his telescope, looking back over the stern. 'They're doing what I'd have done long ago in their place!' he cried, without looking round at the others. 'They're lightening ship.'

'What does that mean?' asked Munk.

'They're throwing ballast overboard,' explained Jolly. Her voice was unsteady.

'What ballast?'

'The cannon!' cried Walker. 'They're rolling some of their guns overboard.' He lowered his telescope. 'They have us now. They'll catch up.'

It was a labyrinth.

A labyrinth of rocky needles, shapeless grey hilltops, stone ridges as sharp as a knife and a few densely wooded islets.

The *Carfax* reached the outskirts of this strange island

group just as they all thought the *Palomino* would draw level with them at any moment. Even with her few remaining cannon, the bounty-hunter had more gun-power than the *Carfax*. Captain Constantine had loaded his sloop up with enough weapons to win a whole war on his own. Muzzle after muzzle stuck out of the open gun-ports. Smoke rose between them. The torches were already burning, the gunners were waiting for their captain's order to fire.

Just as it looked as if there could be no escape now, Walker manoeuvred the *Carfax* through a narrow channel into the labyrinth of islands. Constantine had to turn away to avoid running aground – the passage between the rocks left no room for two ships.

'How much time will this gain us?' asked the Ghost-Trader.

'Not much.' Walker seemed neither relieved by his skilful manoeuvre nor proud of it. 'We can't cruise among these rocks forever. The winds are treacherous here, and as for the currents . . .' He broke off, shaking his head. 'And if we lie at anchor they'll get us all the sooner.'

'So?' said the Trader.

'So we can only hope that Constantine's angry enough to pursue us at once. That's our one chance. If I really do know my way around here better than he does, then perhaps I can lure him on to a reef or a sandbank.'

'In the dark?' asked Jolly sceptically. Bannon had known about such manoeuvres too, but he had always avoided sailing through very narrow straits by night. The risks were many, and were not to be sneezed at.

Walker nodded grimly. 'I'm afraid we have no choice.'

Darkness had fallen now. The moon looked almost circular, shining like a silver coin among thousands of diamonds laid out on black velvet. The beauty of the sky above was in strange contrast to the fear that held them all in its grip. Even Buenaventure was panting louder than usual. Jolly wondered how, after so many hours without sleep, he was in any condition to carry out Walker's orders so precisely. And yet she was sure that, of all her companions, the pit bull man was the one most aware of his own limitations. He might be an old warhorse like his friend Walker, but there was a wisdom in his doglike eyes that could compare with the Ghost-Trader's. As long as he was steering the ship she wasn't afraid that they would run on to a reef, or break up on the ice-grey rocks.

The moonlight drained the craggy island landscape of all colour. By night, even the few wooded islets could hardly be distinguished from the bare rocky slopes. There must be dozens of small islands all crowding close together here in a small space, the peaks of a rugged underwater mountain range. The winding narrow channels reminded Jolly of the tangled alleyways of seaports that she knew. Here too an enemy might be lurking somewhere to one side of you. They had shaken off the *Palomino* for the time being, but at the same time they had lost sight of their enemy. Had Constantine ventured into this maze of islands too? Was he waiting for them hidden by the next hill, the next cliff?

Creaking, with whispering sails, the *Carfax* made her way past steep rocky walls and peaks, through waters that looked deceptively calm but had currents and unknown depths below the surface. The few sounds were thrown back from the rocks, sometimes as an echo, sometimes as if a living being were imitating the sound and calling it out into the night.

Griffin had climbed to one of the yards of the foresail and was sitting there with his legs dangling, looking at the nocturnal island landscape.

'There!' he cried suddenly. 'There they are!'

'Bring her about!' shouted Walker.

Buenaventure turned the wheel, ghosts clambered among the masts. The *Carfax* began to position herself across the narrow channel. That meant they could receive the *Palomino* with a broadside whether she came into their line of fire from right or left at the next meeting of the waterways.

The bounty-hunter's masts rose above the top of several rocks, and then the whole sloop came in sight. She did not turn into the ravine where the *Carfax* was waiting for her, but sailed past it to bar the way out.

'Fire!' shouted Walker.

And 'Fire!' roared the captain of the enemy ship.

Seconds later the air was full of iron. Acrid gun-smoke got into Jolly's nose and throat and restricted the view on board to a short distance ahead. Cannonballs broke through the walls of billowing smoke, scattered them and brought down ropes and sails. Wood exploded with an ear-splitting noise. All of them on board lost their footing, some fell to the deck, others caught the shrouds or rail in time to stay upright. The Hexhermetic Shipworm in his onion-dome cage screamed louder than anyone, although he was the only creature on board still in the same place.

Jolly looked up.

The yard where Griffin had been sitting was empty.

'Oh no!' Her heartbeat raced as she ran to the rail.

Walker kept shouting orders, ghosts were scurrying

everywhere. Soledad and the Trader had disappeared behind the smoke, but Jolly had seen them just now. And Munk . . . yes, there was Munk still setting out his shells.

'I'm going to look for Griffin!' she shouted, clambering over the rail.

'Jolly! No!' Walker's voice made her hesitate only for a moment. 'These waters are full of coral reefs. The whole place is teeming with –'

Sharks, she added in her mind, and jumped. There wasn't time to tell the captain that the sharks wouldn't hurt her. Griffin, on the other hand, was defenceless against them in the water.

Her feet made contact with the churning sea as she fought to keep upright. The foaming crest of a wave broke right between her legs. Jolly lost her balance. As long as she was on her feet the sharks wouldn't notice her; if she was lying down, however, they could identify her by her outline.

She was back on her feet like lightning. In all the gun-smoke she could see only ten paces ahead of her. She saw the hole that a direct hit had made in the hull of the *Carfax*, but it was too high up to put the ship in serious danger for the moment. From here she couldn't see what state the *Palomino* was in; the bounty-hunter's ship was invisible behind the walls of yellow and grey smoke. But it couldn't be long before the next salvoes swept over the water.

'Griffin!'

She called his name into the acrid fumes, but there was no reply. The yard was high enough for Griffin to have broken his neck when he hit the water, but she wasn't even going to think of that.

Again and again she called to him. The cliffs and island slopes on both sides of the passage were hidden behind clouds of smoke too, and she had only the hull of the *Carfax* to give her a sense of direction.

It was terribly dark now that smoke had swallowed up the moonlight. The oil lamps on board the ship gave a faint light, but it didn't reach down to the water; they were hanging over the rail, a dull yellow, like hazy stars in the darkness.

And Jolly knew something else: when Walker decided to stop fighting he would have the lamps extinguished, so that the *Palomino* would lose their trail in the darkness. Jolly must be back on board by then at the latest, or she would be wandering blindly through the smoke forever.

'Griffin, for heaven's sale!'

He was the best swimmer she knew. But if he had lost consciousness when he came down on the water . . . or even worse, if a cannonball had hit him while he was up there . . .

May I? he had asked. *You know what – may I kiss you?*

The idiot. If he'd simply done it, then perhaps she . . . oh, nonsense, of course she'd have resisted.

Or would she?

'Griffin, where are you?'

Her foot caught on something in the water. She stumbled, fell forward, and caught herself just in time. She was on all fours. At the same time a wave rose beneath her, shot up and struck her in the face with the force of a blow from a fist.

Everything didn't suddenly go dark before her eyes – the smoke and the night had already seen to that. Instead, lights flared behind her forehead, so bright that she closed her eyes, lost her sense of which way was up and which was down, and fainted away for a moment.

Or at least she supposed so, for when she opened her eyes again she was drifting on the waves like a piece of wood. With every rocking movement of the water her head came up against something soft, and the roots of her hair hurt – something was pulling them.

Her face felt swollen.

Her head hurt.

Something shot past her, a dark triangle cutting through the waves like a sword.

Cursing, she tried to jump up and avoid the shark. But it wasn't attacking her yet, perhaps it was being cautious because of the noise on the surface, afraid of the turmoil the intruders were creating in its waters.

Swaying, Jolly stood up. As she did so she disappeared from the shark's field of vision. She looked searchingly around her.

Smoke everywhere, darkness everywhere.

And no *Carfax*.

The ship had gone.

'Dammit!' she shouted into the fumes – and then she saw what she had come up against just now.

Griffin was drifting in the water beside her, clinging to a splintered plank with jagged edges. Her hair had caught in them a moment ago. His braids were dancing on the waves that slapped around his head and shoulders.

He was face down in the water.

He wasn't moving.

Jolly leaned forward, pulled his head out of the water, hauled him up, desperately shouting his name.

'Don't *do* this to me!' she cried helplessly. 'You're not going to die, understand? You can't just go and die now!'

A movement beside her swept her mind empty all of a sudden. It wasn't just one shark in the water around her any more.

There were several sharks, six or seven of them.

And the circles in which they were swimming round Griffin and Jolly were closing in all the time.

THE DECISION

The *Carfax* had turned and was now ready to sail back on her original course through the labyrinth of islands: away from the far end of the passage through the rocks, away from the *Palomino*.

'We shall have to leave Jolly and Griffin behind,' said the Ghost-Trader tonelessly into the deathly hush, as the companions stood side by side at the rail, looking at the swirling smoke and the black waves. The water seemed to be boiling, as if all the hidden currents had suddenly decided to come to the surface.

'No!' Munk's cry made the others jump. 'We must look for them and get them on board.'

'If they don't turn up of their own accord . . .' Walker left the rest unsaid. His face was running with sweat. He bore the responsibility for all of them, and command of the ship was wearing his strength down.

351

'Jolly's out there somewhere!' Munk's face was still burning as if he were in a fever, but the anger in his voice left them in no doubt that he was in full control of himself. 'Jolly's a polliwiggle! She can't just drown.'

'In seas like this? Who knows?' But Walker wasn't about to embark on an argument with Munk. Instead, he turned to the Ghost-Trader. 'You're saying we ought to leave them behind?'

The Ghost-Trader's face could only be guessed at under his hood. It was like talking to a gaping black chasm. 'It's not an easy decision. But we must get at least one polliwiggle to Aelenium alive at any cost. Otherwise,' he said, lowering his voice, 'otherwise it will all have been for nothing. The whole mission, our voyage so far . . .' He turned to Munk. 'Even the death of your parents.'

'You've been lying to me all along!' Munk retreated a step from the Trader, but he held the gaze of that shadowy eye. 'You always knew how it would all end. The shells you brought me . . . your visits to the island . . . all of it just to prepare me and take me to Aelenium some time.'

'What's wrong with that?'

'You made decisions about my whole life, and neither I nor Ma and Pa noticed. But now . . . now I'm going to decide what I do. And I'm not going to Aelenium until

Jolly's back on board.' He hesitated almost imperceptibly. 'And Griffin.'

Soledad shouted Jolly's name into the fumes and vapours once more, but yet again there was no answer. She had tried at least twenty times, always unsuccessfully.

The second salvo from the cannon on the *Carfax* had carried the *Palomino* a little way off course, driving her behind the rocks. That was several minutes ago. The ghosts had worked faster than their adversaries could in making the guns ready to fire, so for the time being they had escaped a second broadside from the bounty-hunter. Presumably Constantine was carrying out a lengthy manoeuvre to get the *Palomino* back in her former position, the only one from which he could turn his guns on the other vessel.

They all realised that this was their only chance to get a head start on the *Palomino* again. They didn't know how badly the two salvoes had damaged the enemy ship – smoke still clung to the rocks, obscuring their view – but it could only be a matter of time before the battle went on.

If they were really going to venture on a retreat, it had to be now.

With or without Jolly and Griffin.

'We have no choice,' said the Ghost-Trader. 'Nothing matters as much as our mission to bring a polliwiggle to

Aelenium. It's the only way we can stop the Maelstrom.'

'*Your* mission,' said Munk coldly. 'Not ours.'

'You still refuse to understand. If the Maelstrom unfolds its full power and breaks the gateway to the Mare Tenebrosum open, we're all lost. The Caribbean. The whole world. And you, Munk, are the key to our salvation. Only you can defeat the Maelstrom. But for that I must take you to Aelenium.'

'Me or Jolly.'

The Ghost-Trader nodded. 'I'd rather have taken you both there. Two polliwiggles can be twice as effective as one. But I'd rather do without half our chances than give up entirely. If we don't retreat now we gain nothing at all. Perhaps we might find Jolly and get her aboard. But then what? The *Palomino* will shoot us to pieces, you and Jolly will die – and the Maelstrom will be victorious.' The Trader went up to Munk and took him by the shoulder. 'That's not just a possibility, boy, it's a fact, and there's no contradicting it. Either we give up Jolly and Griffin now – or the end of the world will soon be upon us.'

Soledad had been listening in silence, and even at this point she did not join the conversation. But the look on her face gave her thoughts away. She wanted to save both Griffin and Jolly, wanted to do everything to keep them from being left to an unknown fate here. But she also recognised the ominous truth of what the Ghost-Trader said.

'Munk,' she said calmly, 'it's your decision.'

Munk was still hesitating. Then he began wearily climbing over the ship's rail. 'I'm going to look for them.'

'No!' The Ghost-Trader's voice sounded quite different from a few moments ago, roaring like a stormy wind and with an icy chill in it. 'Soledad is wrong. It's not your decision.' His hands traced a sign in the air, and at the same moment three ghosts dropped from the rigging and gently but firmly led Munk back to the deck.

He cursed and struggled, but the grip of the misty beings was pitiless.

'I'm sorry,' said the Ghost-Trader quietly, and all of them but Munk recognised the genuine regret in his voice. 'But there's no other way. Don't think this is easy for me.'

'Let go of me!' shouted Munk as the ghosts forced him away from the rail and held him firmly in the middle of the deck. He had tears in his eyes now, and his weary face was full of anger and despair. 'You can't do this! Soledad! Walker! You can't just leave Jolly behind.'

The princess lowered her eyes and said nothing.

Walker went back to the bridge, but his steps dragged, as if the air before him had turned into something solid.

They could all see how reluctant he was to give his next orders.

'Hoist all sails, full speed ahead!' he said, and then – hesitantly – repeated it louder.

Buenaventure did not move. 'The girl,' he whispered. 'What will become of the girl?'

Munk was shouting and swearing down on the main deck. The Hexhermetic Shipworm, on the other hand, was silent and had lowered his head with its horny plate; you might almost have thought he was grieving for Jolly and Griffin like all the others.

'Walker,' said Buenaventure. 'We can't . . .'

'You heard him.'

The pit bull man hesitated, and for a long moment it looked as if he would refuse to carry out the order. Then he uttered a high-pitched howl of pain and despair, put his great hands on the wheel, and did what had to be done.

'Thank you,' said the Ghost-Trader, turning and going to the bows of the ship alone. No one followed him, no one wanted to be close to him just now.

'Jolly!' shouted Munk once more, but the vapours swallowed up his voice.

The *Carfax* began to move, and swiftly left the scene of the battle behind her.

Jolly summoned up all her strength and hauled Griffin's torso out of the water. He was heavy, not just because he was a boy and rather taller than she was, but even more because he was hanging motionless as a corpse under the wrecked plank. To make matters worse, his clothes were soaked with water.

The *Carfax* had disappeared from sight. It was impossible to tell whether she was just lying hidden behind the next wall of vapour, or whether . . . no, the others surely wouldn't abandon them.

But would the Ghost-Trader endanger the lives of both polliwiggles if he had a chance of saving at least one of them? He had never left them in any doubt of the importance of getting them to Aelenium. Or at least one of them.

She gasped for air, and felt she was about to throw up. But then, just as unexpectedly, she regained control of herself. She must get Griffin right out of the water somehow.

The sharks were coming closer, circling only a few feet from the two of them now.

Jolly knelt down, put Griffin's left arm round her shoulders, braced herself and, exerting all her strength, got to her feet. The strain made her let out a cry so loud that in spite of the gun-smoke it echoed back from the rocky ravine. She stumbled and fell on her knees again, tried once more, and this time she succeeded.

She managed to haul Griffin out. With her left hand she held his arm, which was still round her shoulders; she got her right arm under his belt behind him, and held him upright by it as best she could.

She had once before brought a helpless man to safety, one of the crew of the *Maid Maddy*, but that had been on land, and weak as he was the man had had firm ground under his feet. Griffin was not a polliwiggle, and water did not resist his feet. Jolly had to carry his whole weight, and must also take care that his legs didn't sink deep enough to attract the attention of the sharks again.

Somehow or other she managed to drag him forward. With a single exception, the shark fins disappeared into the water, and the last predatory fish lingered only a little longer in hopes of its prey before giving up.

Come on, Jolly told herself grimly, don't think! Just keep going forward.

She must reach the shore of an islet some time. The channel had not been very wide, and although Jolly had lost all sense of direction in the vapours the rocks couldn't be far away.

Forward! Keep going!

'Jo . . . Jolly . . .'

'Griffin!' In her relief she almost let go of him. She craned her neck to look at his face, but it was no use. Had he opened his eyes?

Griffin made retching noises, and then a torrent of water poured over her shoulder.

'We're going to make it!' she managed to say, groaning.

He tried to say her name again. Then she felt him go limp once more.

'Griffin! Come on – you must help me! Hold tight!'

He wasn't moving now.

Yet he was alive.

The relief gave her new strength. She struggled desperately against the rough sea, the smoke in her lungs, her blindness in the dark. The wind had risen and was beginning to drive the fumes apart. The moon showed again, mingling its icy light with the swathes of smoke in an oppressive twilight. All the same, Jolly could see something again.

Rocks ahead!

Several humps rose from the water before them, like living creatures rising from a crouching position. Just beyond the humps of the rocks was a stony slope covered with strange shapes. Only as she came closer did Jolly see that they were tree-stumps.

Iron-willed, she passed the outermost rocks and dragged Griffin on land with a jubilant cry. She wasn't sure if anyone could hear her voice but herself; perhaps it existed only in her head. She felt empty and weak.

Pebbles crunched under their feet, then under their two bodies as they collapsed half beside each other, half on top of each other.

Everything went dark before her eyes again, and, once more, she didn't know later how long she had been unconscious. Perhaps only for a few minutes, perhaps for an hour. Maybe even longer.

When she opened her eyes the smoke was gone.

So was Griffin.

In panic, she felt around her, but touched only stones, debris – and a hand. Fingers closed around hers, and then a face appeared above her. Griffin's blond braids dangled round it, almost touching her cheeks.

His smile was exhausted, but still it was a smile.

'Looks as if polliwiggles can see into the future,' he said. His face was very close to hers, but just now that wasn't unpleasant. He was alive.

'See into the future?' she repeated, as if she couldn't have heard correctly.

'Remember what you said to me?'

'I rather think I've said a lot these last few days.' She tried to sit up, and he moved back a little to give her space, but not much, only as much as was necessary.

'You said I could kiss you if the two of us were stranded on a desert island.'

'Oh, but there were . . . reservations,' she said with an uncertain smile. There were thousands of things she ought to be thinking of: the *Carfax*, their companions, the outcome of the sea battle with the *Palomino*, and what was to become of them now, alone on the shore of this rocky islet.

His smile grew a little broader. He was almost the old Griffin again. But then he left it at looking into her eyes, rose and stretched his hand out.

'Can you stand up?'

His abrupt retreat confused her almost more than having him so close just now. 'I wasn't the one who almost drowned out there,' she said, but she took his hand and let him help her to her feet.

Before she saw it coming he put both his arms round her.

'Griffin,' she said, shaking her head, 'this really isn't the time to –'

He dropped a kiss on her forehead and let her go. 'Thank you for saving my life. It *was* you who got me to land, right?'

She nodded. 'What's the last thing you can remember?'

'The noise of the guns. And I . . . I . . . I was sitting up on the mast, wasn't I? I think I fell off.'

She nodded again. 'I went into the water to look for you. There was smoke everywhere, and when I finally found you the *Carfax* was gone . . . both ships were gone.'

She looked out into the rocky channel. Splinters were drifting on the waves in the moonlight. The breakers washed a few pieces of wood ashore, drew them out again, threw them back. There was no ship anywhere in sight. And they could hear no noise in the distance, no voices, no gunfire.

They were really alone.

'Suppose she sank?' Griffin had followed the direction of her gaze. The pieces of driftwood and the empty water among the islands made them both fear the same thing. Yet a voice inside Jolly told her that her first idea had been correct: the Ghost-Trader had left them behind.

Was she disappointed in him? Or angry? It would take her a while to work out the answer to that.

Wasn't this what she had always wanted? Munk could take the responsibility by himself. Magic, enchantment – that wasn't in her line. She could run over the waves. She was a pirate.

Just like Griffin.

'It's not over yet,' he said. 'It certainly isn't over yet.'

She didn't reply. Instead, she turned. 'Let's get moving,' she said, as she began to climb the stony slope. 'Perhaps there's life somewhere around here.'

Maybe human beings, she thought.

Or a creature like the Acherus.

She shuddered.

AELENIUM

Three days later a dense wall of mist ahead of the *Carfax* darkened the rising sun on the horizon. The fiery red of the sky, shot through with streaks of gold and veined with light, blurred and then disappeared entirely in billowing grey.

'There it is,' said the Ghost-Trader, with barely concealed relief. 'Our journey's end lies beyond that mist.'

'Aelenium?' asked Soledad, who was standing at the ship's rail beside him.

The one-eyed man nodded under his hood. The two parrots on his shoulders let out a shrill screech that sounded almost like human laughter.

'We may be able to shake off the *Palomino* in that mist,' Walker called down from the bridge.

The Ghost-Trader didn't turn to look at him. It was as if he were invoking the rolling vapour that soon filled their entire view.

'We will,' he whispered. 'We will.'

The bounty-hunter's ship was still behind them, damaged and much slower than before – like the *Carfax*. Two crippled vessels, limping and gasping as they ran a grim race.

The onion-dome cage hung over the rail from a chain. The Hexhermetic Shipworm had insisted on being placed there so that he too could see the view and wouldn't, as he put it, 'have to spend all day staring at your stinking feet and a few rotting barrels'.

The mist reached for them with filmy fingers, and had enveloped them within a few seconds. It seemed to Soledad as if it had come to meet them, but the Ghost-Trader knew better. 'The mist lies like a broad ring around Aelenium. It keeps most people from venturing here.'

'What about those who try all the same?'

The Trader himself was only a dark fleck in the grey mist now. 'Some turn back, others stay.'

Shivering, Soledad thought of shipwrecks at the bottom of the sea, many fathoms deep below the surface.

'Has the *Palomino* followed us?' she called up to Walker, to give herself something else to think about.

The captain himself was only an outline in the mist.

'I haven't seen her turn, anyway,' he called back. 'And I'd

be surprised if Constantine gave up after so many days at sea.' He spoke quietly to Buenaventure, then turned back to the others. 'Keep quiet. If they can't hear us they'll probably lose our trail.'

For a while there was nothing to be heard but the creak of the planks and the rigging, accompanied by the faint splash of spray along the hull. Then, after minutes that seemed an eternity, there was an ear-splitting crunching and cracking, followed by a terrible bursting sound.

Soledad waited for a collision that would throw her off balance – but none came.

For a moment she had been convinced that the *Carfax* had run aground. But the sounds had died away far behind them. Those sounds had been carried by droplets of mist like millions and millions of tiny mouths delivering a message.

Cries rang through the air. Wild, pitiful screaming, both deep and shrill, from many throats, every single voice so despairing, every cry so final that there was no doubt what was happening to those poor souls. These were the cries of men in their death throes.

Somewhere behind them, deep in the dense mist, the crew of the *Palomino* were dying. And their ship was dying with them.

'Great God!' whispered Soledad. She stood there rigid, motionless. Even her lips felt frozen.

The Ghost-Trader's hand, a corpse-like outline, clutched the rail.

'That was not the powers of Aelenium,' he said in a toneless voice. 'They are not so merciless.'

And then, as if on a secret cue, both of them looked towards the bows.

Munk was sitting there cross-legged. He had laid out the shells in a circle in front of him. A pearl hovered inside the circle, blazing like the fiery eye of a sea-monster. Munk made a gesture, a much easier, more casual gesture than before. The pearl immediately went back into an open shell and was swallowed up by its snapping jaws.

'Did *he* do that?' Soledad didn't realise that she had spoken out loud until the Ghost-Trader nodded. Only once, very briefly.

'By the gods,' he breathed, so quietly that only Soledad could hear him. For the first time she thought she heard something like fear in his voice. Her knees were trembling, her thoughts were going round and round in circles.

'Munk?' she asked.

The boy raised his head and looked at her. His smile in the mist was triumphant and icy.

She was trying to make herself go over to him when a strong gust whipped the mist up above their heads, turning the white swathes into tiny whirlwinds and almost blowing her off her feet. Something large flew over the deck of the *Carfax* above the wrecked mainmast. Next minute it had disappeared in the mist just as quickly. Only faint, rushing, muted sounds reached Soledad's ears, the rising and falling of mighty wings.

'What was that?'

'It's all right,' said the Ghost-Trader reassuringly. 'That was one of the first messengers of Aelenium. We'll soon reach the other side of the mist. It will thin out any moment now.'

Munk was calmly putting his shells away. Sweat stood out on his forehead and drenched his clothing, but that didn't bother him. Only his fingers trembled slightly, and his breathing came a little faster than usual.

Soledad wasn't sure what frightened her most at the moment: Munk's magic that had dragged the *Palomino* down into a watery grave, or the mighty creatures hovering invisibly around the masts.

She made herself look away from the boy. There'd be time enough to think about him later. What he had done – and how he had done it. And what else he might be able to do, both good and evil.

368

Looking out past the bows, she saw a red-gold glimmer just showing through the mist: the morning sky above Aelenium. A bright panorama like a breath of gold-dust on a scarlet sea. With every wave that broke against the bows of the *Carfax*, the water itself took on more and more of the colour of the sky, until the last of the mist finally drifted away like a coppery red torch.

'Aelenium,' whispered the Ghost-Trader, standing beside Soledad at the rail.

She could do nothing but stare ahead, eyes wide, lips parted. She didn't notice what the others on board were doing, didn't know what Walker was saying or thinking, whether Buenaventure was still at the wheel or what the Hexhermetic Shipworm was up to in his cage.

She could only look.

The ring of mist enclosed a circular expanse of water two or three miles in diameter, perhaps even more. Sunrise glowed and shimmered on a forest of rooftops and towers, a many-coloured medley of low-built dwellings, fortress-like battlements, a whole variety of palaces like cakes decorated with bizarre sugar icing. There were bridges between pointed gables, there were viewing platforms, many of them roofed, others open and as finely worked as if they were made of porcelain. There were halls and citadels with spires, there were stairways floating free, flung like spider's webs between facades, doors and hatches; waterfalls spurting from openings in the walls and disappearing into invisible channels and reservoirs among all the buildings. Scarcely any of it seemed to have any obvious, practical function, as if the architects of Aelenium had indulged their own ideas of beauty and elegance without stopping to think how people were to live in the floating city.

In the middle of all these higgledy-piggledy, cluttered, tangled structures rose the cone of a white mountain, very steep and regularly shaped on all sides. Its peak was flattened as if by the blade of a knife, which made it look like a volcanic crater. Whether there really was an opening up there, or whether the artificial peak ended in a platform, could not be seen from the sea below. Water streamed down deep clefts in the mountainside, forming a golden pattern as it was reflected in the sunrise glow.

Broad landing stages ending in points reached out into the sea around Aelenium. It took Soledad a moment to realise what these landing stages really were: the points of a gigantic star.

Aelenium stood on the shape of a starfish. A starfish floating flat on the water, as big as an island, built all over to the outer rims.

But did she mean *built*?

As they came closer Soledad saw that the star-shaped city had not been artificially built at all, as she had thought at first. All the spires, towers, roofs and walls were made of coral, as if layer after layer had accumulated on the surface of the starfish over millions of years, creating a masterpiece that, at first sight, you might easily take for the work of an over-exuberant architect.

Would it look the same underneath? Was there a bizarre reflection of the upper part of the city down there? Endless suites of empty rooms flooded by the sea, upside-down towers with colonies of shellfish clinging to them and crustaceans searching for plankton; halls where no human trod, where only a few predatory fish swam in majestic darkness and silence?

Well, we're going to find out, it occurred to her, for only now did she realise that they were indeed to be guests in this strange structure. They were allies of its people, perhaps even friends. They had nothing to fear.

Yet there was a bitter aftertaste to her amazement and marvelling, a deep anxiety, almost a sense of panic.

What kind of place was this? Where did it come from?

Aelenium might have grown from thousands upon thousands of tons of coral, but it couldn't have been by sheer chance. The stairways, bridges and friezes had piled up for a purpose at the leisurely pace of the aeons. That purpose was to be inhabited.

But by whom?

She could see even more now. In the air high above the coral cathedrals and sea-spray minarets, she saw huge creatures like giant rays with crimson-veined wings, and human beings sitting on them. The riders were tiny compared to their mighty mounts. Now three of them broke out of the wall of mist at the same time in an explosion like snowflakes. Soledad recognised the sound of the wings again. It was the sound she had heard circling their masts just now.

But not all the riders were in the sky; she saw some on the water too. Human beings were riding bony seahorses with long, pointed muzzles and saucer eyes, bodies covered with horny plates and graceful tails, navigational aids to the creatures as they carried their masters swooping through the waters of Aelenium.

As the princess saw all this, she knew that it was probably only a fraction of the marvels awaiting her and the others in the coral city.

One of the giant rays came down lower over them until it was hovering only about six feet above the deck of the

Carfax, slowly beating its wings and flapping the tip of its tail gently. A man with long black hair bent down from it to greet the Ghost-Trader with a gesture that looked like part of some strange ritual.

'Welcome back, old friend!' cried the rider of the giant ray. 'Your friends and companions are welcome too. They shall live among our domes, they shall eat our food.' It sounded more like a polite formula than an invitation that came from the heart.

Soledad exchanged a glance with the Ghost-Trader before he returned the greeting.

'I thank you, d'Artois, captain of the Ray Guard of Aelenium. I am glad to be back. And I bring you what I promised.'

Where have you brought us? Soledad's eyes asked him, but he only smiled mysteriously as he so often did. There was nothing she could do but keep quiet, and marvel, and try to calm her heartbeat and keep her knees from trembling.

Suddenly Munk was there beside her, staring expressionlessly at the coral structures of the star-shaped city.

'Jolly ought to have seen this,' he whispered. 'She ought to be with us now, here and nowhere else.' His head swung round, he looked Soledad in the eye first, and then he looked at the Ghost-Trader. 'We let her down.'

Then he fell silent again, and looked at Aelenium.

Walker hesitantly carried out the instructions given him by the rider of the giant ray, and with Buenaventure's help brought the ship in to one of the starfish points that reached out into the sea, a good two hundred feet from the city itself.

'We let her down,' Munk murmured again.

Soledad fought the urge to move a little way off, where she wouldn't be quite so close to him. Perhaps then she could have stopped shivering.

Munk stood motionless beside her: a boy who had just drowned the entire crew of a ship in the sea with a movement of his hand. Without hesitation. Without any scruples.

The *Carfax* slowed down, the ghosts reefed in the sails, and at last they dropped anchor.

Aelenium welcomed its saviour.

EGMONT PRESS: ETHICAL PUBLISHING

Egmont Press is about turning writers into successful authors and children into passionate readers – producing books that enrich and entertain. As a responsible children's publisher, we go even further, considering the world in which our consumers are growing up.

Safety First
Naturally, all of our books meet legal safety requirements. But we go further than this; every book with play value is tested to the highest standards – if it fails, it's back to the drawing-board.

Made Fairly
We are working to ensure that the workers involved in our supply chain – the people that make our books – are treated with fairness and respect.

Responsible Forestry
We are committed to ensuring all our papers come from environmentally and socially responsible forest sources.

For more information, please visit our website at
www.egmont.co.uk/ethicalpublishing